A S

Claudius donned his wire-rimmed spectacles and studied the papers. MayBelle owned Pearlygates: three dead mines, twenty-odd unproven mining claims, three hundred structures, a water works, and four hundred seventy-nine unsold and vacant commercial and residential lots. Worth a few dimes.

"Madam, your former husband was a cad," he said.

"That's what you get in anyone named Bertram," she said.

"I am named after a Roman emperor," he said. "Tiberius Claudius Drusus Nero Germanicus. He executed his third wife, which recommends him to posterity."

"You're a man after my own heart, snookums."

"We have about two weeks," Claudius said. "I'll need some expense money. You can't start a gold rush from nothing. There must be the lure, the bait, the enticement, the whispers, and gossip, the thing that excites greed. A little bright and shiny ore that assays, say, nine hundred dollars to the ton."

"We have about fifty dollars between us, my love."

He walked to the verandah and studied the sunbaked silent town below him. Not two years before, it had held two or three thousand mortals, along with all their hopes and dreams. What brought them? Bonanza. Make money, get out. First sign of collapse, head for greener pastures and leave the corpse of a city behind.

MayBelle and he needed a three-month boom to sell a hundred lots and vamoose. He turned to her. "Time's a-wasting, MayBelle. Be ready to travel in half an hour."

"Travel? Where are we going?"

"To start a gold rush, madam."

"I think I'm going to like you, Colonel, in spite of everything."

Also by Richard S. Wheeler

The Rocky Mountain Company
Cheyenne Winter
Fort Dance

THE BOUNTY TRAIL

RICHARD S.
WHEELER

PINNACLE BOOKS
Kensington Publishing Corp.
http://www.kensingtonbooks.com

PINNACLE BOOKS are published by

Kensington Publishing Corp.
850 Third Avenue
New York, NY 10022

First Pinnacle Books Printing: February 2004

10 9 8 7 6 5 4 3 2 1

Printed in the United States of America

For Ken Hodgson, with appreciation

Chapter 1

Claudius P. Raines trudged westward, his dignity offended along with his bunions. The businessman, entrepreneur, friend of all humble people, and scourge of the rich, Colonel C.P. Raines was no longer welcome in Storyville.

The infernal Jake Bowler, the Storyville town marshal, had not even offered him the courtesy of a night's repose before ejecting him. Raines had volunteered to spend the night in custody, but Bowler would hear none of it; that would mean a meal at county expense and the marshal was not about to fill the commodious belly of such as Claudius Raines from the public purse.

What really bothered the pilgrim lumbering through the afternoon was not just his bunions, or his dignity, but his empty stomach and his future prospects, which had been reduced to grim penury. Sundown was approaching, and the pilgrim had not even a blanket. The mountains of northern Nevada were not kind to the unprepared. And even less kind to a refined gentleman traveler attired in a black broadcloth suit, boiled white shirt, paisley cravat, black silk top hat, shiny patent leather shoes, and a ring of gold-plated base metal upon his pinky.

Of lucre he had nothing, which meant he could not purchase passage from one of the passing teamsters or stagecoaches or even a rancher with a wagon. And the night would be cold, cold indeed, with ice forming along the banks of creeks and around his heart, and a bitter wind lowering down from the snowy peaks.

A bad streak had put him in this desperate circumstance. He had a fine lottery going in the Golden Hind Saloon, in which one could purchase a one-dollar chance to win three glistening two-pound gold bricks, six pounds of pure gold in all, which were prominently displayed under glass in the front window.

But then some skeptic from Augustine's Beer Garden next door had pried open the case, stabbed the gold bricks with his jackknife, and found under that lustrous gold surface naught but gray lead. Raines, aghast, had been compelled to refund the boodle, but unfortunately he was not able to cover every ticket, which is when Jake Bowler took umbrage.

Claudius thought back to the palmy days when he and the lovely Dora had made several fortunes without half trying. Dora had drifted into his life at Fairplay, Colorado, a pale, raven-haired young woman with smouldering eyes, pouty lips, and a family resemblance. She was not related in any way to Claudius, but looked to be his daughter. They were both thin, large-boned and patrician-nosed, jet-haired and green-eyed. Those were the days when Claudius was a professional cardsharp and he had surveyed her curves with a shrewd eye and a vision of wealth.

He had found Dora in much the circumstance that he himself now suffered: homeless, penniless, without a future, abandoned at a stagecoach stop. He offered her succor and she accepted for want of any other option. But he discovered she had a nature very like his own, and together they lived quite handsomely for several years, sharing the boodle.

His scheme was to embark upon a small friendly game of poker with men of means, lose steadily all evening, profess to be broke and desperately eager to mend his fortunes with one last wager: for a thousand dollars, he would play a single hand of stud poker, with his beloved and only daughter, fresh out of the convent, as his surety. On cue, she would appear at the green baize table, dressed somberly in gray right up to her pale neck, her demeanor virtuous, her eyes burning with unkindled need, her flesh white, her manner demure but just a tad worldly.

That always did the trick. Those at the table surveyed her, their minds racing, and edged those heaps of double eagles outward and into the game. It was at such a moment that Claudius's nightlong losing streak would miraculously reverse; the cards fell his way, and Dora's virtue remained intact. But occasionally Claudius did lose, and then with much sighing, Dora would vanish into the night with her new master, only to reappear at a preordained rendezvous a day or two later. Claudius never needed a bank so long as he had Dora. He could lose everything and still have a fortune to wager at any time.

Now and then Claudius and Dora would decamp for some new diggings, set up shop, and start over. For this kindly service, Claudius shared 25 percent of his booty with her, except when he could get away with less or gull her into believing the stakes were lower. She received less, he explained, because he assumed the entire cost of her maintenance: lodging, food, transportation, and even her dress, which he carefully supervised, so that she had a wardrobe for every occasion and taste.

It was a pity. One day she accused him of gulling her, and ran off with one of the gents who had won her with a pair of jacks, and Claudius never saw her again. It was a great blow to the purse, and even more to his pride. He had fancied that she took a liking to him, and that they could live in semidomestic bliss the rest of their unnatural lives. He had hunted for a new Dora, but couldn't find the right woman. There were plenty of the shopworn variety, but not even powder and mascara could restore such a creature to the innocence and sweetness and pulchritude of Dora, nor did any of the shopworn variety excite the sort of heated attention that Dora won without half trying.

Claudius looked back upon his years with Dora as a sort of Golden Age, a time when he was the king of the mining camps and his every wish was gratified. It had been downhill ever since. He had opened a brokerage, C.P. Raines and Son, sold shares in nonexistent mines, the gaudy certificates splendidly engraved with flags and nymphs and pickaxes and bullion bars.

He had acquired played-out mines and glory holes, salted them with glistening nuggets, and sold them for splendid profits, but the competition in that game was fierce and he sometimes got licked. Worse, several of those fizzled-out holes in the hillsides promptly yielded bonanzas, and poor Claudius marveled that he had sold million-dollar properties for two or three hundred simoleons.

Now he was an exile, trudging a cold and wet road, the soles of his patent leather shoes soaking up muddy water as he distanced himself from all things comfortable and pleasant and warm. But there was naught to do but continue: this exile encompassed the entire county, and if the marshal found him within its boundaries, Claudius's soft flesh would taste the cat-o'-nine-tails. The city marshal of Storyville really had no such authority outside city limits, but C.P. didn't doubt that the dour lawman would enforce his edict.

Thus bemused by his circumstance, and preparing to expire at some wayside, he failed to notice the approach from behind of a farm wagon until it was nearly on top of him.

He turned to discover a moth-eaten nag drawing a creaking spring wagon laden with sacks and cartons, driven by a freckled rube in a straw hat and mud-soaked boots, chewing on a blade of grass.

"Well, aren't you a sight," the fellow said. "Durned if I know what you're doing here, got up like you're heading for a funeral."

"Ah, my good man, it is my own funeral to which I am heading," Raines said. "That is, unless you could help a poor wretch in distress hold body and soul together."

"If that's a way of asking for a ride, hop on," the cowboy said.

Happily C.P. lifted one leg to the axletree, and another to the floorboard, and settled himself beside the driver, grateful that the fellow was a skinny drink of water and didn't crowd the seat. The gent slapped lines over the cadaverous rump of the ranch horse, and the spring wagon lurched forward.

"You, sir, are heaven-sent, and if it were in my poor powers to bestow largesse upon you, I would not hesitate," Raines said, knowing he had just told a whopper. "For I am a man in dire straits."

"Dire straits? Some sort of disease, is it?"

"No, sir, miserable circumstance."

"Ah, I see. I didn't get the handle."

"Colonel C.P. Raines at your service, sir."

"A colonel, eh? I never got beyond private, myself. I'm Rudy."

"Well, Rudy, you have spared me a calamity. I was fearing my own demise. You should be a sergeant, at least."

"What I am is a drover for the N–Bar Ranch yonder, bringing a load of groceries from town."

"Groceries, did you say? Foodstuffs?"

"Yep."

"Sergeant Rudy, sir, I am not one to beg, no, sir, but could you spare me a little fodder?"

"Ah, I'm beholden to the company, sir. The victuals aren't mine."

"I'm a starving man."

Rudy's Adam's apple bobbed. "You don't look it, nosiree."

"The fact is, I have not eaten for three days."

Rudy eyed him coldly. "Three days? You're four hours from Storyville."

Raines saw his chances sliding away. "A meal, then, my fine friend. A nibble to tide me over."

"Where you going?"

"Sir, I am cast out upon the world, knowing neither hearth nor home."

In this manner, Colonel Raines proceeded east by northeast along the rutted road leading away from Storyville and into the arid mountains. Rudy the cowboy spared him nothing but water, and plenty of that, but felt no obligation to burst open a burlap sack and pour its contents over his passenger.

Still, Raines was at least progressing toward some destiny. Perhaps even the ranch, where he might acquire a handsome meal from its owners.

"Who do you work for, my friend?"

"Oh, Captain Gleeson, sir. He's a regular baron of the range, running three thousand longhorns and shorthorns and a few milch cows twenty-five miles yonder."

"Gleeson, is it? I know the man. Many's the time your employer and I have sat across the round table, poring over our cards. I shall be pleased to greet him."

"Ah, Colonel, he's in Argentina at the moment, buying cows and racehorses and learning the tango."

"What is the tango, Rudy?"

"Well, it's so immoral you have to go there to see it."

"Is Mrs. Gleeson about?"

"No, she's visiting her sister in the convent."

Thus they proceeded into twilight, when Raines discovered what appeared to be an entire town nestled against a cliff, but as silent and empty as a graveyard.

"What's this?"

"Pearlygates."

"A town without a soul in it, it seems."

"Abandoned two years ago when the gold played out."

"Pearlygates! Yes, of course, I remember. Quite the booming little burg once."

"Yep."

The spring wagon rolled hollowly through a tidy but empty town, with silent false-front stores and frame houses lining the road. To the east of town rose a great wall of rock, pocked with mine shafts and derricks and hoists.

Raines spotted two burned-out buildings, others in disrepair, but plenty of structures that looked just as handsome as the day they were abandoned. And above town, on a bench south of the mines, stood a noble white mansion with Doric columns along its facade.

"Entirely abandoned, you say?"

"Yep. Not a soul, give or take a few vagrants and pack rats."

"My friend, thanks for the ride. I'll disembark."

"Suit yourself, Colonel."

C.P. Raines stepped down gingerly, laid claim to Pearlygates, and appointed himself the mayor.

Chapter 2

Colonel Raines stood in the middle of the main street of Pearlygates, absorbing the strange, sad silence. It gave him an eerie feeling. Not so many years earlier, this had been a thriving, bustling town of five thousand. Now it was dead.

A wind scoured the street, blowing a tumbleweed before it. A thousand tumbleweeds lodged against the frame buildings lining the ghostly street. Before him stood Larsen's Mercantile, the name painted in black on white clapboard. Next was Hooper's Hardware. Across the street was Jon Day's Saddlery. And the Mother Lode Café. And Big John's Clothier Emporium. All silent and grave and forlorn. In the next block was a cluster of saloons: the Miner's Rest, Stockman, Mint, Mother Lode.

Raines bestirred himself to take a closer look. He patrolled one side of the street and then the other. Most of the stores had been explored by vagrants. Their doors swung in the breeze. Their windows had been shattered, and shards of glass lay about. The saloons showed signs of occupancy. Every passing tramp had burrowed through them, looking for one last bottle that had been forgotten in the great exodus when the ore ran out.

What had happened to Pearlygates had happened to a hundred mining towns all over the West. A bonanza discovery, bustling mines, a mushrooming town, more strikes and failures, seesawing up and down until the last ore from the last hole had been hauled out. And then, slowly at first, and suddenly in a rush, miners and their families packed their possessions into wagons and drove off, heaven knows where.

Some scurrying thing startled Raines; he saw only a flash of darkness and it was gone. A stray cat, perhaps, or a coyote or a skunk. Probably some poor little tabby abandoned when the town fell to pieces.

Finding provender would be difficult. Hoboes would have gotten there ahead of him, along with low-class scoundrels. At one corner of the town, a whole block of houses had burned, but providentially the rest of the place survived. A hobo campfire, probably. The rest could incinerate at any time, and with the slightest excuse.

The cottages of the miners were in better shape, trim buildings, some of them with gingerbread brightening their porches and picket fences about their narrow yards. Raines thought that these offered more chance of a few cans of tomatoes than the mercantiles, saloons, and hotels along the center of town.

He tried a few, found them stripped of everything, nothing but naked cold rooms in deep shadow, their iron stoves cold, windows broken, doors creaking on ancient hinges. Some had cold cellars dug into the slope, and these he explored, finding them empty, or fouled by strange odors.

Raines suddenly felt sorry he had abandoned the wagon that might have carried him to a sit-down meal ten or twelve hours up the road. He shivered. The first stars bloomed. The twilight faded into a slash of blue in the west. Behind him, a giant mountain loomed. The dead town was snugged into the claws of an arid slope, but beyond lay vaulting gray rock, alpine forest, and naked peaks streaked with pockets of white.

Gold had been discovered here, pockets of rich ore to seduce and beguile the miner, but in between the pockets were veins of shattered quartz that offered promise and gave only fraud. Raines could see the abandoned works scattered all over that arid slope: head frames, hoist works, trestles, heaps of cable, piles of tailings, rusting iron. It was not a pretty sight; mining was not a pretty or an aesthetic business.

All dead now, thousands of dreams shattered, the whole place hollow and forlorn. But maybe not. Colonel C.P. Raines had been born an alchemist, able to transform nothing into something, base metals into precious ones, wastelands into gardens, hopelessness into dreams. A little skill, a little effort . . .

Thus did he survey his kingdom, for he had, in his mind, acquired ownership, in fee simple, of all that he surveyed. A fat orange moon popped over a ridge, bathing the empty town in amber light, so that buildings cast umber moon shadows into the white dust of the street. Not a living person inhabited his empire, save for himself, and if he didn't soon discover a means to appease his rumbling belly, he might not inhabit it for long.

He might make something of it. The thought of all that work made C.P. Raines faint at heart. He regarded toil as the plague upon creation, the curse on Adam. He would rather rot in a calaboose than scrounge some living out of a mine or a ranch or a store or a profession. His detestation of labor had shaped him into what he was: a man who would do anything to escape toil. If a good swindle lined his pockets, he saw it as a means to avoid labor. He would rather bilk old ladies than saw firewood for their stoves at two dollars a cord; rob orphanages or pillage alms-boxes in cathedrals than clerk or farm.

He was very good at avoiding work. Put Colonel Raines

into any crowd and he would soon be milking a living out of whatever lay at hand. He needed only to walk into any saloon or hotel or roadhouse to come up with drinks and a meal: a little wager here, a game of chance there, a shell game, some three-card monte, a kindly word to a barmaid, a random compliment whispered in the right ears, and soon enough he would have good distilled spirits before him, and the esteem of everyone, and refills raining down on him.

From Colorado to California, from Arizona to Montana, they all loved Colonel Raines. In some towns he was Major Raines, and once in a while Commodore Raines, and one time he was the Right Honorable Raines, and even the Most Reverend Archbishop Raines on occasion.

But he confessed to himself that the thought of reviving Pearlygates and profiting therefrom was daunting. He needed a few slaves to achieve what needed to be done. It had occurred to him more than once that he put more energy into avoiding honest toil than he would clerking or banking or locksmithing or farming.

High above town stood that noble house with the Doric pillars framing the veranda. It would be his haven this night. The only house in Pearlygates with style and grace, stood in the last light like Mount Vernon, or Monticello, or any plantation house of the mossy South, looking over the city below it, and guarding the old mines beside it. No light filled its windows, which were black eyes peering out upon Pearlygates.

It would be quite a hike to get there, but he resolved to climb the wayward road. If he could find no succor in the humble quarters of Pearlygates, then he would try the pantry of the rich.

Moonlight lit his way up the slope. He paused to rest midway; this majestic house was not easy to reach, but he was determined. If it suited, he would lay claim to it and spin out the little scheme that was blooming in his fertile mind.

He arrived at last at the shadowed portico of the noble house. A massive door barred the way. The windows were glassed. He turned and beheld below, in the bright moonlight, an entire pocket-size metropolis. All his! Colonel C.P. Raines, proprietor!

He tried the door. A metal latch clanked, and the door creaked open. A black cavern lay within, but he saw beyond the foyer a grand parlor, streaked with moonlight, mostly devoid of furnishings but otherwise in perfect condition.

He stepped inside, noting that this establishment exuded some sort of presence, almost as if ghosts had tenderly cared for it during the years of abandonment. He tiptoed into the parlor, wondering why he did not tread heavily, and there, through the tall windows, lay his city below, and the mines to one side. He felt like a king.

Colonel Raines, he said within himself, *you have just found salvation.*

At that very moment of salvation, he felt cold iron jab into his spine and nearly topple him.

"Hands high," said a soft voice. The command was accompanied by a new jab of cold metal, approximately the size of a muzzle.

Slowly, Colonel Raines complied.

"You're trespassing and up to no good."

"I assure you, sir, I am merely a pilgrim in distress, without means, desperate for shelter and succor. Let me turn around and introduce myself, and you shall see I am but a wayfarer in dire need."

"All right, but don't lower those hands."

"My arms, sir, strain under the weight. Let me lower them slowly."

"Keep 'em high or taste a belly full of lead."

Slowly Colonel Raines rotated and discovered that his captor was a short person holding a double-barreled shotgun and it was leveled straight at him. The moonlight confused him, for the face of this creature was a woman's but the clothes were those of a man.

"You're trespassing, and you'll get out and you won't come back."

Some intuition clutched Raines. "Madam—it's madam, isn't it?—I am naught but a starving gentleman in distress, and mean you not the slightest harm. Could you supply some victuals? If I could but refuel this ancient body, worn by care, then you would have done a great and Christian service to a wayfarer."

"Lord, how you carry on."

"I am at your mercy, madam."

She looked him over. "No, I don't think so. You're a bottomless pit. I could pour a sack of oats into you and not fill you up."

"You're right on that account, madam. I have insatiable appetites. You are most discerning."

"You sound like my husband."

"I take it for a compliment."

She laughed. "How little you know."

The twin bores of that double-barreled instrument of death never wavered.

"I fear, madam, that you'll pull a trigger and turn me into chopped meat."

"That would be tasty," she said.

"Let me introduce myself. I am Colonel C.P. Raines at your service."

"You were never at anyone's service, and now you can march out of town."

"Ah, an apple, a morsel, for the road?"

"Out."

"May I ask, madam, why you are here? All alone in an empty town?"

"I own it."

"Own it! Why, I thought it belonged to no one."

"It's all mine, stranger." She waved the weapon toward the door. "Vamoose."

"Madam, I have upon my pinky a most valuable ring, solid gold, my last asset, and this I will bestow upon you if you would only prepare a humble repast for me, and let me bed down in some remote corner, out of the weather."

She glanced at the ring. "Gold-plated nickel," she said. "Shiny top that mirrors playing cards."

Raines was delighted. "Ah, my little chickadee, we understand each other. Together, we shall restore our fortunes. But first, something for the bottomless pit."

She pointed the shotgun toward the rear of the mansion. He took it for a signal, and headed that way.

"You're going to cook it yourself," she said.

"But, madam, I've never cooked so much as an egg. You have culinary skills and can whip up something in a trice."

"Cook or starve," she said.

Raines sighed, weighing the onerous options. "I think I'd rather starve," he said.

Chapter 3

She motioned him to the cast-iron kitchen range, which still radiated a faint heat. She set down the shotgun and struck a lucifer, lit a coal oil lamp, and plucked up the weapon again.

She was a right pretty brown-haired woman, dressed in dungarees and a flannel shirt. He gawked. What was a woman so magnetic doing here in a ghost town?

"Just what I thought," she said, looking him over. "A sharper. Why else would you be here? There's a sack of rolled oats, there's a pail of water and a dipper, there's stove wood, and there's salt, and there's a cook pot."

Colonel Raines was aghast. "Madam, I could not manage to boil water; it is beyond me."

"Starve, then."

"I confess, my palate rebels at oat gruel, madam. My tongue requires delicate viands, prepared by blue-ribbon chefs or a woman's adroit and charming hand."

She waved her cannon toward the door. "Vamoose."

"Ah, I have bunions. My feet, madam, take pity on my feet. I've walked miles and miles."

"Out."

The awful truth was that Colonel C.P. Raines would

have to perform menial labor if he wished to fill his howling belly. He grimaced, set his silk hat on her battered kitchen table, found the fire door in the stove, opened it, beheld some glowing coals, plucked up some kindling from the adjacent wood box, threw the sticks in, attacked the firebox with a small bellows hanging nearby, saw a small flame catch and expand, closed the door, and stared at the sack of rolled oats.

"Madam, this is quite beyond me. The proportions . . ."

She waved a hand toward a door. "Out."

"Just some advice, please; the measurements."

"Take that tumbler and fill it full of oats. Add two dippers of water to the pot and a dash of salt, and stir."

Colonel Claudius P. Raines complied with great dignity. The things one was forced to go through just for a small repast. The things a gently bred man must suffer.

She settled into a kitchen chair, ladylike in spite of her trousers and boots, except for that shotgun, which never wavered.

"How shall I call you, madam?" he asked, once he had started the oats to heating.

"MayBelle."

"Is that it? MayBelle?"

"I had a last name but it was stolen by assorted males, so I don't own a last name anymore. What you don't know, you can't steal."

"And you're a widow?"

"No, divorced. My beloved husband offered me a generous settlement. This was all his, you see. He wished to share it with me as a token of . . . happier times.

"Bertram was his name. Bertram. Can you imagine I would fall for anyone named Bertram? I'd sooner fall for someone named Alphonse. 'MayBelle,' he said during our final meeting, 'I wish to give you everything I have as a parting gesture. Everything. The entire town and the three mines. Never let it be said that the bitterness of these last months interfered with my natural esteem for your person.'

"He didn't tell me that the mines were six weeks from being empty holes in the rock; that he had frantically run explorations in every direction and come up with nothing but quartz and granite, and the town was three months from being worthless, every building, every lot, every outhouse."

The news thrilled Claudius. "The titles? You have title to all of it?"

"Well, you see, my husband laid out the town site under the preemption laws and sold lots, the titles of which were to be granted once the government surveyed the area and the lots could be legally recorded. He also owned two of the mines outright and had a controlling interest in the third. Those were all patented federal mining claims, and quite valid.

"Well, before the government got around to surveying the country, the mines failed and the people vanished, and I possess the whole kit and caboodle. I own the mines outright, patented and all, and the town site, which can be patented as soon as the survey is done as long as I'm here to do it. Since all the lots have been abandoned, it's all mine." She eyed him narrowly. "And don't you think you can snooker me out of them. That's what the dear man left me, and I'll squeeze what I can out of it."

"The thought never filtered through my mind, madam."

"The water's boiling. Stir up those oats or eat glue."

C.P. Raines stirred mightily, his mind dizzy with joy. Here was bonanza at last.

"Madam, I can help you. If you will but hear me out . . ."

"That's what every vagrant passing through here says."

"Behold a man who is dressed fashionably and in costly attire. Does that make me a vagrant?"

"No, worse."

"Madam—may I call you MayBelle?"

"No, don't call me anything."

"Ah, then I will refrain." He drew himself up and smiled, until he exuded benevolence. "It so happens that I am a man of means, temporarily suffering reverses, but a man quite capable of turning Pearlygates into a bustling, rich, happy metropolis, the gateway to heaven where streets are paved with gold, the queen of Nevada, the lodestar of the West . . . if you'll just give a little leeway and let me proceed."

"Lord, Captain, you sound like my recent husband. Your oats are done. Eat and retreat."

"I trust you'll serve them up. I enjoy a woman's touch."

"There's a spoon, and there's the cook pot."

Raines scarcely knew whether to appease his rumbling belly or continue on his course. He chose to let the oat gruel cool, because there were more important matters afoot.

"I am several things, madam: a world-acclaimed mining engineer, University of Freiburg, quite capable of discovering rich lodes where other men have bored holes into country rock. I am a natural promoter, with the skills of a Barnum and the will of a Vanderbilt."

She laughed. The bores of the shotgun bobbed merrily.

"Give me rein and in six months you'll be a millionaire. You'll retire from these arid wastes to comfort and luxury and plenty. You'll be celebrated as one of the great pioneers of Nevada, of the West, of the world."

"You know, when that gruel cools down, it turns into India rubber."

"You're right, madam, and I stand advised."

He ate some of the stuff, masticating the oats slowly, and swallowing with some difficulty. She watched, a sardonic smile lifting the corners of her luscious lips. He could not remember a more dismaying meal. He had boiled the oats too much, until they thickened into paste, and that was his supper.

"Might you have a little whiskey to wash the oats down?" he asked. "A little red wine? A little beer?"

"Sir, eat and be gone, and count it a woman's charity. I'm tired."

He stopped his chewing. "I'd like to propose marriage."

"What?"

"Wedlock, you and I fondly living out our days in perpetual bliss."

She didn't laugh. He glimpsed the fleeting pain in her eyes, pain she didn't want him to see.

"Here you are, MayBelle, all alone, lonely, pining for better things, the embrace of a worthy gentleman, hanging on to the only wealth you have, which may or may not be worth two cents. Here you are, defending your gracious mansion against every passing vagrant, worried about getting sick when there is no one to help, worried about what some ruffian might do to a lone woman. Think about it. You're lonely. Here I am, your friend and protector, offering you the comfort you crave."

"Mister, eat your gruel or else I'll use it for wallpaper paste."

He did manage to down the stuff, and felt that blessed relief that is attained by a full stomach. He patted his mouth.

"Wash the dishes," she said.

"What? Me?"

"There's hot water in the stove reservoir. Right there. There's a scrubbing brush. On the shelf is some Fels Naphtha."

"But, madam, that surely is a womanly art. The sexes were ordained to perform their separate tasks, and I would not wish to interfere with the Divine Plan."

She waved the shotgun at him, and the black bores crept up toward his chest.

"Consider it done," he said, much put out with her. He had washed only a few dishes in his life. To be exact, two spoons, one tumbler, a cup, and a pot. The task had been so horrendous it had hastened him on his path to living by his wits.

He hastily drew water from the stove reservoir, added some soap, scrubbed the utensils, rinsed them in cold water, and set them to dry.

"Now fill the stove reservoir," she said. "Pump's outside."

He stared at her.

"You still want to marry me?" she asked. "If you do, you'd better start scrubbing dishes and fetching kindling and hauling water, and plan on it for as long as we're hitched."

Amazed at this, Colonel Raines assiduously polished pots and pans and silver, all the while eyeing her furtively. Did the madwoman really mean it? He found the oaken bucket, retreated into the starlit night, discovered the well in the yard, and began pumping the handle until a flow of water splashed into the pail. Then he carried the bucket into the kitchen, opened the top of the stove reservoir, poured in the water, and started to sit.

"It takes three buckets," she said.

He sighed. Never in his life had he suffered such indignity. But here was a plump pigeon, a choice squab, and if he needed to offend his own principles for the moment, he would do it.

Twice more did he thrust into the night and pump water. Then, when the stove reservoir brimmed, he set down the pail, planning to rest from his exertions.

"Try any of those cottages on the west side," she said.

"Madam? I don't follow."

"You're not staying here, that's for sure."

"But I'll just slip under a blanket somewhere and won't trouble you."

She aimed that cannon at his chest. "I will count to three, and then my finger will twitch. One . . ."

Colonel Claudius P. Raines hastened into the cold night.

Chapter 4

A tremor raked her body as she set down the shotgun. Someday she would have to shoot someone. But not this time.

MayBelle watched the man vanish into the night and knew he would be back. He was looking for easy pickings like the rest who had drifted through the silent town.

He reminded her of Bertram, which certainly was not a recommendation. Shifty, hard-eyed, affable when necessary, and without a care in the world for any other mortal.

She had known that about Bertram when she married him but it was a way out of the café life she had come to dread in San Francisco. She was a woman with a past, forming liaisons in the hurly-burly of San Francisco night society, the other woman in several men's lives.

Bertram had rescued her from all that, offered her marriage, made her the queen of a mining town in Nevada, and she had responded eagerly at first. Life in Pearlygates was pleasant, even if her husband was the sort who used everyone he met. If there was a thimbleful of the milk of human kindness in him he had poured it out before he met her. But that was all right: she was the queen of Pearlygates.

The marriage had been barren, which pleased them both. She wondered whether it had been his diseases or hers that had kept them childless. That was the price she paid for the life she had lived but she would have made a miserable mother and Bertram an even worse father.

She stood in the door, making certain that Raines really went down the slope and didn't linger about. She had dealt with other sorts, human vultures drifting into the empty town and finding a lone woman in it. Those were the dangerous ones and her only defense was three derringers kept in convenient places.

She understood the man perfectly. In the cafés of San Francisco she had met a hundred like him. Raines wanted to exploit the ghost town and needed her cooperation, having discovered that he could not simply move in, take over, and begin whatever mining fraud he had in mind. That was what lay behind the astonishing proposal. Marriage! After two minutes of talk, he was proposing marriage!

She smiled. That wasn't such a bad idea, and his proposal was closer to her whim than he had imagined.

Fortune hunters were a predictable lot. They all wanted an easy route to a bonanza. Their lust for wealth was equaled by their aversion for honest work. Raines didn't even want to boil some oats when he was starving. Bertram was one. He had hired a lawyer and surveyor to draw up a town site and then sat back and let the world come to him. The real bonanza was the town site, not the erratic mines.

She turned down the wick and watched the lamp blue out. She rarely burned coal oil; it was an expense. She plucked up the shotgun and headed up the stairs in the dark, the white-enameled banister showing her the way to her room.

Later, under the coverlet, she thought about Raines and hoped he would return in the morning. She needed him. He exuded a certain competence at what he was, unlike the other drifters. Maybe he and she could do some business. She wondered how he had managed to stumble into Pearlygates without so much as a saddle horse. Exile, of course. He no doubt had been booted out of Storyville. Odd how she could discern his history in swift flashes of intuition. She knew him before she had met him and now, she realized, she had found the one man who could revive Pearlygates long enough for her to cash in her divorce settlement.

She awakened early and stood at the window overlooking Pearlygates. The grim mountains to the east blocked the sun until midmorning when it crept around their southern flank, but the town lay somnolent and hollow below her, worthless buildings, empty streets, played-out mines, unless she could bring them all to life and get away from this lonely place with something in her pocket.

It was a fool dream and she had roundly ridiculed herself for nurturing it. Stubbornness was what kept her there, enduring the loneliest time of her life. Pure bullheaded stubbornness. Bertram had handed her a joker for a divorce settlement, a bustling town that emptied itself weeks after he pulled out.

"Here you are, MayBelle," he had said that day. "The entire town site, deed to the house, all my shares in three patented mines, claims to a dozen others. Never say I haven't had your best interests in mind."

He smiled treacherously, the very smile that had always melted her—and apparently a few hundred other women. She accepted the papers and signed the settlement. She had known, somehow, even as she held all that parchment in her hand, that she had been gulled.

Bertram wasn't even much of a lover.

Now she ached for company, for friends, for ordinary companionship, simple kindness.

She looked for Raines and didn't see him and knew

such a man rarely stirred before noon; sharpers and rogues were creatures of the night, not the fresh sweet mornings. If he had been lucky, he would have found one of the well-kept miners' cottages with cowhide bunks intact, and thus spent a comfortable night.

She utterly distrusted him.

She hastened through her toilet, choosing an especially handsome yellow silk dress instead of her usual dungarees, and even made herself some precious coffee to brighten her morning.

She thought of the long procession of drifters, half of them outlaws, a few of them vicious, who had poked around Pearlygates hunting for the table scraps. Misbegotten men.

But Colonel Raines, or captain or major, or whatever he was not, seemed different, as if he could summon rains, or tell flowers to bloom, or point a finger at rock and tell someone to dig right there and eighty feet in there would be a coal seam or a vein of bonanza silver, and the clouds and the flowers and the miners would believe and obey.

That was it. She was going to show Bertram that his little parting joke had come to naught. She intended to walk out of Pearlygates a lot richer than Bertram ever was or could be.

Sure enough, at about eleven, the colonel, rumpled and unshaven, toiled up the sharp grade to the mansion. She was ready for him. Her table was set with linen and Limoges, an opened bottle of cabernet stood ready along with graceful crystal wineglasses, and she would serve up some crepes.

She stood on the verandah waiting for him.

"Colonel, how good to see you. What a lovely day! I trust you slept well?"

He lifted his silk hat and surveyed her, not missing the silk dress. "Yes, madam, good day. I am astonished. You are an apparition. This must be a most auspicious occasion, for here you are, transformed into a divine presence. But I merely wish to perform some ablutions, if I may, and perhaps engage in a little business."

"I was expecting you," she said. "Right this way."

She led him to the downstairs lavatory and brought him a pitcher of hot water and a basin and a towel. She laid a silver-inlaid straight-edge before him, a shaving brush and mug, and didn't forget the talcum and witch hazel and a bar of good English soap.

He beamed at her before closing the door. "I knew it," he said.

She puzzled over that. Knew what? Had he read her mind? Well, she was going to astonish him in a few minutes.

He emerged looking and smelling much better. His black hair had been slicked back and his jowls scraped. His black broadcloth suit had been sponged, and his grubby hands scoured clean. He had the look about him of a worldly deacon. Again, he stared at her in astonishment, as she knew he would. She turned slightly, giving him her best profile. She had taken pains this bright spring morning and had pulled out of the chiffonier some clothing that she hadn't worn in two years. It smelled of lilac sachet.

"Madame, I do believe I have walked into Paradise," he said.

"Pearlygates," she replied. "My town, lock, stock, and barrel. Every lot and every mine and every claim. Do sit, have some coffee, and I'll be with you in a moment."

She retreated to the kitchen, pleased that things were going according to plan. In moments she dished up the hot crepes, added some California peaches, and carried the brunch into the stately dining room.

"Please eat; there's more in the kitchen."

"Ah . . . shall we say grace?"

"Only for your private benefit, Colonel. I am utterly lost in the vineyards of the Lord."

She ate daintily, watching him eye her furtively, and meeting each quick gaze with a bright smile. She filled and refilled his cup with steaming coffee, and when he had polished off the entire stack of crepes save for the one she ate, he sighed, gazed through stately windows upon the silent and solemn town, complimented her cooking, and then cleared his throat.

"I thought perhaps I could do you a small favor," he said.

"I accept."

"Ah, accept?"

"You proposed; I accept."

"Ah . . ." Colonel Raines was clearly nonplused.

"Marriage," she said.

"Gad! Marriage?"

"Right now. Till death us do part."

"Ah, madam, I don't even know your last name."

"Haggerty. The former Mrs. Bertram Haggerty. You proposed, didn't you, about ten minutes after we met? Or did I not hear it right?"

"Oh, I did, I did, your fair beauty inspiring rhapsodies of passion in my bosom. Now, ah, let's examine this." He lifted the cup to his lips and she saw a tremor in his hand.

"Claudius, my own, I own the whole place. I'll share it fifty-fifty."

"What's it worth?"

"Exactly what you make of it. Right now, about ten dollars. If you apply your . . . skills, maybe it'll go for a million."

"I see. You want me to make something of it. Ah . . ." He picked at a molar. "You've come to the right party. It's my calling and my particular talent to make something of nothing. But about this marriage, my dear MayBelle, ah, are there stipulations?"

"Yes, you get all of me and half the land and mines and buildings, and I get all of you and half of what you make of this place, but you'll have to bring in a Chinaman to do your laundry."

"Ah, have you any assets, liquid assets? One needs a little seed money, you see."

"Bertram's wine cellar. It's kept me going."

"Wine cellar?"

"In the cliff behind the house. In a played-out glory hole he owned. He abandoned that. He had two hundred bottles of vintage French wine in there, Bordeaux, Beaujolais, Rhine wines. I've traded them for the things I need, but there still are a hundred."

"Well, my little partridge, where can we tie the knot?"

"Who needs a preacher? You just move in, Claudius, and we'll sign a little contract, common law marriage, and then . . ." She smiled. "We'll just do what married people do."

The scoundrel stared at her, hooked like a fat trout.

Chapter 5

Colonel C.P. Raines devoted an appropriate amount of the morning to cooing and clucking, but MayBelle seemed slightly bored, and he surmised that a hundred suitors had cooed and clucked ahead of him.

"Now, my little turtledove, we must begin our bold enterprise," he said, rising from the horsehair settee where he and the grass widow had sealed their bliss. "And the first step is to examine your bank."

"Bank?"

"The wines, the wines."

She trilled. "Bank indeed. I'm selling five bottles a week, but now that you're here we'll need to sell more."

"How is this arranged, my little canary?"

"I have a buyer in Storyville, and once a month I send a few bottles to him. I know some ranch hands who always like to do my errands when they ride through." She smiled wryly. "Now that we're attached they might be less inclined to be gallant."

"Ah, the price for the wines. What does this buyer pay?"

"It's Mr. Mobridge, the harness and tack merchant.

He pays six bits a bottle and resells it to the hotels and saloons. It's his new sideline."

"Six bits? French wine? Ah, perhaps that's a bit low, eh?"

"The other option is to drink it ourselves, Colonel, and starve to death."

"And when this runs out, what?"

"I don't know. That's for you to figure out. Maybe you could sell me instead of wine. Do you suppose that's the road to bliss?"

"Ah, if we could only roll back the clock twenty years we would both prosper, my little tootsie."

"You know how to needle a lady."

"Forgive me. Both wines and women are better aged a little."

"You're getting into big trouble, Colonel."

"I am examining assets. We are in this together. Let us examine the other side of the ledger. What are your expenses?"

"Food for me and hay for my nag, a few odds and ends, and now food for you."

"MayBelle, let's inspect your wine cellar and find out how much time we have."

"Oh, Colonel, we've very little time."

She smoothed her yellow silk dress, primped her hair, and headed for the kitchen where a brass key lay hidden in a cupboard. Then she led him out the back door of the manse and angled along a path toward the vaulting cliff thirty yards distant. There, just north of the house, was a tunnel drilled into the orange-colored stratum of rock that overlooked much of Pearlygates. An iron door on thick hinges barred entry. She slid her key into a small hole, twisted, and pushed. The door squeaked open and a rush of cold air boiled out.

Raines peered into the gloom. The shaft didn't go far, perhaps forty feet, and ended in a blank wall. Lining both sides were racks, mostly empty. But along one side were bottles, tipped cork down in orderly rows. Claudius and MayBelle pushed toward the rear of the old mining tunnel and examined the liquid assets. There weren't very many left. Swiftly, Raines counted the bottles: sixty-six, not a hundred. Not ten weeks of succor. How could he start a gold rush in ten weeks?

He lifted the chilled bottles and examined the labels and condition of the wines. These included fine Bordeaux, including such Medoc wines as Château Lafitte, Château Latour; some sauternes including Château D'Yquem, and Burgundies such as Côte D'Or and Close Vougeot. Others came from the Rhone Valley and the Loire Valley.

"My little hummingbird, these are excellent houses and fine vintages. Perhaps we can get more for them."

"In northern Nevada?"

"I'd almost prefer to drink it than sell it."

"Colonel, the clock is ticking."

Raines sighed. The clock was ticking fast. "This is it? We starve when these are gone?"

"Unless you strike gold," she said.

"I'll just pluck a bottle for our nuptial night," he said, his fingers clamping on some Vougeot.

She smiled and patted her hair and took his hand as they walked out of the tunnel.

"What was this? An abandoned glory hole?"

"This was Bertram's own little tunnel," she said. "He had some men blast this until it was plain there was nothing but red rock. All the gold, you see, was over there, around the mines across the gulch. He knew nothing about minerals. He used to laugh about it. This was his foray into hard-rock mining."

She pointed to the abandoned mines, which lay across a gulch that bisected Pearlygates. The same stratum ran along the side of the mountain over there, but perhaps a hundred feet lower than here. The gulch carried a creek that watered the town, but the gulch itself had been formed from a giant fault rather than erosion, and the orange stratum was higher here on the bench where the mansion stood. No wonder Haggerty chose this place to build his manse; it overlooked not only the town, but the mines off to the south. Everything below him was his.

Raines spotted workings all over the slope above and below the gold-bearing iron-stained rock, each hole punched into the slope, and each with a pile of rubble below its mouth. There had been a lot of determined and costly exploration of the whole area. It would be very hard to crank up a rush to such an exhausted, mined, and explored area that people had fled only after they had run out of options.

Raines carried the bottle into the kitchen and watched the sunlight filter through the ruby wine within. He was eager to uncork it, and uncork her, but restrained himself. There was much to do.

"The papers, my little chickadee."

"You mean the mine patents and things?"

"All of them, and the town site papers."

These she had stuffed into her husband's rolltop desk in the spacious parlor. She extracted them from various cubbyholes and spread them over the mahogany dining table.

"I'm looking for the letter transferring them to you in the divorce settlement," he said.

She squeezed the colonel's hand, and vanished. He heard her rummaging upstairs and when she returned she bore an envelope.

He pulled a lengthy document from it, and discovered a straightforward assignment of title to MayBelle, including the ownership of the mines, ownership to four mining claims located just behind the mansion, none of them proven up, the town site papers, water rights, the mansion and its furnishings, and stock in an ore milling works that had never been built.

The only thing of value was MayBelle's remaining furniture. But by the time it was shipped by ox-team to Storyville and sold, there wouldn't be much left.

He donned his wire-rimmed spectacles and studied the papers. The town lots reverted to the town site company if they were abandoned before they were paid off. Except for a few lots purchased outright, MayBelle owned Pearlygates: three dead mines, twenty-odd unproven mining claims, three hundred structures, a water works, and four hundred seventy-nine unsold and vacant commercial and residential lots. Worth a few dimes.

"Madam, your former husband was a cad and a bounder," he said.

"That's what you get in anyone named Bertram," she said. "I hoped he would be the exception that proved the rule."

"I am named after a Roman emperor," he said. "Tiberius Claudius Drusus Nero Germanicus. He executed his third wife, which recommends him to posterity."

"Have you been married?"

"Never. But we shall know bliss: a cottage filled with laughter, where lilacs and hollyhocks grow, and a picket fence around the yard."

"Is that what you want from life, Claudius, dear?"

"No. I'd settle for a little brick pile on Nob Hill with fifty servants, a harem, and a yacht or two."

"You're a man after my own heart, snookums."

"We really have about two weeks, not ten weeks. I'll need some expense money, and that means converting more of your assets."

"Expenses?"

"You can't start a gold rush from nothing. There must be the lure, the bait, the enticement, the whisper, the gossip, the thing that excites greed. A little bright and shiny ore that assays, say, nine hundred dollars to the ton."

"We have about fifty dollars between us, Claudius, my love."

"It's a small difficulty, yes."

She sighed, and ran a veined hand up and down his arm.

He ignored her, rose, walked to the verandah, and studied the sunbaked silent town below him. It shimmered in the morning air. Not two years before, it had held two or three thousand mortals, along with all their hopes and dreams. What brought them? Bonanza. Some were prospectors, hacking at rock; others miners, better paid than most laborers. Others were the sleeve-garter men, calculating how to get the edge. Brokers, merchants, teamsters, children, bawds, saloon men, whiskey drummers. Make money, get out. First sign of collapse, head for greener pastures and leave the corpse of a city behind without even turning back for one last look as they rode away.

MayBelle and he needed a three-month boom to sell a hundred lots and vamoose.

He turned to her. "You have a nag, but do you also have a wagon?"

"Not a wagon, a buggy. Bertram's buggy."

He headed toward a carriage barn nestled against the ochre cliff. There indeed was a shining black buggy with a folding hood, and in a stall a fine-looking dray horse munching hay from a manger.

"Time's a-wasting, MayBelle. Kindly carry all those bottles to the manse—your kitchen will do—and harness the horse."

"Me?"

"I need to think."

"What are we going to do with the wine?"

"Drink it. Ah, the touch of vintage grape upon the tongue . . ."

"Drink it!"

"Why sell such treasures?"

"But that's the bank."

"No, that little tunnel is the bank. You just haul those bottles out while I look at a few of your papers. And be ready to travel in half an hour."

"Travel? Where are we going?"

"To start a gold rush, madam."

"I think I'm going to like you, Colonel, in spite of everything."

Chapter 6

The road to the Amalgamated Climax Gold Company was a tad rougher than the colonel preferred, but he negotiated the two-rut trail up the arid canyon slowly, sparing the horse.

Beside him sat MayBelle, dressed in her yellow silk dress again, smashing and wildly seductive. Claudius supposed he didn't look half bad himself, freshly shaven and well scrubbed.

In a leather portfolio were certain of MayBelle's papers. They would come in handy. The Alagamated Climax Mine was eleven mountainous miles from Pearlygates, but was actually supplied from Storyville. Year after year, it produced several hundred thousand dollars of gold and was considered one of the prize mining properties in Nevada. A hard-nosed ham-fisted Irishman named Flannagan managed it for eastern owners, and received regular bonuses for keeping costs down and production high. Raines knew there was no tougher, more skeptical, or more savvy man in the mining business.

The road topped suddenly on an arid alpine flat, and there stood a hoist works and several ramshackle tin-roofed buildings. Smoke billowed from a stack beyond the hoist works. Mule-drawn ore cars collected at a tailings dump. A great thunder seemed to rise from underground.

Raines steered toward the one building that obviously was an office of sorts, and brought the buggy to a halt at its door. He smiled at MayBelle, helped her down, and dusted her off. He patted the alkaline dust from his black broadcloth suit and then escorted her into the offices.

These were scarcely offices at all, just grimy log rooms jammed with cabinets and tables.

"Yes?" said a burly gent in a mining jumper and felt hat.

"Mr. Flannagan, please. Colonel and Mrs. Raines here."

"I'm Flannagan. Is it important? I'm just heading down to look at a . . . some trouble. A hanging slab of rock."

"Why, sir, as important as can be."

"Come back later."

"We've come a long way, sir, on business."

The manager looked annoyed. "All right. I'll send Bowman down to look at the slab. Be quick, please."

"I'm C.P. Raines, Bryn Mawr, Pennsylvania, sir. This is my bride, MayBelle. We have a little business to lay before you."

"First time in the West?" Flannagan asked.

"It is indeed, sir. I've made a speculative purchase and have come to look over my property. We now own, sir, the entire district of Pearlygates, the mines, the claims, and the town site."

"Sorry you got into that, Mr. Raines. It's been dug over every which way. I went myself and found not the slightest prospect left. If that's what this is about—then I'll spare you the refusal you'll get from me by bidding you good day."

"Ah, of course, quite right, Mr. Flannagan. But my proposition would earn your company some profit regardless. I'm looking for a contract mining crew."

"On speculation, I suppose."

"No, sir. Cash payment for each ten feet of exploratory tunnel you complete. I want to drive a certain horizontal tunnel two hundred seventy feet."

Flannagan looked ready to bolt. "Waste of your money, sir. That district . . . well, the best mining men in the West have all had their crack at it. You won't even find any low-grade worth hoisting."

"Professor Hodgson thinks otherwise, sir."

"Who?"

"Kenwood Q. Hodgson, geologist. You're familiar with the district, right? Then you know that the gulch dividing the town is really a fault, and the stratum on the north side is the same as the south side but a hundred-some feet higher. That north-side stratum has never been explored, sir. The recent owner drove a short tunnel back forty feet or so, but Dr. Hodgson says the ore, if there is any, would be two hundred back. No one else has explored that section, because the owner had claims on all of it. But now I own it. And my man Hodgson tells me it's worth the gamble."

"Who did you say you are?"

"Colonel C.P. Raines, Bryn Mawr, Pennsylvania. I'm a babe in the woods here, sir. My background is investments and railroads and Latin American ventures. I've started up a banana company, a mahogany company, and a pineapple venture. Don't know much about this. But I would treasure your instruction."

"And you want us to drive your tunnel. No, sir. I don't know you."

"You have the means?" Raines asked.

"Certainly. Means and men."

"What's the obstacle, then?"

"I don't know you; that's the main one. And if we did drive that tunnel it would be for cash in advance."

"Cash, certainly, sir."

"Ten feet for a thousand dollars, payment in our hands before we drill."

"Ah, sixty a foot's all I'm willing to pay."

Flannagan had the look about him of a man who would like to get rid of his visitors. "It'll be a hundred a foot, sir."

"I'm forced to consider other options, Mr. Flannagan."

"Go right ahead. This is scarcely business I want."

"Ninety, then."

"If there's rail laid, if the drift's timbered, if the grade is more or less horizontal, and a there's a handy dump and ore cars, maybe ninety."

"What about schedules? We're in a hurry, Mr. Flannagan."

"Everyone in the mining business is in a hurry. Who knows what we'll run into? Do you know how long it takes to shore up an unstable stretch? What a hung charge does to a schedule? What happens when we hit water? Especially hot water? Or deadly gases?"

"I have an inkling. Suppose, sir, we simply agree that you will bore with all deliberate speed, letting nothing keep you from the task."

Flannagan stared. "Colonel Raines, you're a newcomer and you're about to throw away a lot of money down a rat hole. If I take you on, it will be at a profit for Amalgamated and without the slightest prospect that you will strike ore. My advice is, don't. Or put your money into an existing, paying mine with proven reserves. This is no business for the novice. Now, if you'll excuse me, I really must get down there. Trouble at the third level, and I have some decisions to make."

"Mr. Flannagan, send a face crew tomorrow. Start right in. Use the barracks at the old mines. I'll post a performance bond at McNaughton Trust in Philadelphia for whatever you require."

"A bond won't do, not at first. Cash. Nine hundred in gold or greenbacks."

"That is no problem, Mr. Flannagan. I'll make the arrangements. Could you suggest the best place?"

"Miner's and Stockman's Bank in Storyville. Now, if you'll excuse me . . ."

Flannagan pumped the colonel's hand and fled, obviously glad to escape.

MayBelle sighed.

"Progress, my little parakeet," the colonel said.

There was no one else in the building save for a clerk with a green eyeshade poring over ledgers.

"Did you bring that nugget?" the colonel asked.

"What nugget?"

The colonel smiled. "The one, my dear, we found beside the gopher hole."

"Oh, that one! Bigger than any I've ever seen, that's for sure. All that gold!"

The clerk was pretending not to listen.

"I thought to leave it with Mr. Flannagan. You know how it is. Bona fides always help."

"I wish I had brought it. You were in such a hurry!"

"Well, never fear. I'll do a little banking and we'll have our face crew. My only thought is that maybe we should have two crews, night shift too. You know, there's something about this gold business that drives a man. It's worse than the pineapple business. Do you have any idea what can be made from pineapples?"

"A very good salad, Colonel."

Raines wandered over to the clerk, who peered upward and smiled.

"My good man, you tell Mr. Flannagan that Colonel and Mrs. Raines will be back shortly with the necessary surety."

"Oh, I'll tell him, I surely will, the moment he hangs his jumper in the closet, sir."

"Good. It's an easy job and some quick contract money for Amalgamated Climax."

"What's the name of your company, sir?"

"Why, we have none. We're new at the game. We've a ghost town and some dead mines and a sheaf of unproven claims, and we're just having a little fun out here in the Wild West. The money's in mahogany and bananas, you know. And I might try kiwi fruit."

"I didn't know. I'll pass it along, sir."

"Come along, MayBelle, we've some banking to do." He shepherded his bride toward the door.

"Colonel, sir," said the clerk. "I think I know of a crew that would work for less than ninety dollars a foot."

"You do? My word, what have you in mind?"

"Some fellas I know would work on shares. You hit ore, they got something."

Raines frowned. "Sir, I'm so new at this business I scarcely know whether that's a bargain or not. I'm a little leery of just hiring on fellows for some percentage. How do I know what sort they are, eh? I could be bamboozled."

"Good hard-rock miners, Colonel. They can advance your face three feet a day."

"Well, I'll think on it. I've moved into that old mansion there for a few days just to look around. I'm always willing to dicker. You just send some fellows along and let me size them up, and we'll see. I like the idea of having Amalgamated do the bore, but your company does charge plenty."

The clerk in the green eyeshade smiled. "I'm Gilbert N. Sullivan," he said. "At your service."

"Indeed you are, sir."

"You'll be hearing from me."

Colonel Raines nodded and led his bride to the buggy.

"Better than I'd hoped," the colonel said to MayBelle.

Chapter 7

At one o'clock the next afternoon, Colonel C.P. Raines's honeymoon came to an abrupt anticlimax. A churlish lot of miners arrived in Pearlygates, along with a noisy wagon. Their presence in the silent ghost town seemed almost a sacrilege.

But there they were. Raines stuffed his nightshirt into his trousers and met the miners at the veranda door.

"You Colonel Raines?" asked a bald one.

The colonel nodded.

"Gil Sullivan, he sent us. You are needing a face crew?"

"Ah, my fine fellows, you have come to the right door. Indeed, your fortunes shine this hour. I will join you in just a tad, but meanwhile, hie you around the manse to the cliff behind, and examine if you will, the drift bored into the earth."

The burly crew headed for the ochre rock while Raines hastened to his boudoir and donned his black broadcloth suit.

"Claudius, love, you are my salvation," said MayBelle, staring up at him from under the bedclothes.

"Is that what you call it?" he said.

He pulled his shirt over his head, climbed into his well-blacked shoes, and brushed his black locks.

"I'll set them to digging, my little robin," he said. "And that will attract others. And soon we'll be selling lots."

She sighed. "It was so private here."

"It's starting, MayBelle. We've launched our own little gold rush."

He pecked her fevered cheek and headed down the long curved stairs, across the foyer, and into the kitchen. From there he could see the crew collected around the head, puzzling at the iron door and shelves within.

"Ah, gentlemen, welcome," he said. "I am Raines, and I'm looking for a face crew to advance this drift."

"What's the iron door for?" asked one.

"This, sir, was the previous owner's private wine cellar. Those shelves were laden with the finest French wines money could buy. Had the fellow not been such a novice at this complex business, he would have known that this bore, which he took only forty feet in, points straight at the lode."

"How do you know that?"

"I've had it examined. The world-renowned geologist, Kenwood Q. Hodgson, spent two weeks tramping this exhausted district at my request, and noted an odd thing: this is the very stratum that enriched the mines across the gulch but it is a hundred twenty feet higher here than on the other side. We'll drive the drift a hundred and fifty feet farther, which is where the ore body should be, according to Dr. Hodgson."

"That's what you want? A hundred fifty? That's a month's work for one shift; ten or twelve days for two shifts."

"Yes, all of that. You're contract men, right? Pay by the foot?"

The bald one stepped forward. "Milt Hoag," he said, offering a calloused paw. The colonel shook it. "I don't know about this: you start pulling rock out of here and you'll have a tailings pile. We start blasting in there and that house of yours, it's going to dance on its foundation, and you can kiss the windows good-bye. We get some rail in and muck out rock and dump it here, it's going to sound like ten railroad trains at once. This fancy house . . . it's done for. You sure you want this?"

"My friends, this little woodpile here is of no consequence. What matters is gold. We'll get out. Use it for an office or a dormitory; store your blasting powders in the kitchen. Sleep in the bedrooms. Knock it down when it's in the way."

Hoag stared. "That's some house to be knocking down."

"Mr. Hoag, it's no house at all. A man in my shoes who has certain pineapple, banana, kiwi fruit, and mahogany plantations would scarcely call this a house. My managers have better."

Hoag scratched his belly. "Well, let's see what's here," he said. He and the colonel and the crew penetrated the cool tunnel, past empty racks, deep into solid, dull ochre rock, showing not the slightest mineralization except maybe the iron oxide that tinted it. They stared at the face, an abrupt wall that seemed to hide nothing but more of the same.

"That's as far as the owner went," Raines said.

"No timbers, no rails," Hoag said. "Cost you plenty just to put in some timber sets and run some rails. We could wheelbarrow the rock out, but that would be slow."

"Well, be about it. Money's no obstacle."

"Yeah, well, that's the next question. How we going to do this?"

"How do you want to do it? Amalgamated Climax wanted a hundred dollars a foot, and I refused. I can contract it for sixty a foot. Beyond that, I'm open to offers."

"You own those dead mines?" Hoag asked.

"Every last one."

"Salvage would cut costs. Rails, ore cars."

"You're welcome to all of it."

"We brought fuse, powder, drills, and our gear. You mind if we move into some of these cabins?"

"For the moment, go ahead. I own the town site including these abandoned buildings. When the time comes I'll sell you houses dirt cheap, a special bonus for your exploratory work."

"Yeah, well, what are you offering?"

"I can shell out sixty a foot, six hundred every ten feet, payable in ten-foot increments, or you can speculate if you wish. . . ." Colonel Raines let the idea slide gently into their skulls. "Of course, it could be a bust. Professor Hodgson might be wrong. Might be nothing here but red rock. Then you'd lose. Some men don't want to take chances, you know. Cash on the barrelhead. Others take a few chances and often reap a reward for it."

"A percentage of anything in there?" Hoag asked.

"Percentages are messy. They lead to conflict and that leads to lawyers and pretty soon the legal profession is the sole inheritor of the bonanza. Let's just say, if you strike ore, you take away the first ten thousand from the smelter, and then it's all mine."

Hoag squinted. "Why so much? You can hire face crews for sixty a foot."

"Incentive, sir. A man working for a pot of gold is a demon with the sledgehammer and drill."

Hoag grinned. "You mind if we talk this over private?"

"Go right ahead," the colonel said.

The miners retreated into the bore, while the colonel gazed upon the silent sunbaked city. Then, at last, they emerged.

"We're not quite gamblers," Hoag said. "That's a lot

of work for maybe nothing. We'd like something for expenses, anyway. A thousand dollars right now, some surety that we walk out of here with something."

"Why, you're prudent and intelligent men and I admire that. I myself would not want to risk a month's labor on what could be nothing at all. . . ." He gazed at those blank faces, those men with hardened muscles, big boots, ragged clothes, and an assessing gaze, directed at him. "You know," he said, "I can do better than a thousand. I will give you each five bottles of some of the best wines in the world, wines extracted only yesterday from safe storage in the bosom of the earth, right in there; wines so rare and desired they command anything a man might ask for them. Do you doubt? Ah, here's the heart of it. You delegate one of your men to carry your thirty bottles to Storyville and make the rounds of the better saloons and restaurants, and see! I'll entrust this precious cargo to you and not require a lick of work until you're entirely satisfied."

They looked skeptical.

"Come, come," he said, and led them into the kitchen where the bottles stood in disarray.

"Look at this! Look at this!"

He thrust bottles into calloused hands. "Take your pick; take the ones you think will fetch the most, eh? Be connoisseurs, examine the vintage, look at those labels, eh?"

"We should get cash," said a slope-shouldered one.

"Cash you can have, as swiftly as I can get it here. That takes a few days, of course. But I'll sweeten the deal. Take six bottles apiece, thirty-six, and send one of your own to Storyville with them, find out what they're worth, and then make your decision, eh?"

They never formally acquiesced. Instead, each of them began studying labels, most of them choosing the oldest vintages, and soon they had their bottles.

"How we going to get them there?" asked a miner.

"Aw, hell, let's knock out ten feet and then we'll decide."

"My buggy," said the colonel. "Right in the carriage barn, and a good nag too. You send someone to Storyville and sell the wines, and maybe hire some more for your face crews, speed everything up, eh?"

"You'd lend us the buggy?"

"Least I can do. And while you're in town, let people know you're going after a bonanza."

"Joe," said Hoag, "you're elected. Let's pack these bottles nice and tight and off you go. The rest of us, we'll salvage what we need from them mines over there and maybe lay some rail and put up some timber sets."

That settled it. Hoag was the straw boss and his word seemed to settle issues.

Swiftly they harnessed the dray horse to the buggy, loaded the wines, and sent Joe on his long journey. They watched Joe drive the ebony buggy down the grade, through the town, the clop of the hooves echoing hollowly, and then over a hill and out of sight.

"I guess we'll drop our gear in the houses down below and start to work," Hoag said.

The colonel gave Hoag a hearty handshake and a clap on the shoulder. "Remember, I'm here to help. You need anything, just summon Colonel Raines. That's the word. Don't hesitate. Mrs. Raines and I will be right here."

He watched the miners hop aboard their wagon and ride it down into town. They stopped in a street lined with gingerbreaded cottages and began probing them.

Colonel Raines felt an odd hollowness. He always did at the very moment of his triumph. It was as if his life wasn't complete or right, and he had no way to improve it. He hated the sadness that engulfed him just when he should be elated.

He found his bride sitting in the parlor, awaiting him.

"Buttercup," he said, "we're rich."

Chapter 8

An enormous whump awakened Colonel Raines. The house vibrated. The chandelier swung. He bolted upright in the four-poster so he could see out the window. A whirling cloud of dust and debris swept by.

"What?" asked MayBelle, sleepily.

"A blast," Raines replied. "They've fired a shot. That was probably good for three feet."

MayBelle tugged him down and kissed him.

"Buttercup, we've got to get up. Put on your dungarees."

"Why?"

"The land office."

She yawned.

Yesterday, Colonel Raines had explored Pearlygates and found what he was looking for. The offices of the Pearlygates Town Lot Company were intact, save for a broken windowpane, but coated with dust. Within, the place was empty save for a naked counter. He was delighted. With a little scrubbing and brooming, he could be in business.

"Up, up, up," he said, prodding her. "The rush will start today, and we've got to be ready."

She yawned.

An hour later, MayBelle was hard at work mopping and dusting and cleaning windows and brooming while Raines busily decided where chairs and furniture gotten from the manse would go.

She glared at him. "You could help, you know."

"Madam, I am engaged in exhaustive mental labor. There is nothing more crucial to this enterprise than a proper land office. It must be substantially furnished, inviting, and sublime."

She leaned on her broom and grunted. MayBelle was not averse to hard work so she tackled the old office with vigor, sweeping pack rat leavings, dust, and debris out upon Nevada Street, the town's main thoroughfare.

Raines paced, stared, and muttered to himself.

"Now, MayBelle, when you're done with that bring the papers. The ledgers, the plat maps, the receipt forms, the sales forms for the lots, and don't forget the ink bottle and a pen."

She shot a hard glare in his direction but he pretended to be oblivious.

"You could carry them yourself," she said.

"I am engaged in important considerations."

"Are we having our first tiff?"

"Madam, you are my own buttercup and my tasty lollypop, and if there is the slightest abrasion I beg your forgiveness."

She laughed and patted him on the hand.

The previous evening, Joe the miner had returned from Storyville. The rare wines had gone for only thirty-seven dollars, purchased by the Hotel Peckingham.

"You told us them Frenchy wines were worth a fortune," Hoag said.

"My dear sir, they are, anywhere but here in wild Nevada where most miners wouldn't know lager from champagne. At any rate you've got cash in your britches now. Come, come, let's see you advance the bore. . . .

Ah, did your man Joe happen to mention where he went in Storyville?"

"Oh, sure, he spent the night touring the saloons."

That was all Colonel Raines needed to know. The rush was on.

By noon MayBelle had put a gloss on the land office and carted the ledgers and papers to its shelves while Claudius studied the forms, tested the nib pens, and made sure the ink bottles were available on the counter. By midafternoon, Maybelle had dragged two chairs from the manse down to Nevada Street.

"Now, then, my little hoot owl, we're open for business," the colonel said.

They settled patiently in the chairs, listening to the roar from the hillside above. In the space of two days, Hoag's crew had run rail into the bore, erected some timber sets at five-foot intervals, and dragged an ore car from a dead mine to the new works.

While all this was going on, two drillers were steadily jacking holes deep into the face. That morning they detonated the first charge, which rolled red dust and rock out of the tunnel and shattered three windows in the manse. Now the muckers were shoveling ore into the one-ton ore car and making a racket that could be heard all over Pearlygates.

Which suited Colonel Raines just fine. Noise was what sold lots. Let a pilgrim arrive in Pearlygates and hear the rattle of rock, the screech of ore cars on rails, the thud of blasting, the hammering of the drill bits, and that pilgrim was sold before Raines even opened his mouth.

MayBelle returned with a picnic hamper full of lunch.

"Some honeymoon," she said, slapping it down on the counter. "Red dust and sweat."

"Why, my little prairie hen, you've prepared a sumptuous repast to delight the soul and body of your beloved."

She shot him a surly glance.

He burrowed into the picnic hamper, finding fresh bananas from Storyville and a sandwich wrought from tinned ham and Storyville bread.

"You have outdone yourself, my canary."

"Where's the customers?" she asked.

"It's a tad early."

"Then why the hurry to put the land office in shape?"

"Because when the rush comes, MayBelle, it will roll like a tide through Pearlygates. And we must be ready. Be of good cheer. We might be on our way to the orange groves of California in a week or two. And with a satchel full of greenbacks to lighten the heart and lift the spirits."

She eyed him darkly. "We'll see," she said.

All that day they waited but no one showed up. The road into Pearlygates was as empty as ever.

The next morning they were awakened by another whump, which took four more windows out of the mansion and boiled red dust through the building.

"How am I supposed to get my beauty sleep?" MayBelle asked.

"Fear not. Soon you will have enough money in your satchel to stay beautiful forever. You will even be able to purchase a makeover from your undertaker."

She elbowed him and got up.

An awful rattle filled the air as the muckers unloaded an ore car just outside the kitchen window.

"How long can we last?" she asked, wheezing in red dust.

"We can't move. Not yet. The world has to realize that we are the king and queen of Pearlygates, and that requires staying here until a blast flattens our parlor."

She shook red dust from her dainty negligee and disappeared into her dressing room.

Claudius shook the dust out of his black broadcloth suit, noted that his boiled white shirt was turning pink, and thought perhaps he should look for another house and turn this over to the miners. But not yet, not yet. Tomorrow, maybe, after the rush clogged the land office with eager gold-seekers.

But that day no one showed up except a couple of ranch hands driving a spring wagon, en route to Storyville for supplies, curious about the uproar in the ghost town.

"Just a little exploration," Colonel Raines told them. "I've had a mining geologist locate some new prospects. Unfortunately, they're all within a few hundred feet of our home."

"Found anything yet?" asked a kid.

"Oh, nothing spectacular, my boy. A little color, just half an inch wide, but it's looking better every time we blow another three feet of rock to kingdom come."

"Could I see it?"

"Sir, the whole thing is a proprietary secret. No, of course not. I'm not going to show the world a thing."

"I'd sure like to see the ore."

"Never. And you can tell the world they won't see a thing, and that we're posting armed guards to keep trespassers out."

"Yeah?"

"From now on, young fellow, the Wine Cellar Mine is closed to the public. And don't try to get any information from my crew. They are loyal, high-paid men dedicated to my company."

The kid shrugged. "I was just asking."

"Well, secrecy is vital to business. When we're ready to make an announcement we will, and we'll invite the press and half the politicians in Nevada and show them the quartz. We'll hand the first gold bar to the governor for a paperweight. We'll throw a champagne party and invite the whole county. Meanwhile, there is absolutely nothing for you to see, and nothing for you to tell anyone in Storyville."

"Sure. I wouldn't know gold ore from cow manure. You need anything in town?"

"Not a thing. I'm afraid that if I gave you a draft on my bank the whole world would soon know who's doing the exploration here. But you're most kind to offer. I've been sending my manservant along to make purchases privately for us, and that's all we need for now."

The kid took one last look at the red dust rising from the bench behind the manse, shrugged, waved, and rolled out.

The days repeated themselves, one by one, and still no one came. Colonel Raines fretted. Had he not baited the mousetrap? Started rumors? Hinted at bonanzas? Where were the speculators? Wasn't there one greedy soul in Nevada?

He knew what the trouble was: Pearlygates had been mined and probed to a fare-thee-well, and everyone knew it. No one had found more ore. No one expected any more to be found. And no one came, even to snoop around, ask guarded questions, bribe the face crew for information. No one.

The mansion was a shambles. Most of the windows had surrendered to their fate. Red dust lay thick over the noble furnishings. MayBelle had taken to glaring at her swain and muttering things. She was stained red. Their only solace was to uncork a bottle of rare wine each evening to wash away the grit on their teeth.

The miners blew ten feet out of the tunnel and then another twenty feet, without discovering much change in the ochre rock.

Then the straw boss, Hoag, showed up at the door.

"The boys are quitting," he said. "There's nothing in there, and the promise of splitting ten grand looks more and more like a joke."

"But we have an agreement!"

Hoag shrugged. "I can't keep men working for no pay. We'll be pulling out tomorrow."

"All of you?"

"Me, I'd stay on for the full one hundred fifty to get my hands on good ore. I think your geologist is right. There's ore in there. But that don't cut ice with the rest . . . unless you want to start paying, day rate, sixty a foot, cash at the end of each shift."

"Yes, yes, perfectly natural, perfectly natural," Raines said. "I'm sure I'd want cash too, but of course if it's cash, then you don't share in that moment of victory. . . ."

"Sorry," Hoag said, and wiped red dust from his face.

Chapter 9

A desolate silence lowered over Pearlygates. The sun rose and set upon a barren town, so distant from its brief life that it did not even harbor memories. Colonel Raines would have welcomed a ghost or two for company but the best he could manage was a pack rat and a rattlesnake.

Raines had not neglected to proselytize every passing ranch hand and teamster with rumors of a new gold strike in Pearlygates. Everyone on the road had seen the furious activity at the new mine. Word had spread through every saloon in Storyville. But no rush had materialized. Where were the miners, the throng at the land office, the merchants eyeing abandoned stores along Nevada Street, the clamorous fortune seekers bidding up the price of all those claims in the colonel's folder?

MayBelle painfully cleaned red dust out of the manse, tacked pasteboard over the broken windows, dusted and scrubbed and restored some semblance of order. But the old mansion would never be the same: now a heap of gritty tailings filled the rear yard almost to the kitchen door and she had to step over wobbly shards of rock just to get to the pump and draw some water.

After the crew pulled out, Claudius and MayBelle had gingerly poked into the mine, which now extended thirty feet deeper into the cliff. The crew had left without mucking the last of the rock, and it lay in a heap at the face. The last dozen feet was not supported by timber sets. The rails stopped ten feet short, and the ore car stood forlorn and empty. Rock dust lay so thickly over everything that it rose in whirls as they stumbled toward the face.

Mostly the rock was the same ochre stuff the drift had bored through from the beginning but at the face there was some thin black material webbing the ochre rock. Colonel Raines could not tell one stone from another. The slight change in texture certainly hadn't excited the veteran miners who had come and gone and given up hope.

Raines had tried to dicker with Milt Hoag, but the man simply shrugged. The colonel had watched the men pack their tools and powder, drive their wagons down the grade, load up what had been spread through a few cabins, and rattle away. Ever since then, a vast silence had descended on the dead town.

"Some gold rush you started," MayBelle said, crossly. Everything she wore was streaked with rock dust.

"I'll start another."

"What'll we live on? Rattlesnakes?"

"There must be some beans in one of the cabins," he said. "A pound or so left by Hoag, maybe."

She laughed sardonically.

"Maybe we could mine it ourselves," he said. "There's some old drills around."

"By 'we' you mean me. Unless you know of some way to move rock by thinking on it."

Colonel Raines drew himself up, intending to reply, but he was feeling too melancholic, and instead wheeled down the grubby road. He had turned the Pearlygates Town Lot Company office into his refuge, a hideaway from that annoying woman.

There in his office he pored over papers: he knew every claim, every lot, every standard clause in the contracts. He knew what lots had been paid for and belonged to others. There were only seven in the whole town. The rest had reverted to the town lot company because the owners had abandoned them. He knew which mining claims were patented. Most weren't. They had yet to be proved up.

While he was thus engaged, and escaping the snapping turtle tongue of MayBelle, he chanced to observe a lone prospector wander into Pearlygates. This man was a miner without a doubt: he led a gaunt mule that was heaped with gear and half a dozen canteens; the gentleman sported a beard that had not seen shears for months. A straw chapeau protected his weathered face from the worst of the Nevada sun. And he was so skinny that the colonel didn't doubt that the man subsisted on cactus and rattler half the time.

The man squinted this way and that, peering into empty stores, studying the silent mines, pausing to examine the manse on the hill.

Colonel Raines stepped outside the door, onto the plank walkway shaded by a gallery roof.

"At your service, sir. May I show you around?"

The man's gaze slowly focused on the colonel, as if Raines weren't quite there. "Where's the diggings?" he asked.

"The mines are all closed, sir. But there's plenty of prospects I'd be delighted to show you."

"The new one."

"Oh, up yonder, behind that house on the hill."

"That's it, what I've been hearing about."

The miner shuffled toward the mansion, while Raines hastened to catch up.

"I'll have a look. That's what interests me."

"You met the crew."

"Yep. They said you didn't have a plugged nickel and they quit."

"Why, sir, I have pineapple plantations, coffee plantations, banana plantations, an entire mahogany forest—"

"And not a thin dime."

"I also own the entire town, give or take a few paid-up lots."

"That's not worth a plugged nickel either."

The mule reached the sharp grade and quit.

"Come on, Agnes."

The mule laid back her ears.

"She's contrary. You got some hay up there?"

Raines nodded.

"Come along, Agnes. Hay."

But the mule lowered her head and locked her legs.

"All right, all right."

The prospector untied the half dozen canteens and thrust them upon Colonel Raines, who stood there, astonished by the weight he was holding.

"All right, Agnes."

The mule started up.

"She's a hinny and they're temperamental," the prospector said.

Colonel Raines followed meekly behind, carrying unaccustomed weight.

"You're the colonel," the prospector said. "At least that's the rank you hang on yourself. I'm Cracker."

"Cracker?"

"Front and rear name. Now that's the glory hole there. I can see the rock, newborn. Rock when it comes out of a hole is prettier than when it gets weathered and bleached by the sun. It sure don't look like it's got any mineral."

Cracker abandoned the mule at the portal of the tunnel and stalked in. Raines lowered the canteens and followed.

"That bunch didn't do you any favors, leaving all this rock around," Cracker said, crawling over huge angular chunks until he reached the face.

In the dusty gloom Cracker picked up pieces, licked them, studied the wall of stone, picked at some of the darker material threading it with his thumbnail, and carried one or two samples back to sunlight.

"Damn fools," he said. "All right. I'll mine it, take three-quarters, and you get one quarter."

"What? What are you talking about?"

"We strike ore, I get three-quarters of every penny of revenue."

"Why, sir, I own this ore."

"That's debatable. You want to go for it?"

"Sir, I'll hire a dozen others."

Cracker laughed. "They'll take you good, burn your town lot papers, and pitch you into the desert."

Colonel Raines's pulse climbed. What was happening here? Was this desert animal, this scorpion, about to pull a fast one?

"It just went up to eighty percent. I'm taking eighty percent of everything out of this mine," Cracker said.

"No, no, I'm not interested."

"Well, that's what you'll get. Now help me unload Agnes and feed her."

"Do it yourself."

Cracker grinned darkly at Raines. "Put on your dungarees and help me. It'll go faster. You muck out the rock and I'll drill."

The thought of physical labor made Colonel Raines nauseous. "I left my work clothing in a trunk in San Francisco twenty-seven years ago. I haven't seen it since."

"Then muck in that baggy black suit. When we're done, you'll be able to afford a hundred suits, partner."

Cracker had untied the load that heaped over Agnes's back, and was easing it to the ground. "I haven't got much powder and even less fuse," he said. "But I can shoot a little round."

"I'll hire a helper," Raines said.

"With what? Some of that French wine?"

The commotion drew MayBelle out of the manse.

"Ah, Cracker, ah, this is MayBelle, my beauteous queen of the city of Pearlygates. MayBelle, this is Mr. Cracker."

The prospector nickered.

"Mr. Cracker believes that our salvation is not far off."

"I didn't say that. What I am saying is that I need help. Someone to muck the rock out of there."

"MayBelle, my little partridge . . ."

The mistress of the manor eyed her paramour, then Cracker, then the rock littering the tunnel, and retreated into the house. When she emerged, she was wearing her dungarees, gloves, a bonnet tied under her chin, and a mean look in her eye.

Cracker grinned.

"I will prepare a little agreement for us to sign," Claudius said. "That will keep matters straight."

"Eighty-twenty."

MayBelle had already begun lifting rocks, one by one, and dumping them into the ore car. It would take her the whole day to fill that car, and most of those stones would be too heavy for her. But she had a look in her eye that inspired awe in the colonel.

Cracker, wheezing with joy, extracted his drill bits from his pack and began single-jacking holes into the face.

"Let's hope one charge does her," he said, "because that's all the giant powder I got."

Chapter 10

All that afternoon, the colonel listened to the steady tap of Cracker's hammer and the occasional rattle of the rock that MayBelle was tossing into the ore car.

The thought of all that exertion made Raines dizzy so he repaired to his offices on Nevada Street and awaited customers. But the ghost town baked silently in the summer sun, the home of lizards but not of mortals.

The colonel did pen a little agreement and made a second copy. There was something about Cracker that required putting things on paper.

Then, when the sun began to settle in the west, the faint tapping from upslope ceased, so Raines trotted to the manse and the mine head behind it, and then gingerly pierced to the rear of the tunnel, his eyes adjusting to the dim light. MayBelle had managed to load the ore car with all but the rubble she couldn't lift or break up, and Cracker was gently loading three sticks of DuPont into each of the five holes he had bored, pushing them home with a wooden stick.

"We'll blow it in a few minutes," Cracker said. "Still some things to do."

Tucked into the final five sticks were copper-clad fulminate of mercury blasting caps, and these in turn were clamped to lengths of fuse, which dangled down from each hole.

"The center hole's got the shortest fuse; that'll blow first, and then the ones above, and then the ones below, all in order. The last two should push rock away from the head if I do it right," Cracker said. "When I get the charges loaded, I'll push a little wet clay into each hole to increase the power of the shot."

Raines watched with wary fascination, half afraid Cracker would make a fatal mistake and blow them all to oblivion.

"Help me push this ore car out of here," MayBelle said. She looked dog tired. Her hair was coated with rock dust, her face streaked with gray.

"My love, my honeybee, you've spent a most profitable afternoon loading rock," the colonel said. "What a triumph for a woman. You'll take pride in finishing the mighty task yourself, shouldering that heavy car out of the mine. Then no one can take away from you your rightful glory, the first of your sex to load an ore car and remove it from a mine."

"Queen bees sting their mates," she said, pushing at the car, but it wouldn't budge.

"Ah, Mr. Cracker, I'm sure you'll lend a hand," Raines said. "I just sponged off my suit and I need to stay presentable for customers. I'm expecting a crowd any time now."

Cracker grunted.

"By the way, we've a little agreement to sign. I didn't know your first name, and left it blank."

"It's Arnold. My friends call me Safe."

"Safe Cracker? Ah, that's rich."

"There's nothing I can't break into, including this ore, Raines."

Cracker finished loading the charges, pushed the ore car out of the drift with a great squeal of wheel on metal, and then urged the colonel and MayBelle to stand well back and far off to the windward side.

"But, Mr. Cracker, you'll want to sign the agreement. It's for your benefit, of course. It guarantees your right to a share—"

Cracker plucked the papers out of the colonel's soft hand, read carefully, and tore them to bits.

Raines was aghast. "But you can't!"

"It was eighty-twenty my way, not your way," he said. "I read you right the first time I saw you."

Raines sorrowed. He thought Cracker wouldn't read the agreement all that carefully.

"Maybe I'll just keep it all," Cracker said, sizing up Raines. "I like this hole in the ground. You can sell town lots to suckers. I'll sell ore and pocket the checks."

"You drive a hard bargain, Cracker, and I'll have none of it. Pull the charges out of the holes. Or fire off this shot and be gone. Pearlygates isn't big enough for the two of us."

Cracker wheezed and spat. "Pull charges out of holes? That shows how much you know about mining. The only thing you know how to do is talk."

Colonel Raines contemplated a rejoinder, but Cracker wasn't done.

"Now, I'll light the fuses and come hurrying out and don't you be in the way. I've got a spare thirty seconds and that's all. I'll come walking, not running, because I don't want to stumble, and you might just hold your ears or get inside that house of yours and kiss the Bible and make out your last will and testament. Get a kerchief over your nose unless you want to eat dust, and don't stand near glass."

"Sir, I refuse to budge," Raines said. "I will stand right here at the portal and you will not light those charges. You're discharged. We have no agreement."

Cracker laughed nastily and cut a two-foot piece of

fuse off of a roll with his jackknife, and notched the fuse.

MayBelle tugged at Raines, and together they retreated well to one side of the old wine cellar.

Cracker watched them, lit the fuse with a lucifer he held to it until it was spitting sparks, and then vanished into the mine. It seemed forever before he strode out, walking with great but relaxed determination. The instant he reached sunlight he wheeled to his right and walked another fifty feet along the side of the ochre cliff.

A violent whump, whump, whump shattered the peace, and a great cloud of dust and debris boiled out of the mine head, up and around the mansion, off to either side. A red haze blurred the air.

"All right, we'll let her settle," Cracker said.

"Whatever is in there, sir, is not yours."

"You'll make your wad selling town lots to suckers, Raines. Me, I think I'll just see what's in here."

"Can we go in?"

"Not for a couple of hours."

"Two hours!"

"Try it. It's your lungs and eyes and throat, not mine."

"An eternity, sir."

"It's a short drift and there's fresh air close by. You should see what it's like in a deep mine with no air."

MayBelle vanished into the manse, looking begrimed. Cracker settled on the bare earth and the colonel lowered himself to the ground, a position he was unaccustomed to assume. And there they sat for a while, watching the shadows crawl out from the buildings down below as the sun lowered. Sometimes there was a disconcerting rattle from the mine, as debris tumbled.

Raines was getting itchy. "Ah, Cracker, my friend, let's talk man to man. This place is hers, you know. She was clinging to it. All alone. It was her husband's and he unloaded it in a divorce settlement. Of course he knew the mines were played out, but she didn't and he thought it was a good joke on her. I came along and proposed to bail her out by reviving the town for a while, start a little rush with some blasting and a few hints carefully planted and watered and fertilized here and there, keep it going long enough to sell lots and claims, and cash in."

"I think maybe she's bailing you out."

"No, I have prosperous pineapple and mahogany plantations, sir, and I dicker in bananas and kiwi fruit. She appealed to my charity, and I obliged her. Now, Mr. Cracker, it occurs to me that you might wish to join us. Clearly, you have abilities we lack. If you'll just keep blowing rock out of that hole in the hillside and be very public about it, we'll all profit. The world will see we're up to something. That is, if we can work a little arrangement . . . such as thirds. A third for her, a third for you, and a third for me."

Cracker eyed the colonel. "Well, Raines, that's not so bad, as long as we each do a third of the work. You muck rock while I jack the drills, and that gal can cook and clean up and keep an eye out for visitors, sell lots."

The colonel felt trapped. "A third of the toil? Ah, oh, Cracker, sir, Arnold, old friend, you must understand I was wounded in the war long ago, my torn-up body simply can't stand the stress and strain of that sort of thing. My left leg, sir, you would not believe it if I showed it to you. No, my task is to plan and manage and spread the good word. That is sublime work, sir. Every enterprise requires a brain and a heart as well as brawn."

"Which war?"

"Ah, the Crimean. Bloody fight it was, too. I was helping out the British, Colonel of Hussars, you know, attached to the Queen's Own Welsh Guard."

"Never heard of it. No dice, Raines. I guess I'll just operate this glory hole myself. If you don't like it, file a lawsuit and we'll see who owns it. It ain't gonna be you."

"Ah, Arnold, what did you before you took up this trade?"

"Before or after I was in the pen?"

"Ah, before."

"Cracked safes."

"And after?"

"Cracked heads. I was a mine guard until I cracked the wrong heads. Namely, those of the owners. Now I prospect."

"And crack rocks."

"And heads too. Yours would crack very nicely."

"Have you struck any ore?"

Cracker looked annoyed. "What do I know about ore? What I do is steal mines. Like this. If you want to stop me, put up your dukes and try me."

"Ah, what pen?"

"What state?"

"Ah, California?"

"San Quentin."

"Montana Territory?"

"Deer Lodge."

"Ah, Arnold, I think we have come to an agreement. You get the mine. We'll sell lots. I'll arrange it with MayBelle."

"No, I'll take a cut of the lots, too, Raines." Cracker was grinning darkly but then he slapped the colonel on the back, almost staggering him.

Raines drew himself up with dignity. "Is the dust settled?"

"One thing I've learned about life. The dust never settles, Colonel. We'll pretty near choke and probably won't see six inches in front of us. But sure, put a wet cloth over your snout, and we'll have a little look."

Raines fled to the manse, found a dishrag, soaked it in tepid water, and returned to the mine head. Arnold had pulled a bull's-eye lantern from his kit and lit the candle. He had tied a water-soaked red bandana over his face, and looked all the more like an outlaw.

Together they proceeded into the drift, through clouds of choking dust and acrid powder fumes, clambering over rock. Cracker went ahead, poking at the roof for loose rock, but the top of the drift seemed solid enough. Near the face the rock lay heaped, forming a barrier Raines could barely see over.

Cracker started to crawl over that rock, moving cautiously and carefully, carrying his lantern with him. There was naught to do but follow, so the colonel gingerly clambered over the rubble, bemoaning the awful effects on his black suit. But at last they stood at the face.

There, before them, was a two-foot-wide seam of glistening quartz, and along the bottom edge of it, a one-inch seam that glittered yellow with native gold.

Chapter 11

Arnold Cracker was in a jovial mood. The prospector sat at MayBelle's kitchen table, polishing and licking the dozen ore samples he and the colonel had pulled out of the mine.

Maybelle watched him sourly, not sharing his elation. Gold! She should be overjoyed but she wasn't. She had fed Cracker and Raines a mountain of flapjacks she had cooked from her meager store of flour, and they had scarcely noticed. She knew where this was leading: she wouldn't get one cent out of it from a confidence man and a safecracker.

The house was a ruin; rock dust coated everything, including the kitchen, where it got mixed into the food. She could no longer keep clean. The dust coated her hair and flesh and clothing, caked under her fingernails, gritted in her mouth. But she could endure that if she had to. What she couldn't endure was Cracker.

"It's the big bonanza. I'm rich!" he said for the tenth time.

The colonel sighed. He was coated with rock dust and for once he looked unkempt. She doubted he could ever cleanse the stuff from his black broadcloth suit or wash it out of his hair.

"We're all in this together, Arnold, old friend," he said.

Cracker laughed nastily. "I blew it open and it's all mine. This here rock's worth a thousand a ton. That's how it'll mill out; one thousand simoleons for every ton of ore we run through the stamps. There's a pretty good mill ten miles away; I'll have them stamp it and amalgamate and cast it into gold bricks. They take a little percentage for that, but so what? Lots more where it came from."

"You've bared a seam, but you've hardly explored," MayBelle said, wearily rinsing dishes in water laden with rock dust. "It could be a pocket."

"Lady, them mines yonder pulled a million dollars of gold out of this same seam, and that's a fact."

He examined each sample, clucking at the thin wires of gold running through the quartz, some of them thickening into bands of the precious metal.

"See this? It'll mill right out. Hardly needs amalgamation. Stamp this quartz and get the gold. I could pretty near do it myself with some simple equipment. I'm gonna take over this mine and get it running right, hire some muckers. I'll do the blasting myself."

The colonel looked peeved. "Arnold, old friend, we're in this together. This mine happens to belong to MayBelle here. . . ."

Cracker's amusement lit his face. "It did. It don't now."

MayBelle put the dishes in a rack to dry, knowing they would soon be coated with dust. She was tired. She eyed the pair of males at her table. Cracker was the dangerous one, capable of anything, including murder. The colonel was merely a con man and she rather liked him even if he hadn't done a lick of honest work in his parasitic life.

"Let's make some plans," the colonel said. "Now, while you're getting the mine up and running, I'll see to it that this bonanza's well publicized."

Arnold stared. "I don't want a rush. I don't want nobody around here. And I'm taking over the rest of the claims along this cliff, right straight along this formation. Where's the papers? The ones your husband left you?"

He was staring at her but she ignored him.

He rose suddenly, loomed over her, and grabbed her arm. "I said where are the claims?"

They were in a cubbyhole in her husband's rolltop desk. "I'll find them tomorrow."

"Now."

The colonel intervened. "Arnold, old friend, we won't make money unless we have us a little gold rush and sell the lots and the buildings all over again. There's more wealth to be had from that than from a dozen mines."

Cracker ignored him. "Now. Give me those claims."

She felt his steely grip on her shoulder. It hurt. He was hurting her and the colonel. They had offered this man a fair share, his cut in some valid claims, and he was plainly about to get all the papers in hand and push them out into the night.

"I'll get them," she said. "Have some coffee."

He let her go. The places where his cruel fingers had twisted her flesh still hurt.

She stood stock-still, brushing rock dust off her dress, her mind on the months and years she had kept vigil here in an empty town, looking for some way to turn the whole of Pearlygates into a paying proposition. She thought of the times stray prospectors had drifted in, most of them harmless and cheerful. She thought of the vagrants hunting salvage, anything that might be turned into a meal, or money, or advantage. She thought of the dozens who drifted to the mansion, the few she had turned away with the shotgun, the few she had fed or helped. She thought of the lonely nights and hollow days, walking the empty streets like some wraith, desperate for some way out.

Cracker was leering at her, his eyes hot with lust. Not sensual lust, but lust to possess the world. "I'm coming with you," he said.

"You'll be bored. I'll be hunting through piles of papers my husband left behind. If you want to make yourself useful, go feed the livestock. They haven't gotten a scrap of hay all day."

"Hey, Colonel, go feed the nags," Cracker said.

The colonel sat stock-still.

"Oh, hell, I'll do it. Agnes is hungry." Cracker vanished through the kitchen door and into the night.

She watched him go.

"Colonel, get out of the way," she said.

She headed through the dark house, feeling the grit on the floors under her feet, until she reached the front door where she kept her over-and-under shotgun. She waited in the shadows until she heard Cracker return. The kitchen door banged and she heard voices, and knew that Cracker was heading her way.

She stepped into the hall, raised the shotgun to her shoulder, and waited.

He appeared.

"Stop or I'll kill you," she said softly.

He paused momentarily, chuckled, and headed straight toward her.

"One more step and you're dead."

He laughed. "Put that thing down."

"It's got two barrels and both are loaded."

"Hey, sweetheart, I'm your new fella." He started toward her.

She lifted the barrels slightly and pulled one trigger.

The violence rocked her back. The roar was magnified by the hallway. It battered her ears. Plaster fell from the ceiling.

"Jaysas," he said.

"Next one won't miss."

He believed her and stopped.

"Put that thing down, sweetheart. You don't have the guts to kill me."

"Try me."

"Hey, what I came back here for is to work out a little deal. Get rid of that lazy pup that's sucking on your rear teat."

"Turn around and walk into the kitchen. And if you try for the colonel, to use him for a shield, you'll be dead before you take two steps. I'd shoot you both if I have to."

"Be careful with that thing," he said.

She knew she had won.

"Sit down at the table. And stay clear of the colonel."

"Hey, don't get into an uproar. Me, I'm just a lonely prospector."

He retreated to the kitchen and sat down gingerly, his gaze never parting from the black bore of the shotgun that was relentlessly pointing straight at his chest.

"Colonel, stay well away from him," she said.

Raines edged away from the table entirely.

"Reach into the pocket of my apron and take the derringer," she said.

Raines did exactly what he was told to do and soon had a deadly little brass-framed forty-one-caliber cannon in hand. He pointed it straight at Cracker.

"You have some choices," she said. "You can pack up and get out of here. You can try to kill us both and take over. Or you can work on shares, keep your greed in hand, and take an equal share out of all this, a third apiece."

"MayBelle, my little goose, don't—"

"Colonel, this man works, which is more than you do."

Cracker was watching the both of them, looking for

something to exploit, some division. She saw it and lifted the shotgun a bit.

"Don't get ideas," she said. "I'll tell you this just once. You try to kill us or cheat us and you'll end up dead in one of those glory holes all over the slopes, with a ton of rock to seal your carcass from the world."

He stared, expressionless.

"I've dealt with your kind," she said. "All you understand is the bore of this shotgun, so take a good look. It's got twelve buckshot down there and maybe a little extra powder for good measure."

His gaze slid away from her.

"What'll it be?"

Cracker's trapped-rat gaze shifted to her, to the colonel, to the glittering prizes on the kitchen table.

Suddenly his face lit up. "Guess I'm a partner."

"No, you'll never be a partner. The colonel and I will make all decisions. But you'll get a third cut . . . if you behave."

"A third?" Raines was aghast. "Not of the town lots! He shouldn't get those. A third of the mine."

MayBelle glared at him.

"A third of everything, Cracker. That'll keep you as honest as you ever get."

"Let's shake on it," Cracker said.

"No, we won't shake on it. I'm always armed. If you ever come closer than ten feet I'll kill you, and I won't ask you to stop before I do."

"A third," Cracker said. "It's a deal."

Chapter 12

The gold-shot quartz glittered in the center of the kitchen table. Raines, Cracker, and MayBelle stared at it. The gold changed everything.

"We need food," she said. "Tomorrow we run out."

"I need giant powder, blasting caps, fuse, and other stuff," said Cracker. "And some help. I can't dig ore alone."

"One of us will have to go to Storyville," she said.

"I, ah, am not welcome there," Raines said. "A little misunderstanding with the town marshal."

Cracker laughed. "I ain't going either."

"Why?" asked MayBelle. "You could trade that ore for food and supplies."

Cracker whickered like a horse. "Woman, you don't know nothing."

That riled MayBelle. "If that's how you think, get your skinny butt out of here."

Cracker looked annoyed. "I got reasons. First is the hardware man, Gildersleeve, grubstaked me. He's got a third of everything I find. Everything. Not a third of my third but a third of this whole potful. And that's just the beginning. The grocery man, Lomax, he grubstaked me so he's got a fifth. I owe the assayer eighty-seven dollars, and I got saloon tabs all over town need paying up."

"You mean to tell me that some storekeep in Storyville thinks he has a third of this mine, and another thinks he's got twenty percent on top of the thirds we have?" asked the colonel.

"That's why I ain't going to Storyville. No one needs to know I got a piece of this mine. If I don't go there and don't trade any ore for food, they don't figure it out."

"But how are we going to start a gold rush? I want a thousand miners crawling over this old town. I want gold-crazy people chopping holes in rock. I want a bunch of merchants moving in and setting up shop. We own the land under them. We'll sell it to them at a fancy price and they won't even quibble. I want a line two blocks long waiting to buy from the land office."

"We ain't gonna start no gold rush, Colonel. Not now. We don't want a soul to know about it. This gold changes everything. It's not a confidence racket anymore."

"Cracker, you're not a partner. MayBelle and I will decide these little matters."

MayBelle didn't like the colonel's peremptory tone. "Arnold, what are you saying?" she asked.

"Everything's different now. Before, we needed to start a rush with a few pieces of good ore for bait, and sell lots. Now we found gold, real gold, a whole mine full, and we gotta keep it quiet as we can."

The colonel looked ready to explode but MayBelle hushed him.

"You show that quartz gold around Storyville, you'll start a stampede and I'll tell you what'll happen around here," Cracker said. "All them fortune hunters come rolling in here, half crazy, and they stake claims and take over every building in town, and you ain't gonna sell one lot or one claim.

"You'll sit there in your land office just sputtering away whiles them gold-minded miners snatch every room. And what's to stop them? Have you got a sheriff here or a bunch of hard cases to enforce things for you? You gonna say, 'You can't move in there, it ain't yours'?

"And what about them that abandoned houses here and come a-running back and move into their old place? You gonna throw them out? You'd need a howitzer to get them out. There aren't enough lawyers in Nevada, and enough town marshals, to toss them out of the houses they quit just two years ago. And no matter what their contracts say about abandoning their place, in their minds it's still theirs.

"You gonna take 'em to court with Bullfrog, the county seat, seventy miles away, or pay ten lawyers and a dozen hard cases with money you ain't got to defend your title and chase off trespassers and claim jumpers? The skinny of it is, we gotta rethink all of this."

MayBelle saw the truth in it. She also saw the empty pantry. They had no more fancy French wine to trade for food and they were down to a few cups of cornmeal and a little molasses.

"Why, drat it," said the colonel, "I'll handle the crowd. They're chumps. I'll just sign 'em to long-term land contracts, no money down, payment later. Or rent by the week. Easy terms will do it: Step this way, gents, get the land you want, the house you want, anchored down with a deed, nothing but a one-dollar down payment to seal the deal, just take two minutes to make sure you've got a legal right to your land so no one jumps your claim or pushes you out the door. . . ."

Cracker jeered. "All right. You go on into Storyville and start laying that quartz on the bars and see what happens."

"The ore is the only real asset we have," MayBelle said.

"And little enough of that. It wouldn't fill two burlap bags," Cracker said. "We just nicked that seam."

"We need to have it assayed," Raines said.

"Naw, that stuff, you don't need to do that, not at the moment. It needs to be milled and amalgamated. That's rich ore. There'll be maybe a hundred dollars just in a couple of bags of that quartz. Listen, I've been around this mining business and I know what to do. We'll take what ore we got over to Amalgamated Climax and have them mill it. Only I'll take it over there on my mule, not your buggy, so they don't know what's what.

"Maybe I can trade the gold for some supplies, some giant powder and all, with nobody the wiser. I'm just a lone prospector, see, and all I did was find a little pocket of quartz that I'm cashing in. Get it? If some bum follows me, I'll just drift away from here and shake him."

MayBelle scarcely understood the technology but it didn't matter. She trusted Cracker's judgment. "That's the best we can do," she said.

Raines stared at him and at MayBelle. "I can see I'm outvoted," he said. "I still think MayBelle should spread a little ore around Storyville, like cheese in a mousetrap. . . ."

But no one had a better plan than Arnold's. MayBelle knew good and well that Arnold Cracker was right: now that they had a real gold mine going, her town lot company and mining claims weren't worth the paper they were written on.

"I'll start in the morning. I'll fill a couple of bags with quartz right now," he said. "There's enough light left."

"You'd better hurry before we start eating my horse," she said.

"Colonel, you want to help me pick up some ore?" Cracker said.

"Ah, no, your practiced eye will spot the true goods, especially by the light of that lantern. No, you're the expert, and I would only toss barren rock into your gunnysacks. Besides, my friend, I should spend time putting our papers in good order. If there's a rush, we'll need to defend our title."

Cracker was amused. He stood, lit the candle in his bull's-eye lantern, and vanished into the dark.

"I wish he had gotten here ahead of you," MayBelle said. "At least he works."

"Madam, there is no toil more exhausting or rewarding than the exertions of the mind. Trust me, when the dust settles you will see the firm and inspired hand of your friend and colleague Colonel Raines showing the way."

MayBelle started to laugh but Colonel Raines looked so wounded that she stopped abruptly. She needed Raines, too.

They all slept well that night.

Cracker was ready at dawn, his hinny bearing three gunnysacks of quartz ore and glaring at her master. He was once again a wandering prospector.

"I'm going to take me a roundabout way coming back, just to keep people away from here," he said. "It may take me a few days. They don't exactly stop milling their own ore just because someone wanders in wanting a custom job. With any luck, there'll be enough gold to buy some powder and fuse and caps."

"And food," MayBelle said.

"You better not count on food. I'm heading for a mine, not a grocer."

"And hay," MayBelle added.

Cracker shook his head. "You solve your problems and I'll solve the mining problems. Least you could do is muck out that last blast," he said to Raines. "I can't get at that seam until you do. It was all I could do to crawl over the rubble in there and get two or three bags of ore, and not very good ore, either."

"I'll put MayBelle right on it," Raines said.

Cracker glared, and tugged on his lead rope. "Come

along, Agnes, sweetheart," he said. The mule followed along behind him as he trudged out of Pearlygates.

"I hope we've seen the last of him," Raines said.

"How can you say that!"

"Why don't you go in there and find a few bits of ore that he missed? I think maybe if I slide into Storyville at night and keep a sharp eye out for the marshal, I might be able to spread a little ore around a few saloons, just enough to whet a few appetites."

MayBelle stared at him. "Cracker's not even half a mile away and already you're scheming to undo everything."

"Well, MayBelle, my little magpie, you can't take a man like that at his word. I'd be surprised if we ever see his skinny mug again. He's got maybe a hundred dollars of ore, and that's what he was after. Enough for a swill of whiskey and a tart. We have to continue with our own little plan, which is to unload Pearlygates to any pilgrim coming down the pike."

"But the gold mine!"

"A little pocket of gold just helps us do it."

MayBelle made up her mind. "I'm going into Storyville but I'm not taking any ore. And I'll come back with some fodder for you, me, Safe Cracker, and the livestock."

"You have money?"

"I have other assets, Colonel."

The very thought sent an awful tremor through Claudius P. Raines.

"You'll be here alone," she said. "I don't know why I worry about that."

Chapter 13

MayBelle paused outside Storyville to freshen herself. It had been a long hard ride, most of a day, and dust had settled over the buggy and her clothing.

She looked sensational in her silk dress the color of burnished gold, with her black silk hat and feather boa. The colonel had observed all this with a thin-lipped glare, no doubt thinking the worst. She smiled. Let him think.

She shook dust out of her clothing, washed her porcelain face at the creek, rouged her cheeks, shadowed her eyes, and proceeded into town. She knew her mere passage through woman-starved Storyville would be a sensation, which is what she intended. She lacked so much as a dime but managed to look like an heiress, which is also what she intended. Not even a harsh life in a ghost town had ruined her golden flesh.

She steered the dusty trotter past wagons and buggies, and sure enough, men turned and stared. A few trips down the boulevard would do it. She eyed the hotels wistfully. For the moment, anyway, she would not have enough loot to pay for one night. But what did it matter? She was achieving exactly the effect she desired.

Men stopped in their tracks. Some whistled. Others grinned. One yelled a welcome.

"Hello, boys," she said, and smiled sweetly.

"You need help, lady?" one asked.

"Any time, any place," she said.

She reached the far end of Storyville, turned around, and ascended Mine Street once again. She had been through this town several times, and knew it well. But she wanted to check out the cabarets and saloons. In time, she negotiated the three business streets of Storyville and eliminated all but two bistros, the Silver Star, and the Stockman. It was time to deal.

She parked her buggy, dropped the carriage weight, and sashayed into the Stockman. It took a moment for her eyes to adjust to the gloom. But she discovered a long bar with a brass rail along it, poker tables, and at the rear an elevated podium.

"Madam—" said the barkeep, about to begin the process of booting her out of male precincts.

"Sonny, are you the manager?"

"No, he's in back. Ma'am, I don't think—"

"I don't think either," she said. "But I sing."

A half dozen miners and boozers gawked, which was fine.

She swished and rustled her way to the rear, noting the sour smell of whiskey and cigars. The stage would do if they lit it. An upright piano occupied one side. She would need a piano player.

"If my eyes weren't crossed, I'd swear that was a woman," said one lush.

"It's got the right shape," said another.

She found the manager in a tiny cubicle with a desk and a black safe with pink nymphs crawling over the enamel.

He was chewing a yellow cigar butt.

"You're in the wrong place," he said.

"Sonny, I do one-night stands."

He smiled, baring tobacco-yellowed incisors.

"I'm a chanteuse."

"Whatever that is."

"I sing, dear, I warble sweetly and every male within ten miles comes to listen . . . and drink, and wish."

"So sing."

"Get me a piano player and I will."

He eyed her slowly, up and down, his gaze missing nothing. She didn't mind. She had what it took.

"One night. Tonight. You get a piano player, and put out word around this burg."

"Five dollars," he said.

"Ha!"

He lipped his slimy cigar. "Then what?"

"Half."

"Of the till? You're crazy."

"See you," she said. She swept out of the joint, gasped as sunlight blinded her, and walked fifty yards to the Silver Star, a fancier joint by far.

She discovered a larger crowd here, and stopped conversation entirely as she stepped in. One moment, babble; the next, utter silence. This one was better lit, with a six-lamp chandelier, cherry-colored bar, and some poker tables and a faro layout.

She approached the barkeep, a black-haired gent polishing tumblers. "You want a one-night stand?" she asked.

"If you pay me well," he said.

She laughed. "Where's the boss?"

"I'm the boss."

"I do little numbers onstage."

"I bet you do."

"You got a piano player?"

"When he's sober."

"This is a one-nighter."

"I never was much for marriage, sweetheart."

"Half the gross," she said.

He laughed. "You can sing for tips."

"All the tips? Everything that gets tossed to me?"

He supplied a feline smile, and she smiled back.

"You pay your piano player, right?"

He shrugged.

"Okay, nine o'clock."

"Start earlier," he said.

"You got a little room for me?"

"Upstairs, when it's not in use." He cocked an eyebrow into a question mark.

"Eight to closing, and I get all the tips, and a room, and you can pitch me booze and meals too."

"Yeah, well, who are you?"

"Madame Chanteuse. I'm on the road."

"Maybe I better listen to you warble."

"I charge by the minute."

"I got nothing to lose but my patrons," he said. "Okay; I'll spread the word, baby."

"You can start with dinner and a glass of wine."

The barkeep eyed her a long time, shrugged, and began pouring some red.

"And you can put my rig in the livery barn and feed my nag."

"It figures," he said. "Give an inch and surrender a yard."

Customers sighed. She ignored them, sipped red wine, and eyed the dark stairway going up to even less respectable quarters. She didn't much mind. She had not crossed that line, exactly, but she was never far away from it. A lady does what she must.

She plucked up her sheet music, ascended into a cloying world upstairs, populated by sad females in kimonos who eyed her without curiosity.

"I'm doing a one-nighter," she said.

"I do about twenty a night," said the blonde.

MayBelle slipped into an odorous little room and closed the door behind her. She needed to look at the sheet music. She had forgotten lyrics, and even some melodies. She had tried the game once in San Francisco and had been laughed out of various saloons. She could barely hold a note in any range between soprano and contralto. But she had survived with a few gimmicks. She had learned to shed her feather boa, a few gloves, a hat, some shoes, and fiddle with her buttons, and that always got her a rain of coin at the end. But it was a vile living, if sometimes amusing, and she chose to survive in other fashions.

Long ago she had a different and very ordinary dream: a good marriage, a cottage with lilacs on a shady lane, a boy and two girls, a good tradesman for a husband. But she had always had man trouble, and at the same time, she had always liked men better than women. Those were things that changed her. She still liked men, even if she didn't trust a one of them. And along the way she had discovered money.

It wouldn't really matter whether she could sing, or whether the drunken piano player could hold a tune. A little bit of temptation would win her some coin, in fact a heap of it. She knew how to do that. She had made a career of tempting.

She memorized lyrics, hummed, tried a few scales, and when eight o'clock rolled around, she descended the stairs in full feather and beauty, and was met with a wave of whistles. The joint was packed. She sashayed to the makeshift stage, where a gnome of a piano player leered. She dropped the music in his lap, but he scowled and pitched it aside.

Word had gotten out. Plenty of miners and ranchers and clerks had crowded in to see this novelty. They packed the tables and lined the bar, and stood along the walls. Smoke blued the air. The odor of unwashed bodies laced the room, along with the sour smell of stale beer.

She smiled too brightly, hummed a bar of "When Roses Bloom" for the little rat at the piano, and started to warble. The keyboard monkey picked up on it, and they soon had a melody going. But her voice, never good, wobbled and careened and hit flats and sharps with percussive effect. Still, she had polite attention, and when she finished she was rewarded with a collective sigh.

She tried "This Dear Old Hearth" next, and the mean little punk at the keyboard slowed her down and hit some clinkers. He was enjoying his little sabotage. But she persevered, even as she sensed attention wandering. She was not exactly galvanizing this entirely male crowd. Maybe that was too sentimental, but miners were a sentimental lot, dreaming of homes and wives and babies even while squandering their pay in bawdy houses.

She could sense where this was drifting, and how much grace she had left before they all turned away.

"Gents," she said, "this one's for you."

She started in on "A Stolen Kiss at Twilight," and as she sang, she pulled the feather boa off her shoulders, baring some neck, twirled it in rhythm, snaked it sinuously over her body until it was a living, writhing thing that seemed to possess her, and then suddenly she whipped it away and finished with a breathless whisper. In the silence that followed, she blew them a kiss, and another.

A whistle greeted her. Good.

"At least they like your curves," said the nasty little piano player.

She glared. Then, sotto voce: "You wreck one more number and I won't share a dime with you, you little rat."

"There won't be any dimes, unless you take it all off. That would get you two cents, or maybe they'll want some coin from you."

"You go to hell."

She smiled at the miners, and got a few whistles.

"Like that one? I was just warming up."

"Keep on warming up, babe," said a spectator.

"It's pretty hot in here," she said. "How about 'I Shed a Tear Last Night'?"

"That's all you're gonna shed?"

She plunged into the melancholic music, which the gnome at the ivories soured as best he could. But this time she didn't care. She tugged at a glove and pitched it, warbled some more, and then tugged the other glove off, making a sensuous act out of it.

But her voice was failing her. She heard it crack twice that time, and with each bad note the piano player added a trill.

"Okay, fellows, one last little number," she said, breathing heavily. 'Daisies on my Mother's Empty Bed.' "

She tossed her slippers and undid her sleeves and worked some buttons loose on her bosom as she trilled the sad old ballad, and then she wound up the song with a deep bow.

They booed and hooted.

"That's all for now, fellows," she said.

"Thank God," someone yelled.

She bowed low, and bowed again, and they whistled.

"You should be paying them to listen," the nasty piano player said.

"Encore," said someone. "Ten more buttons."

She grinned and undid one.

"Show them your vocal cords," whispered the piano player.

"You wrecked it," she said.

She found her black hat, waved it, looking for coin.

A few coins did clang onto the stage, but no folding money.

"Hey, guys, fill the hat," she said.

She hated this.

Oddly, they did toss some coin and a few bills onto the little stage.

"You gonna cheat me?" the piano player said.

"You cheated yourself, playing like that." She tossed him a dollar.

He grinned nastily.

She collected the coin while the miners drifted away or ordered rounds.

Later, in that noisome cubicle upstairs, she counted out thirteen dollars and twelve cents. She could have made an easier living that night, but a lady had to have principles.

Chapter 14

Arnold Cracker was called into the mill office sooner than he expected.

"Well, sir," said Atkins, the mill manager, "that's rich ore, all right, maybe two thousand to the ton, based on your small sample, of course. We milled and amalgamated one hundred seventy-one dollars of gold, at fourteen an ounce. And we're charging twenty-eight fifty for the custom work. I assume you want to pay us in gold?"

"Yeah, sure."

"And a check for the rest?"

"Naw, I just want to head out to my ledge again. You think the company would trade me some giant power and stuff?"

"You could get it cheaper in Storyville."

"That's a long way."

"That ore, I must say, it looked like Pearlygates ore. . . ."

"Well, it's out of a ledge I found, and it's nobody's business where it is."

"Pearlygates district, I'll wager. We did the custom milling for those mines. Same red stains in the quartz, iron oxide. Very unusual. Might be some refining problems in it. Well, now. A receipt. And your name is . . ."

Cracker was getting annoyed. "A man can't get some milling done without everyone poking into his business. Now are you gonna let me trade that gold for some supplies or not?"

The mill man ran a bony hand over his bald head. "I'll give you a receipt," he said quietly, "and you take it over to the company stores building and ask for Flanders. Maybe he will, maybe he won't. It just means Amalgamated's doing a business it doesn't want."

"Well, then, give me the gold and I'll go where I'm welcome."

The mill man ignored him and wrote out a receipt. "Try that," he said. "And we're always looking for ore. You need help developing that ledge, you come to me, and I'll see what I can do. We do like to know who we're dealing with."

"Yeah, well, anyone follows me, he's likely to get perforated right between the eyes."

The mill man glazed over, and produced the receipt.

Cracker hiked over to a storehouse building, found a slope-shouldered oaf, traded off the receipt for a case of dynamite, caps, Bickford fuse, twelve drills of varied sizes, some candles, a new shovel, a flask of mercury, some gloves, and a pick.

He still had twenty-odd dollars to spend. "Give me a greenback," he said. He figured that was his, for hauling the ore so far, and his partners didn't need to know about it.

He loaded sweet old Agnes, headed into the desert, climbed a ridge, waited to see if he was being followed, decided he wasn't, and headed toward Pearlygates and the mine. The mule left prints in the yellow dust, a track easily followed, so Cracker circled far north into barren rock before he switched directions. He studied his back trail, knowing he wouldn't fool anyone for long.

The mill man had figured it out with one glance at

the ore. No one had to follow him to know where it came from.

Cracker rued the day he got into this deal. He would do a lot of backbreaking work and for what? A lousy third. That sharper Raines would do nothing and walk away with a fortune if the vein didn't peter out. And that MayBelle, she'd get rich because of some shaky no-good claim to the place. At least she would work up a sweat, lift rock, which was more than Raines would do.

"Agnes, you're the only friend I got," he said.

He led his burdened mule across a desolate mountainous land, seeing not a soul, knowing he would not talk to another human being this day and the next. He hoped MayBelle would be around to greet him. There was a lady he liked. He wouldn't mind beating her out of her third, and then taking her to Cuba or some place. He had spent too many years staring through bars and dreaming about women like MayBelle, who knew all about men, and liked them just the same.

Eleven years he had spent behind bars, and for what? Looking for the big deal, the big hand. Looking for the one killing that would set him up for life. Then he would lay off, retire, find some port in South America where he could have a raven-haired sweetheart on each arm. One big one. And maybe this was it, if it didn't peter out on him. He'd blown safes from Buffalo to San Francisco, but never hit the big one, the safe so full of gold, so stacked with greenbacks, that he never would have to work again. Once he'd blown a safe in the middle of Green Bay and found only twenty-seven dollars in it. But maybe this mine was the big one he kept looking for.

Cracker avoided the usual route into Pearlygates, and chose instead to look things over from the heights above town. When he reached a good vantage point he studied the slumbering city below, saw no movement, heard no noise, and only after he was satisfied that he was not in danger did he descend the gulch that brought a tiny creek into town. Nothing had changed. The mule snapped at grasses alongside the creek.

Cracker hiked up to the mansion, tugging Agnes behind him, found no one, peered into the mine, and discovered that not one stone had been mucked out. He cursed. It would take most of a day to fill an ore car, dump it, fill it again, and shovel enough rock out of the way so he could put up a timber set and start drilling.

He paused, fighting down an itch to keep on walking, head over the next hill, and leave these partners of his eating his dust. Either that or bury them in some little cave-in around here and have it all to himself. He put the mule in the pen, fed it some hay, rubbed Agnes's nose, and unloaded his gear, gingerly carrying his giant powder and caps well away from the blasting area and the mansion to a neighboring glory hole he would use for a magazine.

He ransacked the silent kitchen looking for some chow, and found nothing, which irked him. A man couldn't even count on his partners for a bite to eat. MayBelle was gone with the buggy. She had better return soon, or there would be hell to pay.

Enormously offended, he stormed through the mansion, one floor at a time, and discovered the colonel asleep upstairs, his handsome face unstained by rock dust, his shiny shoes parked neatly beside the bed, his immaculate black broadcloth suit coat hanging unrumpled from a clothes hook.

Never in Safe Cracker's colorful life had he felt such loathing and contempt and hatred and rage.

Cracker started to yell and thought better of it. No amount of hollering would extract a lick of labor from the confidence man. Not one pebble had been removed from the mine, and none ever would by Raines's soft white hand.

Cracker stormed down the stairs, tried the empty pantry shelves again, found nothing but a dusting of flour in a bin, and decided he and his partners had come to a parting of the ways.

Well, he would teach the colonel a thing or two about partnerships.

He headed for his cache of mining supplies, extracted a waxy red stick of dynamite, found a copper detonator, clamped a two-foot segment of Bickford fuse into it, cut open the dynamite and pushed the fuse into the soft explosive, and headed for the mansion.

He let himself in, studied the downstairs parlor, which lay directly under the slumbering colonel, and finally decided to set the stick in a red silk and mahogany love seat that had orange tassels around its cushions. He'd blow the love seat and the partnership all to hell, and if he collapsed the damned mansion all the better. The stick wouldn't have a whole lot of force, detonating like that in the middle of a large room, but it would sure wake up the colonel.

Satisfied with his labor, he dug into his shirt for a lucifer, scratched it on his sole, and watched it flare into fire. He gauged his exit route, deciding to leave the way he came, through the kitchen, and reach the safety of the mine shaft. He would have ample time, an entire minute.

He lit the fuse, which was reluctant to spark at first, but then it hissed handsomely, and Safe Cracker slid easily out of the parlor, through the kitchen, outside, across the few yards of moiled ground, and into the shaft.

The earsplitting blast shattered the rest of the glass, which flew like shrapnel in all directions, and that was followed by an enormous bloom of smoke and debris from each downstairs window. The mansion shuddered, bulged, groaned, and started to cave, at least where the parlor once had been.

"Ha, ha, you bum, I guess that woke you up," Cracker howled.

The building belched smoke, groaned on its timbers, and tilted precariously toward Pearlygates, but did not collapse. A vast silence settled over the structure, broken only by the creaking of timbers, the occasional tinkle of falling glass, and the whine of twisted floorboards.

"Ha, you bugger, now maybe you'll work!"

He received no reply.

"Good, you're dead!"

Only a sullen silence greeted him. But then he heard a noise, and another, and finally the sound of a man slowly and carefully descending the tilted stairs, step, by step, by step.

So the bugger lived.

At last, Colonel Raines emerged from the creaking ruin, an apparition immaculately attired, his silk top hat adorning his black locks, his suit unrumpled and utterly devoid of dust and debris, his shoes glinting sunlight.

"Ah! Cracker! I thought it was you. A very good idea. It was in the way. Now you can mine."

"I can mine! I can mine! You didn't move one rock out of there."

"My dear sir, the object of life is not to toil like some brainless brute, but to get others to do your toil for you, so that you may enjoy a life of ease and comfort. We succeeded in getting you to hammer and drill and expend your energies, you see, which you seemed willing to do, though I will never fathom why."

"Somebody had to do it! You can't sit around and dream of getting rich!"

The colonel looked nonplused. "Why not? There's no other way to do it."

"If it weren't for me you'd be desperate and starving," Cracker said.

The colonel smiled, patted Cracker on the shoulder. "That's a good fellow," he said. "You just have at that rock, and pretty soon you'll have the mine cleared out and you can drill again."

The wounded mansion creaked, snapped, whined, and collapsed in a great whump of dust and thunder.

Chapter 15

MayBelle arrived at PearlyGates just in time to see her mansion heave, buckle, and collapse in a tower of yellow dust. It was amazing. One moment she had a home on a hill; the next moment she gaped at a heap of boards and debris, with dust and smoke boiling out of it.

She snapped the lines over the rump of the dray horse, hurrying it up the sharp hill to the ruin. Breezes swept away the cloud of dust, and she beheld the colonel and Safe Cracker talking as if nothing bizarre had just transpired.

"My house!" she cried.

The horse labored up the final grade. MayBelle wheeled the buggy into the yard, riding over stray planks and debris, and a heap of smouldering rubble.

"What is this?" she cried.

"Ah, madam, you have come at a most appropriate moment," the colonel said. "We're hungry, and here you are, with abundant succor."

"What about my house?"

"It was in the way," the colonel said. "Good riddance."

"I blew him out of his bed," Safe Cracker explained.

"He hadn't moved one pound of rock. He had not even lifted a pebble. So I taught him a thing or two."

"Ah, my little turtledove, I see you have a fine lot of sacks and crates. Let us eat."

"But my house!"

"It had to go. Dust everywhere. Every blast from the mine made it harder to live here."

"Where are my things? From the house?"

"I blew 'em to kingdom come," Cracker said, picking at his teeth.

"Then starve!" she snapped. "You get everything you can rescue out of there right now. I'm going down the hill."

"Cracker blew it; he'll run the salvage operation," the colonel said.

"You are both going to salvage my kitchen; every pot, every pan, every knife. You are going to get my wardrobe, and my furniture, and right now, before this catches fire. You are going to haul it down into town and settle me in a place down there. If you don't, don't expect me to feed you."

They eyed her sacks of beans and flour and tins of food contemplatively.

"How can we do that when we can't hardly stand up, for the want of food?" Cracker asked.

"Feel lucky that you'll get fed. I can't feed you anyway until you give me my kitchen back."

Cracker nodded, surrendering.

She glared at the colonel. "You didn't even ask how I got that food, the food that sustains body and soul, the food that has you transfixed. I'll tell you how I got it, I sold my body, that's how I got it."

"You didn't!"

"I did. My golden flesh."

"Ah, to a former swain?"

"To the general public, in front of everybody."

"My little peach, wasn't that a bit drastic?"

"I work for a living, which is more than you can say. Now get busy and bring me a kitchen."

"My prairie hen, don't ruffle your feathers."

"What about my clothes? You could at least have removed them before blowing up the mansion. And beds? And furniture?"

"He didn't lift a damned finger," Cracker said. "So I blew him out of bed."

"Well, you two get your little chores done, and I'll scout around Pearlygates for a suitable house," the colonel said.

"Get things done, get things done, while you stroll," the prospector snapped. "You don't even ask about my trip. You don't want to know what the gold was worth. You don't care. You don't even know what I bought with the gold. Well, I won't tell you. What that ore's worth is my business, and you'll never know."

"What's it worth?" asked MayBelle.

"It's worth so much that I'm cutting you out. This here is my mine now."

"Then starve," the colonel said.

"Starve! Starve! Who does all the work around here, and you tell me to starve!"

MayBelle sighed, wheeled the buggy around, and headed down the steep slope to Pearlygates. She knew several pleasant houses that still had stoves in them, and some even had stacks of stove wood sitting unused. She didn't miss the mansion, which had been ruined by dust and debris. It was nothing but a burden, and would have been impossible to live in once Cracker started blasting again. But that annoying Cracker could have pulled a few dresses out of her armoire first, and a mattress or two, or paid some attention to a lady's needs before he decided to blow things up.

She pulled up in front of a nice two-story house on D Street, one that had belonged to August Marlow, the banker, and dragged her burlap sacks inside. She had more houses than she knew what to do with, and this one suited her just fine. She had known these people. Now, as she wandered through the forlorn rooms, her footsteps hollow on the plank floors, she felt an odd sadness. Life had fled not only Pearlygates, but each dwelling, each room, each comfortable and cozy place where people lived out their lives in joy or sorrow.

Maybe she would insist that Colonel Raines pick his own house, since she was forced to pick up after him.

Well, the look on his face when she told him she had sold her flesh was worth the whole trip to Storyville. She thought she would rub it in a little.

MayBelle emptied the buggy, and drove up the slope to the tumbled heap of rubble, glad to see that Safe Cracker was digging around in the mess, salvaging what he could. She spotted a pile of kitchen things, a chair, two mattresses, a divan, a bedstead, some coal oil lamps, and even an undamaged mirror. She also spotted her shotgun lying under a plank, and quietly retrieved it. Her armoire was unscathed, so she would have clothing.

The colonel was staring at her, no doubt imagining all sorts of sordid things. It did her heart good to have him thinking it. For once he had met his match.

"Aren't you glad I took all the records and papers and deeds to the land office?" the colonel asked. "They'd be confetti if I hadn't. And then where would we be?"

She ignored him. Silently, she and Cracker loaded what small things they could into the buggy, pots and pans mostly, and she headed down the hill to off-load the stuff. It took several trips, some of them with furniture balanced precariously on the small buggy. This alarmed the horse, but eventually MayBelle was able to set up house below with clothing, beds and bedding, some half-ruined furniture, drapes, cracked mirrors, and most of her former kitchenware. She even salvaged a set of plates, cups and saucers, and random pieces of flatware. It would do.

About the time she had some semblance of a functional home, Colonel Raines strolled in.

"Ah, what's for supper?" he asked.

"You can grub your own supper, and cook it in your own house," she said. "There's enough houses around here, and you can salvage whatever you need from the ruins."

"But, my dear little partridge—"

"No work, no food."

"But I've been hard at work ever since you went to Storyville, and I know exactly how I'll handle the gold rush when it starts. You'll rejoice!"

"Out of my house."

"Ah, where is your devoted swain to lay his head?"

"Storyville?" she asked cheerfully.

The colonel drew himself up, sad-eyed. "Is this to be a parting of the ways?"

"Not if you work."

"But I have engaged in strenuous mental labor, exhausting me to the point where I can hardly keep my head up, thought ceaselessly for the benefit of all three of us, and have devised a scheme to bring us all into the lap of luxury. You can hire a maid and a cook and a scullery to do the grubbing. I now have in mind a complete plan of operations that will yield a fortune for us."

"Cracker and I are going to mine gold. Tomorrow I will muck out ore. You do whatever you want, and feed yourself by your own means, but not at my table."

"Mucking ore is beneath your dignity. You should hire it done, turtledove."

"Colonel, hit the road."

He stared sadly about the kitchen, noting the sacks of beans and flour, the fruit, the tins of vegetables, the fresh eggs and produce, the loaves fresh from the bakery.

"Well, we have come to divorce, sugarplum, you and I. And you, the light of my life, the beacon of all my dreams, too. You are the noblest and fairest of your sex. Never was there a fairer lady. I admire your boundless courage, sticking here like a nettle long after the town collapsed, determined to make something of your paltry divorce settlement. Ah, madam, there is none to match you for courage and tenacity among all of the fair sex. . . . Ah, something for the road?"

"I'm sure a passing cowboy will help out."

"If it wasn't for me, proposing we blast out the wine cellar and make a great show of it to attract interest, you wouldn't have any gold. It was my idea that led directly to a fortune. But thinking doesn't count. The world puts no value on thinking. My thoughts led to a bonanza, but here I am, destitute and starving. The world overvalues toil and ignores genius. But I bid you sweet adieu, noble lady."

"Yes, thank you. Now I'm going to cook, and I'm busy. I want to settle this house."

"Madam, I depart in utmost sorrow, filled with fond memories of happier days, when hope blossomed upon the bosom of Pearlygates, and we dreamed of joys unspeakable."

She relented a little, and kissed him on his smooth and perfectly shaven cheek. "I think you could get some ranch work," she said.

He looked like a lost puppy. "I will depart, with fondest memories of you, turtledove, and if we should meet in the next world, where I surely will be shortly, for want of anything to sustain my flesh, I trust it will be a joyous reunion. And if I do not perish, out of love and respect and sweetest memory, you will receive my entire estate to have and to hold, in the fullness of your years."

"What estate?"

He eyed her sadly and wheeled away. But he did not proceed down Nevada Street, as she expected, but toward the ruins of the mansion. As she built a fire in the cookstove and set water to boiling, she watched him labor up the slope to the heap of rubble. The low sun in the west lit the cliff, shooting light into the mine.

He stood, small and distant, before the hole in the cliff. Slowly, the colonel doffed his black silk hat and broadcloth coat and stood in shirtsleeves, the late-hour sun highlighting his dark hair.

And then he vanished, clambering over rock and rubble as he worked his way back into the sunlit tunnel. He would either start mucking ore for a while and plead that he had worked, look for some rich samples to peddle for food, or concoct some little scheme. He amused her. He would work a little for some samples of quartz ore. He would even carry a gunnysack full of samples down the road, it if came to that. He saw it as a form of cash, negotiable for some beans or whiskey.

She heard a knock, and found Safe Cracker without.

"What's he doing up there?" he asked.

"He's looking for some samples. I've sent him down the road."

"Samples? I don't want him spreading samples around. He'll start a stampede. How'm I gonna mine if I have three hundred claim jumpers trying to push me out of there?"

"Well, he's not welcome here. Go take the samples from him if you have to."

"Hey, MayBelle, we can't let him outa' here. You know what's gonna happen when he shows up somewhere with quartz like that? Quartz threaded with gold so thick it looks like jewelry? Quartz so crumbly you can crush it with a hammer and pick up piles of gold with your fingers? Stuff we can mill ourselves without no one horning in? You want some cash out of Pearlygates or not? Because we're no match for what's coming up the road if you cut him loose."

She sighed. "Cracker, go tell the lazy bum he's welcome for supper."

Chapter 16

For two weeks Colonel Raines watched Safe Cracker and MayBelle blast and muck. It flabbergasted him that two intelligent mortals would stoop to such misery. Cracker, he could understand. The low brute didn't know better. But MayBelle knew that all that grunting and groaning could well be disposed of.

Each morning she climbed into her dungarees, which she had salvaged from the manse, and shoveled rock into the ore car until she was so tired she obviously could barely stand up. They managed to fire a round about every other day, with Cracker not only drilling, but timbering and laying rail. Sometimes he did the mucking too, when the rubble was too heavy for MayBelle, or it needed hammering down to a size she could handle.

Each night they returned to town so worn they could hardly down a meal. But the heap of gold-bearing quartz grew, and threaded through it all were wires and nubs of gold. Most of it would be taken to the mill. But they segregated the choicest quartz, and brought it into town. Sometimes, after MayBelle had spread beans and canned tomatoes on the table, they recovered from their toil enough to hammer the quartz and pluck those threads and nuggets of shining gold out. Gradually, they filled a little bottle with threads of pure gold.

The colonel watched all this aghast.

"Hire it, hire it," he said.

"We'll hire you," MayBelle retorted.

"I can make you a fortune ten times larger, ten times faster, and without you lifting a finger," the colonel said.

"Raines, this seam's getting bigger and richer. It started at one inch, and now it's five inches more or less. But it's trending down about twenty degrees now, and we won't be able to push out the ore pretty soon . . . unless you lend a hand. We could hook up my mule and you could drive it up the tunnel," Cracker said.

"Cracker, old fellow, it's time to hire a few brutes with low brows and vacant stares," Raines said, after lapping up some flapjacks. "Mining's hard work. I get exhausted just looking at you. There are better ways. Think, Cracker, think. You weren't made to drill and muck; you have a head on you, a fertile little brain somewhere behind that sloping forehead, and a noble will that works through steel safes to reach the ill-gotten loot of commercial pirates. Be sensible."

"You're lucky to get beans," Cracker snapped.

"Cracker, you're not using your gray matter. Be a sharper. A man with all your skills could have anything. The object is to gather the world's wealth without lifting a finger, and the way to do it is to harness other people's greed. Once you get the knack, it's quite simple."

"Yeah? Then where's all this gold coming from? That's food and hay for the livestock. That's a bottle of rye for me when I want one."

"Cracker, you're no different from all the world's working stiffs," Colonel Raines said. "You spent time in the pen for nothing. Here you are, dead broke, and nothing to show for your years behind bars. You lack the true talent of a confidence man."

In truth, the colonel didn't much care for this bonanza. A little gold would have been fine. Enough to bait the traps, lure the suckers. A nice little ledge to clean out and use for larger schemes. How grand it would be to foist off an entire ghost town on unsuspecting rubes.

The very thought of it quickened his pulse. Sucker a thousand fools into buying up lots in a dead burg, and then walk out! They would talk about it for a century! But now there was a real gold strike, not a phony, and he would be reduced to selling lots and claims that had actual value like some ordinary salesman. The whole turn of events depressed him. This was the cruelest cut, being robbed of a chance to swindle people who deserved the swindling.

"Gad, I don't know how I got in with two working stiffs," he said.

"I don't either," MayBelle retorted.

Pearlygates slumbered through the autumnal days, life within it barely noticeable except for an occasional boom, or the rattle of ore sliding out of a one-ton car and down the slope near the heaped ruin of the old manse. The world knew nothing of all this, which Raines thought was a great pity.

Now and then the colonel slid a few pieces of gold-wired quartz into his pockets, just for publicity purposes if someone wandered in, but mostly he bided his time. There was always the moment to seize and the opportunity that came knocking.

This heavenly event occurred the very next day, when a ranch wagon rattled into town with a gawky young cowhand aboard.

Raines at once set foot upon Nevada Street to greet the fellow.

"Hey, where's MayBelle?" the lad asked.

"Up at the mine, my good man."

"Where's her house?"

"We demolished it. The mine lies right behind that heap of rubble."

"You got a mine?"

Ah, there was the question, and the colonel was well supplied with fishhooks.

"Young fellow, look at this!" He plucked from his pocket a particularly winsome specimen of quartz bristling with loops and strands and nubs of native gold. He dropped it into the cowboy's hand.

"Have you ever seen the like?"

The boy pushed back his hat, turned the quartz over and around, and squinted at it. "Man, that's some specimen!"

"Boy, there are tons and tons like it. Now, I wish I could just give this to you, but this is a secret. We don't want the world rushing in. No one in Nevada thinks there's any more gold left in Pearlygates, but we've uncovered a bonanza that will make the Comstock Lode look like poor diggings."

"Man, I can't believe it!"

"I suppose you could keep that if you want. Lots more where it came from. . . . But, boy, don't you tell a soul. Not one living soul."

The cowboy studied the strands of gold and licked them.

"Tastes like gold," he announced. "You can taste real gold, you know."

"I'm afraid you'll have to give it back, fellow. You made me no promises, and I can't let a specimen like that fall into the wrong hands."

The youth silently handed it back, which startled Colonel Raines.

"Yeah, well, I like herding cattle myself. Someday I'll have a nice spread," the young man said. "Anyways, I just thought I'd see if MayBelle, maybe she wants something and wants me to take some wine into town or fetch her some provisions."

"We're quite nicely furnished, thank you. Now remember, not a word."

"Me, I don't care about gold one way or the other," the boy said. "Just shorthorn cows and blue heeler dogs."

Flabbergasted, the colonel watched the youth drive the spring wagon away. He tucked the sample into his commodious coat and headed back to the land office wondering why he couldn't even start a gold rush with gold in his hand.

He slipped into a funk. Maybe his palmy days were over. Maybe fate had turned against him. He had known nothing but the dregs for weeks, and here he was in a rude rural camp, devoid of civilized people, with nothing to do and no one to skin out of a nickel. He peered at himself in a cracked mirror, observing that the crack separated his fine clean jaw from his neck. He moved slightly, and mended the separation, and felt better. He was, by God, the Adonis he always was, though his black suit showed signs of stain and dust.

Heartened by his suave image, he sallied forth into the empty streets, intending to discover his own luck. And much to his delight, he espied two prospectors standing at the brow of a hill yonder, watching MayBelle and Cracker shoulder the ore car toward the tailings pile and release the country rock within it.

These two gents watched a moment, consulted, and proceeded down a long sagebrushy slope into town, each leading a cadaverous mule. Judging from their gaunt frames, they had not enjoyed fat times in recent memory, and their beasts of burden were not any better off. That delighted the colonel, who examined them with a shrewd eye. Here were pigeons for the plucking, and the more starved and desperate, the better the plucking.

They seemed not to have laid eyes on Pearlygates before, and proceeded into town gawking this way and that, pointing at silent and empty houses, stores with no glass in their windows, and heaps of dun tumbleweeds banked along the windward sides of most buildings, shivering with every breeze.

He met them in the middle of Nevada Street, these sun-stained, bleach-eyed, squint-bagged gents, and found them entirely satisfactory.

"Welcome, brothers, welcome to Pearlygates," he said.

They paused, surveyed him up and down and up again, their gazes fixated on his black silk top hat.

"Colonel Raines here, at your service."

The taller one raised a battered hand. "They find anything up there?"

"Ah, gents, I wish I could convey happiness and good luck and joy, but my partners have had little success. A little color, elusive, a kiss and a promise, leads them further into the bowels of this godforsaken and abandoned slope, but no, sirs, not enough color to gild a lily."

"And you? What do you do?"

"Raines, sir. Colonel C.P. Raines, mining broker, financier, capitalist, and entrepreneur. I'm drilling a test bore in an overlooked area. You can see the mines over there, dead as carrion, abandoned two years ago, exhausted after massive efforts to find new reserves. But look up the slope. There stood a great mansion, now that ruin of plank and rubble, and there, in the very yard of the former master of Pearlygates, we are pushing steadily into the cold, mean rock. . . . And what, sir, is your occupation?"

The taller one smirked. "Grave digger," he said.

"Assistant grave digger," said the other.

"Excellent! You know exactly how to bore into the cruel earth. Perhaps I can hire you? I pay the prevailing wage, with bonuses and emoluments for sterling performance."

The pair looked at each other. Raines knew they were deciding whether to work for a day while they decided how to loot the place and bury the previous tenants in a glory hole. One of these gents sported a long-barreled hogleg, while the other carried a bandolier loaded with shells. The butt of a good rifle poked from a sheath on his flap-eared, yawning mule.

"Raines here; and you are . . ."

"Godfrey Whitebread," said the nobler of the two. This is my brother, Clyde Whitebread."

"Ah, gents, welcome. You must avail yourselves of our hospitality. We have a fine sheaf of claims to sell, and deeded lots and houses—we own the town, of course. And if you feel adventuresome, sink your pickaxe into the hills outside of town, where no claim has been filed. But meanwhile, there is sustenance and provender, comfort and escape from the weather, right here in Pearlygates."

"Mind if we look at that operation up there?"

"Why, Mr. Whitebread, that is the one request I cannot grant. That, sir, is a very private development, and not opened to public scrutiny."

Clyde stared. "You fixing to keep us out?"

"If you are qualified miners, sir, and I have your surety and guarantee that you will speak not a word of what you might see, upon your sacred honor, I would consent. Examine the tailings, if you please, but not the bore. You'll soon see what sort of rock we are bringing out."

The Whitebreads looked at each other, tugged on their sullen mules, and headed upslope.

Chapter 17

The colonel and two prospectors were climbing the slope. MayBelle watched them, annoyed. She pulled the lever on the ore car that opened the chutes, and the country rock within it roared out and down the slope. Two weeks of mining had built an impressive heap of rubble below.

"We got company," Safe Cracker said. "I thought he was supposed to keep people outa here."

"The colonel talks to his own set of angels," MayBelle said.

"Yeah, and they're all moochers," Cracker said. "I'll head these sourdoughs off. I don't want them to see the ore."

MayBelle nodded. She ached. Two weeks of grueling labor had not made the job easier or built her muscles or wiped away her pain and exhaustion. She wiped her brow, pushed back some strands of dusty hair, and waited.

She watched Cracker confront the three visitors. But the sourdoughs didn't stop; they just kept walking, and in a moment they were all gathered there at the tailings heap.

"Ah, turtledove, this is Godfrey Whitebread and his

esteemed brother, Clyde, doing a bit of scouting here. I told them we're doing a little exploration."

MayBelle sized up the armed pair in a hurry. If they were prospectors, they got their wealth by shooting it out of the earth.

"This is as far as we go," Cracker said.

The Whitebreads surveyed MayBelle, studying her dungarees, her caked hair, and the curves that not even loose work clothes concealed.

"This is yours?" asked Godfrey.

She nodded. "I own the town, most of it, all that wasn't purchased outright from the land company."

"How come you own it?"

"My husband owned the land company and the mines, or most of them. The lots reverted to him, and so did the mines."

"Ah, my friends, examine the prospects here," said Raines. "Feast your eyes upon the future. We'll dicker for anything, land, claims, houses. Buy now, buy cheap, get in on the ground floor."

"Where's the gold?" asked Clyde.

"Gold? Why, what a question. You may as well ask, where's the champagne and caviar? My friends, as you well know, the development of new wealth takes time. We have a most promising circumstance here, a bit of color, a tiny, glittering promise, not enough to matter, but it fills the bosom with hope and rainbows and visions of angels and archangels and bliss."

"It's nothing, we got nothing," Cracker said, glaring at Raines. "He's trying to push lots, sell dead claims is all."

"Why, Mr. Cracker, you take a most jaundiced view of it. I think in different terms, of inviting these fine young men to share in the future, to build upon hard work, faith, and yes, luck too."

"That your ore pile up there?" Godfrey asked, nodding toward the heap of quartz at the mine head.

"That's going to an assayer, yeah, but we're not counting on much," Cracker said. "Now, you've seen what we got here, maybe we'd like to get to work."

"My dear Cracker, don't be hasty. These fine fellows might just be the hard-rock miners we're looking for, so you and our dear MayBelle can get back to the important things, such as the happy future of Pearlygates."

"I'm gonna have a look," Clyde said. He handed the lead rope of his mule to Godfrey and headed straight for the quartz pile. Godfrey shrugged, and followed leading the two mules.

"Hey!" snarled Cracker. "Don't you take one damned step!"

But the Whitebreads would not be put off, and neither MayBelle nor Cracker had any way to defend the place against two big, armed hard cases.

The Whitebreads reached the mine head, leaned over the quartz pile, and plucked up samples.

"Jaysas," said Clyde, rubbing the quartz and then licking it clean. "A whole damn pile of gold."

Godfrey studied one lump after another, tracing the wires and bands and nubs of native gold. "Son of a gun," he said. He stuffed a sample into his jumper, and then another.

"Hey!" yelled Cracker, but neither Whitebread paid the slightest heed.

MayBelle knew the game was up. The secret was out . . . if she and Cracker and the colonel survived the afternoon. And she didn't even have one of her damned derringers in her pockets.

The colonel, however, saw things differently. "Ah, gents, stuff your pockets! Show the world! Pearlygates lives! The dawn of a bonanza lies before your very eyes! Show this in Storyville! Buy as many claims as you wish! We'll give you one free, and auction the rest three days from today. Tell the world that Pearlygates is alive and bursting with life and wealth."

The Whitebreads ignored him. They poked through the mound of quartz, studying sample after sample, pocketing the choicer ones, as if they were alone.

Cracker pulled her aside. "Your scattergun inside your house?"

"At the door."

"I'll get it."

"Fat chance," she said, as Godfrey turned and surveyed them.

Clyde found the bull's-eye lantern, lit it, and headed into the mine.

Cracker hastened toward the mine head, only to discover the bore of Clyde's hogleg pointing his way.

Cracker backed away.

Godfrey smiled. "You were saying, you found a little color, Raines? Nothing but a little promise?"

"Ah, my fine friend, it was our design to mine a little before making our finds public, but actually I'm delighted it turned out this way. You'll go to Storyville, show those splendid samples around, and start a rush, and we'll all prosper. You need only sign a small agreement to pay for lots, houses, and whatever you wish to speculate on, and you'll reap a bonanza, even if this little pocket of quartz goes the way of all things."

Godfrey grinned darkly. MayBelle had seen those sorts of smiles before. Her husband was the master of the dark, smug, knowing, all-commanding smile, and she knew who held the aces then, and now.

"This would mill at three or four thousand a ton," he said. "It's so pretty. I think gold's pretty, don't you? The way it sort of threads through there? A regular Tiffany jewel, I'd say."

Clyde reemerged, blinked, blew out the candle.

"Jaysas," he said. "They're only eighty feet in, five-inch seam, a foot of likely quartz above it, and they've been chasing it for forty feet, getting thicker all the way back, with no laterals yet. They don't even know how wide it runs."

"We're millionaires," Godfrey said.

MayBelle had a sickening feeling that he was right.

The Whitebreads' hands were never far from their revolvers, and they glanced cheerfully around, as if looking for the opportunity to shed some blood.

Cracker shrank into himself, and edged backward. Only the colonel seemed unruffled.

Godfrey addressed MayBelle: "Where's the papers?"

"Ah, what papers?"

Godfrey laughed. "What papers, she asks. They're down in the land office. Where else? Let's just have a little look."

"Why, I'll show you the very claim," Raines said. "Let's just wander down into town."

The sourdoughs herded the colonel and MayBelle ahead of themselves after collecting their mules. Cracker stood stock-still, and soon was left behind, momentarily forgotten.

"Not just one claim," Clyde said. "Every claim. And the lots. We've just bought the town."

"That takes my signature and a witness," MayBelle said.

"Oh, that can be arranged," Godfrey said. "Or maybe not. Your choice."

"Yes, it is my choice," she said.

They laughed.

She did not glance backward. She did not want them to remember Safe Cracker, who was standing stock-still.

The law was far away. And it probably wouldn't lift a finger anyway, especially if the sheriff learned that Raines and Cracker were her partners. She wondered how good her claims were, whether they could be defended. Few claims in the Pearlygates district had been patented, and none of those behind the mansion had been developed and patented through the federal government's office in Carson City. The town lots probably were better protected by the preemption law; she knew her husband had taken pains to follow the correct procedures when setting up a town, and had filed the platted and surveyed town site with the federal and state governments.

But what difference would it all make? She was well acquainted with ownership acquired at the point of a gun. There wasn't a cop within seventy miles, nor a judge, nor a sheriff.

"There's more boodle to be made from lots, my fine friends," the colonel said. "Gold comes and goes; today's thick seam is tomorrow's borrasca. But land is forever. Now, my partners and I have had a little disagreement. I'm in favor of developing the town lots, believing there is more to be gotten from the sale of an entire town, while they prefer to blast rock. And here you are, right in the middle of our little controversy."

The party reached the foot of the grade, and started across the flat, past rows of miners' cottages, straight toward the town lot company offices.

"Gentlemen, welcome to the Pearlygates Town Development Company," Raines said, as he stepped up to the door.

They shouldered past him and peered about the gloomy pine-paneled office.

"Where's the claims she owns?" asked Clyde.

The colonel pointed at a folder on a desk.

"And the town lots?"

The colonel pointed. "And on the wall, gents, is the plat map. Every lot. Yonder, on that wall, is a mining claim map, all plotted out. Now I believe the claim that interests you, and we are negotiating, is—"

"Negotiating," Godfrey said. "Negotiating."

He and Clyde yanked open the file drawers, hefted the folders out, and carried them into the middle of Nevada

Street. Records, receipts, deeds, contracts, claims, ledgers, and mining patents. These they dumped in a heap. They made a fine little pile, wavering in the zephyrs.

The colonel stared, aghast.

Clyde returned to the land office, grabbed a coal oil lamp, yanked off the glass chimney, opened the reservoir, and poured coal oil over the heap, while Godfrey flicked his thumb across a lucifer and touched off the conflagration. Deeds, titles, sales agreements, federal patents, surveys curled into ash and rose to the heavens as blue smoke.

Godfrey started laughing, and then the colonel joined him.

Chapter 18

Safe Cracker waited quietly until the Whitebreads were out of sight, raced to the pen where he kept Agnes, threw his packsaddle over the mule, led it to the glory hole where he stored his powder, and loaded the mule.

He dreaded carrying unstable blasting caps in the same load as a case of dynamite, but it couldn't be helped. Swiftly, he added fuse and other items, and then cautiously led Agnes along the cliff to the edge of the gulch, and down a precipitous grade.

His object was a small, snug cabin built there out of sight of town. He had stayed in it several times in his wanderings. It could be seen only from the defunct mines, looked like a toolshed rather than a residence, and would provide him with the base he needed now. He gingerly unloaded the dynamite and carried it inside, and then just as gingerly divided the blasting caps, putting some in a lean-to behind the cabin and the rest in a crack in the steep rocky cliff.

He unburdened Agnes and set her loose. She would forage and drink along the bottom of the gulch, never wandering far from where she had been unloaded.

Then he set to work. He cut three two-foot lengths of

fuse and crimped them onto the copper-jacketed blasting caps. Then he slit a stick of dynamite open, exposing the soft kieselguhr and nitroglycerin paste within, and gently slid a blasting cap into the stick, and bound it with a bit of wire. Now he had a bomb. He gently manufactured two more and placed them far apart outside his cabin.

He would show the Whitebreads what toast was made of.

He tucked a candle stub in his shirt pocket next to the lucifers and started out. Bickford fuse resisted ignition when held to a match; a candle would do the job better. He took two of the armed sticks of dynamite with him, and crept down the gulch until he was well into Pearlygates. He didn't know where the Whitebreads or his mates were. He discovered a pile of ash and burnt paper in the middle of Nevada Street and surmised what had happened. It all figured. He knew the Whitebreads by reputation; they were almost as hard as himself, and dangerous as vipers.

He avoided his friends, cut through shadowed and empty streets looking for the Whitebreads, and finally discovered that they had moved into a miner's cottage at the foot of the grade leading up to the Wine Cellar Mine. They had piled their gear inside and taken their mules upslope to the mine head. There they were loading some gunnysacks with ore. So they were planning on getting some cash. One would stay to guard the mine; the other would take a few bags to the mill, or maybe even to Storyville.

Good. There were things to do.

Cracker swiftly examined the one-room cottage. Heaped within were the Whitebreads' camping gear, clothing, kitchenware, bedrolls, and tools.

Cracker slid around to the side not visible from the heights where the sourdoughs were loading ore into sacks. He soon found a hole in the rough stone foundation and pried it open until he could reach well under the building. Gently, he slid one of his charged sticks under the building, pulled out, calculated the distance to the nearest place to hide himself, which was an abandoned store, Prosperity Men's Clothiers, fifty yards distant, and decided it would do. He lit the candle with a match, held the flame to the fuse until it sputtered, and then dashed across the dusky field to the sagging wooden false-front mercantile, and ducked into the recessed doorway.

He barely made it. A thunderous crack shattered the silence and smacked his eardrums, a flash and boom. He watched the cottage erupt into a fireball, debris flying. He saw a skillet sail high and plummet. Wood flew everywhere, like shrapnel. Flame engulfed the place. Every window in the store was blown to smithereens, leaving holes grinning in the walls. There was no wind, so fire would not sweep Pearlygates unless something freakish happened. Not that he cared whether the ghost town burned or not.

A giant column of dust and smoke billowed from the ruin of the cottage. He peered around the edge of the clothing mercantile and saw the Whitebreads staring in disbelief from the mine head.

"I'm saving the next one for you," he yelled.

They heard him. Revolvers materialized in their hands.

Let them come, let them come, he thought.

"You're up to no good, and I like it," said the colonel.

Cracker whirled to find the colonel crouched behind him. "Get back. This is a charged stick in my hands."

"Got one for me?"

"Where's MayBelle?"

"Holding her ears."

"She got that shotgun?"

"In her hands when she's not holding her ears."

"You armed?"

"I have MayBelle's derringer, for what good it'll do."

"You're not armed, then."

They watched the Whitebreads slowly stalk into town,

revolvers in hand. These two weren't giving up without a fight.

They left their loaded mules up at the mine head.

"Colonel, can you run?"

"Not if I can help it."

"Then you'll blow yourself up. Now watch."

Cracker knelt at the foundation of the clothing store, pulled some loose sandstone out, and inserted the charge until only the fuse remained in sight.

He thrust some matches and a candle stub at the colonel. "You set this off when they get close. Real close. This here fuse don't ignite easy, so light the candle, hold it to the fuse until it spits, and that'll start it. Make sure it's spitting good and then get out. Out! Move your butt! They won't see you; we're behind the store from where they're coming."

"Where will you be?"

"I've got one more of these little poppers hidden away. I'll get it and make use of it one way or another."

"You're a Napoleon, my esteemed friend and sainted colleague."

"No, but I've dodged a few coppers and I know a few tricks."

Colonel Raines was softly cackling and Cracker thought maybe the man was demented.

Cracker slid away, running nimbly from building to building, but the thickening dark hid him well. The Whitebreads reached the foot of the grade and immediately spread apart, even as the colonel waited behind the mercantile.

The Whitebreads suddenly split. They were going to round the false-front store from both sides, and the colonel would be in trouble.

Cracker didn't have time to get his third stick. "Hey, Clyde, I'm over here," he yelled.

A shot snapped the quiet.

One or the other of the Whitebreads turned toward

Cracker and began trotting. The second Whitebread stayed on course, heading for the dark and silent mercantile.

"Godfrey, old fellow, I'm over here," announced the colonel.

A Whitebread headed in the direction of the sound.

Cracker saw a sudden light flare behind the building, saw lights dance a moment, and then sparks.

He saw shadow and light and shadow.

"Godfrey, get back!" Clyde yelled.

The yellow blast lifted the whole front of the mercantile, shattered it into kindling, shot debris everywhere, loosed lethal glass shards and nails and wire, and set the rear half of the store on fire.

Cracker saw no movement at all. His ears rang.

He waited. The fires flared, casting shadows on the surrounding structures, hiding ruin in the darkness.

The Whitebreads, both armed, would be particularly dangerous now. The colonel was probably dead.

There was nothing to do but wait. Cracker was three blocks from his own miner's cottage and the revolver he had in his kit. He was even farther from the cabin out of town where he kept the dynamite. So he lay beside tumbleweeds next to an abandoned building, hoped he was not getting too intimate with rattlers, and settled down for a long wait.

Nothing happened. The fire cast eerie bobbing light and moving shadows on the surrounding flat. Cracker saw no movement he could identify as mortal, and finally concluded that there were three bodies lying there. But he wasn't about to crawl in and get shot in the head by some possum.

He waited awhile longer, growing itchy, and finally faded down the silent streets of Pearlygates, which were silent and serene in moonlight, as if mayhem had not occurred on the skirts of town. He peered right and left, forward and back, and saw no one stalking. He finally reached MayBelle's house and was astonished to find the kitchen lamplit, and within it, MayBelle and the colonel sipping something that looked a lot like some whiskey.

Like the rest of Pearlygates, her house now lacked an intact pane of glass.

"Hey, Colonel," he yelled. "Is it safe?"

The colonel and MayBelle scarcely looked up from the table. "Come right in, Cracker. All's fine."

Cracker fearfully sidled across the verandah, avoiding moonlight, slid inside, and headed for the kitchen. There they were, sipping amber fluid with satisfying exhalations.

"You're crazy, sitting in front of an open window with a lamp lit," he said.

"Oh, tut, Cracker. We were a tad concerned about you. I suspected a rattler."

"Where are they?"

"Gone, Cracker, gone."

"I didn't see a thing."

"How could you? The fire drew your stare. But I watched from close at hand. After a few minutes, our erstwhile customers, the Whitebreads, picked themselves up from the earth, which they hugged for some while, and limped away. Yes, limped is the word. I believe Clyde was carrying Godfrey, who seemed to have suffered some sudden arthritis of the left knee. I strolled away from the fire to another storefront where I could purchase a fine view in the moonlight, watched them gather their livestock, lead the mules down from the mine, with some of our ore in the sacks of course, straight down Nevada Street, and over the hill. They are now two or three miles in the direction of Storyville."

"I got our mine back," Cracker said. He wanted some credit, some fawning, some slavish adoration, if not a kiss and a hug from MayBelle.

"If you don't quit blowing up Pearlygates, I won't have anything to sell," MayBelle said, crossly. "I should bill you for the windows."

Chapter 19

Colonel Raines was in an uncommonly cheerful mood.

"What are you gloating about?" MayBelle asked.

"The rush. Tomorrow will tell the tale. Tomorrow we'll get rich. Tomorrow, the whole world will descend on Pearlygates and I will be selling lots until midnight."

"How can you do that? I can't even prove I own a thing around here."

Colonel Raines sighed, happily. "That's the sport of it. I never much cared to peddle things I owned."

That evoked a short bark from Safe Cracker, who sat at the kitchen table wolfing MayBelle's flapjacks and side pork.

MayBelle had been in a nasty mood for days, slapping their meals down, cooking carelessly, muttering to herself. The burning of all those legal records and deeds and sales receipts and claims had set her off.

"Ah, turtledove, tomorrow your ignoble toil ends and bliss begins," the colonel said.

"Yeah, well then, wash the dishes."

"We'll hire it done. The world is full of chumps."

"I don't see you getting a living, and you sure aren't working," she replied.

He swallowed the flapjacks, which was all she felt like cooking these days, and wiped his mouth gently. "Have faith," he said.

For two days after they had chased the Whitebreads out of town, they had worried about what might come. Safe Cracker had opined that the Whitebreads would return with a small army of toughs, far more than one safe blower and a confidence man and a moll could handle. But the colonel would have none of it.

"I know the type," he said. "They'll show that ore from one end of Storyville to the other. They'll blabber and bellow. And tomorrow half of Storyville will arrive on our doorstep. And then the dance begins."

"I can't even prove we own the mine," she said, snatching the colonel's empty plate from him.

"Oh, that. If it troubles you, go claim anything you want. Claim all the glory holes. Write a claim, put it in a can, put the can in a cairn at the corner, and that'll take care of it."

"I suppose we oughta," Cracker said. "Like maybe tonight."

MayBelle didn't acknowledge the colonel's wisdom, but he could tell she had agreed.

After she had dried the last dish, the trio wandered the silent and haunted streets until they reached the land office, where various pads and forms remained, along with pen and ink. Together, they manufactured a dozen claims, signed them all, and headed out into the moonlight. It took only a couple of evening hours to insert each claim into a can, and pile rock over the can at each claim.

"It ain't gonna do any good against a mob," Safe Cracker muttered, but he wasn't objecting to it, either.

The colonel was singing melodies he hadn't remembered since he was a boy and his opera diva mother, Matilda Noble, sang them to him, especially when he had been good about using the thundermug.

"You're getting on my nerves," MayBelle said.

The colonel was humming "The Battle Hymn of the Republic."

They retired, each to his own abode because MayBelle was not in the mood for company. The colonel slept soundly. The next morning he shaved with extra care, anointed his face with witch hazel gotten from Storyville, donned his newly scrubbed and boiled white shirt, put on his newly sponged black broadcloth suit, blacked his scuffed shoes, and headed for the land office looking more like Beau Brummell than ever.

They were laughing at him, but they had no experience with a gold rush. He fussed with his blank sales pads, receipt pads, and so forth, sharpened pencils, checked his nib pens and ink, and sat back.

About noon he heard a commotion on the road, stuck his head out the door, and saw a dozen horsemen pushing their sweated and flagging mounts the last half mile to Pearlygates. Behind the vanguard, he saw a hundred stragglers, whipping carriage horses, flagellating mules, even trotting heroically with nothing but a knapsack. He sighed, cheerfully.

At last.

They stormed into Pearlygates, scarcely bothering to examine the silent buildings baking in the sun. The colonel watched them from his window as they debated, pointed, waved, argued. A cluster of them threaded through the old ghost town toward the dead mines, whose head frames pierced the blue sky. Others pointed to a hundred little glory holes poked into cliffs, while others simply studied the surrounding country, without an inkling of where anyone might have struck gold. Some discovered the still smouldering heap of the clothing store, and the foundation of what had been something or other, whose shattered wood blanketed a wide area.

He saw bearded prospectors among them, but these people were mostly city men; one, with a black sleeve garter, he recognized as a clerk in a Storyville hardware store. The gent who had punished his trotters half to death was a dentist in Storyville. Others were hard rock miners in blue jumpers. A silver-haired fellow in a black suit was a mortician the colonel knew of. Quite a few were callow youths, pimpled and pocked, expecting a stream of pure gold to flow from the rock wherever they struck a pick.

Few had tools of any sort, and colonel considered the ones with tools the dumber members of the species. He spotted not a single woman, but they would show up shortly to mine the miners. And soon there would be a few sturdy widows to cook and sew and run bedbug establishments. In fact, he knew his first solid sales would be to doughty women setting up boardinghouses in these empty frame buildings.

The whole lot peered about, expecting to see a rainbow's end somewhere. But there was only a boiling sun, a dusty town of abandoned board buildings, and silence.

The colonel was in no rush. Let them first suffer confusion. MayBelle and Cracker were hard at work in the mine, and not visible, and would not be discovered for some little while. So it was a hundred or so fevered argonauts wondering where the gold mine was and how they could stake a claim next door to it.

Raines was so vastly pleased with events he began humming "Yankee Doodle." It was just about then that the mob discovered a live store and land office, and a dozen crowded in and stared at the colonel, who was taking his ease behind a counter.

"Good afternoon, gents," he said.

"Where's the gold?" asked a bug-eyed boy.

"Why, sir, there is no gold."

"I saw it. I saw quartz threaded with gold."

"Someone was pulling your leg, young fella. This old town's been slumbering away for nigh two years now."

"What're you doing here, then?"

"Oh, the owners pay me a bit to keep an eye on things. Not that they'll ever earn a cent from a place like this, with exhausted mines in it."

"There's got to be gold. Several people said it was Pearlygates quartz, with the iron oxide in it."

That came from a seasoned prospector, whose vast black beard hid all but two jet-black eyes and a chestnut-colored forehead.

The colonel shrugged. "You go home now. Or look around. I don't much care."

"He's hiding something. He don't want people poking around," said the clerk in sleeve garters.

The colonel sighed, sadly. "Young man, I don't mean to shatter your dreams, but neither do I wish to mislead you. If you insist that there's gold here, then in your mind you will see gold, and you will no doubt want to purchase claims or lots or whatever, but I would rather not sell them to you and end up with an angry man on my hands. No, no, go home to Storyville."

"Ain't that the colonel?" said one.

"It's the colonel. Don't believe a word he says. Them gold bricks he was raffling, they were lead is all."

The colonel peered soulfully at the assemblage. "Why, yes, I am the man, banished here to sell lots for want of any other income. Lots in a ghost town. I can remember better days, yes, sir, better days."

"If he says there's no gold, then there probably's gold all over heah," said a southern fellow.

"What do these houses and lots sell for?" asked a sharp-eyed man of some education.

"Regularly, sir, a hundred a lot and two hundred with a house on it, and four hundred for a lot with a store on Nevada Street . . . but I must confess, sir, that very recently some of the records were burned—you can see the ash right there, outside the window, and ownership is in dispute. Indeed, sir, on a third of these lots, the papers and deeds have been destroyed, and it will take some little while to work it all out. Now those, if you're willing to gamble, I'd sell cheap, but with the caveat that you might not get clear title. Cheap, but uncertain, that's the word for it."

"Cheap, meaning what?"

"Seventy-five for a lot and a hundred fifty for a lot and house with a clouded title, sah. The owners don't know I'm doing this, but they gave over to me the opportunity to improve our fortunes, and I will offer them for that."

"Yeah, and who owns the town lot company?"

"That, sir, I am not privy to. I was hired by a third party to look after things. Somebody seeking to make a killing by unloading a ghost town, I'd say."

"How do you know what lots are clouded?"

"Why, my friend, we have lost the records." He turned to the plat map on the wall behind him. "Now, take A Street. The truth of it is, we don't have a single deed to any lot or building on A Street." He traced the street with his finger.

"I might take a couple for fifty," the sharp fellow said.

"Fifty apiece? Why, friend, go select your two, come back, and deal privately, because I don't want this getting out. I'll sell you a pair of houses."

"I thought I'd just get in on the ground floor," the fellow said.

"A worthy idea, sir, if there is a ground floor," the colonel said.

The sharp fellow studied the plat map and headed out the door. In the space of twenty minutes, the colonel sold eleven lots and seven houses, all on credit, of course, ten dollars down.

But he closed the day with cash in the till.

Chapter 20

Shouts greeted MayBelle and Safe Cracker as they mucked out the rubble in the drift. They were eighty-five feet from daylight, and could well hear the voices at the head of the mine, even though their own lifting and shoveling made an awful racket.

They headed at once for the mine head, and discovered a mob of twenty or thirty men collected around the ore pile, each examining the gold-threaded quartz.

"Hey, we found it," yelled one.

A dozen others were running up the slope, and still others down in the ghost town were pointing and gesturing.

"Gold!" cried a man in sleeve garters, who appeared to be more of a bank clerk than a hard-rock miner.

"Yes, and this is ours," Cracker said.

"Who are you?"

"This is the Wine Cellar Mine, if that's what you want to know, and it's owned by this here lady."

"Yeah? Who says?"

MayBelle eyed the miners who were pawing through the quartz, looking for the choicest specimens. "I own the town," she said.

Several of the men laughed.

"I own the town lot company, those dead mines, and about seventy claims, including this one and the four or five on either side of it."

"That's not right; any mining district limits claims, one per man, two for the discovers," said a bushy-bearded one.

"This is not a new mining district; it's a ghost town I happen to own," she replied.

Ore samples were vanishing into pockets and sacks.

"Hey!" yelled Cracker.

They ignored him.

"What does it assay?" asked one in spectacles.

"It hasn't been assayed."

"This is rich ore. How thick's the seam?"

Cracker had had enough. "This here is private property, and you can clear out now."

"Man down in town, he says there's no gold around here!"

A dozen men laughed.

"Some of my claims are for sale; why don't you go dicker with him?" MayBelle asked.

"Lady, you say you own this, but where's the proof?"

She had none. The Whitebreads had burned it. But there were those claims in cairns.

She pointed. "There, and in the center of each of our claims."

"How wide are these?"

"Five hundred feet," she said.

"That's too wide. You can't do that. You can't just shut us out like that, hogging the whole bonanza."

"We found it; we'll keep it. You want to work for us? I pay good wages. And I'll give a lot and house to each man I hire. We've got plenty of blasting and mucking ahead of us, and I need mine timbers, rail, and we'll need a hoist soon because the ore is running downslope now. We'll also need teamsters to haul this ore to the mill. I could hire a dozen men right now, today, starting this minute. You fellows interested?"

She would like some help. She ached from the labor. Her clothing was worn out; rock gashed and mashed the cloth on her body. She would like to hire crews, mine by shifts, and turn it into a regular business. She brushed away her matted hair.

"Three dollars a day for good reliable men," she said. "That's high wages. And you get a lot and a house."

She didn't like the looks on their faces. They were weighing the odds. They weren't crooked exactly, but they didn't like this deal, and were calculating the odds. By now, more were flooding in, pawing the quartz, pocketing pieces, peering into the mine, studying MayBelle and Cracker.

"Isn't that the singer?" asked one.

"Yeah, the one that did all that unbuttoning."

"Yeah, that's her. What'd she do that for if she has a mine?"

"And that guy's Cracker. I know him. He's done time. He can blow a door off any safe ever made."

"Yeah, and that colonel down there, he was in Storyville pushing some gold-plated lead bricks off in a raffle."

"What a bunch!"

"This whole thing, it's a crooked deal. They don't own this, or my name ain't Wilbur."

"See if there's ore in there. Hey, Joe, go in there."

The argonaut named Joe, and a dozen others, pressed into the mine, followed by still more.

MayBelle watched the mine swallow half the crowd.

"I wish I had a stick to throw in there," Cracker muttered.

"What are we gonna do?" she asked.

"Maybe a stick or two isn't a bad idea," he said, and wheeled toward his supply of blasting materials.

But then Raines huffed his way up from below.

"Yeah, no gold," someone said. "You said there was no gold."

"Why, it does appear my partners have just discovered some. Let us open some champagne and rejoice."

They laughed.

"I see we've been found out," he said. "I tried to keep it secret, but one must never underestimate the ability of a prospector to sniff out gold."

She watched the colonel stroll easily among the miners, as if this dangerous situation was just the sort of thing he enjoyed.

She wasn't enjoying it. She was about to lose everything, once again. There was something wolfish in this mob. They were circling prey and ready to pounce, looking for just the right opening so they could justify what they had done, maybe even brag about it.

The crowd that had flooded into the mine erupted from it, holding still more samples.

"Thick seam, plenty of it in there," one shouted. "Lookee here. I pulled this right out of the seam." He waved a shining lump of quartz laced with ribbons of native gold.

"Yes, and it's mine," MayBelle said, holding out her hand.

The argonaut grinned.

"Dontcha think these notorious characters should be banned from our mining district?" asked the smart-looking one in spectacles. "A burglar, con man, and . . . sweetheart of the world." He grinned. "Mining districts, they enact rules. They figure out the width of the claims. They limit claims one to a man. They kick out undesirables."

She itched for her shotgun. Not that it would do much good against a hundred twitchy, gold-fevered miners. But if she had it at hand, she would by God lower the barrel straight at them. But she and Cracker didn't even have a revolver.

The colonel rounded into the crowd, lifted his silk top hat, and laughed.

"Ah, gentlemen, there you are, and here we are. You want mining claims; we have them. Let's proceed with a forthright auction. You've seen the fabulous treasure that lies within this mine; you are thinking it stretches to the claims on either side of this one. Maybe you're right! So the fair and proper thing is to sell them to the highest bidder."

"No, that makes you the owners, and we're not buying." That came from the bespectacled one again, who was hunting for some way to legitimize the pillage they had in mind.

These men crowded close, a sea of calculating eyes and frowning faces.

The colonel eased through the multitude until he came to a flat rock, and then he stepped up.

"My friends and neighbors," he said, "behold here a widow of the grass variety, who has clung to this little village, bequeathed her by her perfidious husband as a settlement, even as the mines were dying and the town emptying. My friends, see how she has clung to her pittance, and now has the good fortune to earn a bit from it. Is there any man here who is such a cur, such a scoundrel, that he would rob her of her inheritance?"

"Yeah, and she undoes her buttons when she needs to," retorted one.

"Here we all are," the colonel continued sweetly. "Men of integrity and honor, men of such transparent honesty that I have no doubt that this will all be settled according to all the rules of justice, fair play, and charity. Here you are, eager and willing to be good neighbors, good citizens, upright and noble argonauts, wise as Solomon, as inspired as Moses, filled with saintly passions."

They were grinning at him. "All except you, Colonel," yelled one.

"Ah! There you have it! You will behave in a manner that honors the virtues, while I have sometimes strayed. And having said that, you will see to the welfare of this little lady, this widow tossed in the storms of life, and protect her property as fiercely as you would protect your own, or even more so because she is of the frail sex and needs your manly protection."

"Hey, Colonel, she can take care of herself!"

The colonel turned toward the heckler. "Indeed she can, sir, and she has authorized me to donate one mining claim in a raffle. Which shall it be? A raffle, and one of you will have a claim to mine to your heart's content. Will it be that one there," he said, waving at the cliff, "or the one beyond it?"

"It ain't hers to raffle, pal," said another, the one in the sleeve garters.

The colonel fixed a stare upon the fellow until he withered before the colonel's unblinking gaze. "A pity it is that a good honest clerk like you would rob widows. The next way station upon your road to perdition will be robbing orphans, young fellow."

"Not a bad idea," the clerk said, by way of bravado.

The colonel turned to her. "My little turtledove, which claim would you care to raffle off, entirely for free, to these gents, by way of welcoming them all to Pearlygates?"

"I'll meet the colonel and up the ante," she said. "I'll raffle off the three mines across the gulch, and one claim right here on the bluff . . . let's see, that third one there."

"There!" said the colonel. "An incredibly generous offer from a great-souled lady who fills me with awe, and fills my old eyes with tears. Let us begin, and may you all be lucky!"

She marveled. Silver-tongued Colonel Claudius P. Raines had won, at least for the moment.

Chapter 21

Colonel Claudius P. Raines was proud of himself. He had swiftly raffled off three exhausted mines, and one live and potentially valuable claim three hundred feet away from the Wine Cellar Mine. All of this business had quieted the clamor, but more to the point, it had tacitly established MayBelle's ownership of the town and the surrounding mining claims and patents.

Four lucky argonauts had whooped and pranced when the colonel pulled their names out of his silk hat. For the moment, MayBelle still owned Pearlygates.

But more were coming. Even as MayBelle, Cracker, and the colonel retreated to MayBelle's house at dusk, the road from Storyville was clogged with fortune seekers and adventurers, and they were spreading through town, claiming houses, exploring old glory holes without a by-your-leave.

Cracker wasn't impressed. "You gave away a good claim, probably the same vein as ours," he said while sipping some barleycorn malt. "And tomorrow they'll be demanding the rest. Whole new mob coming in, and grabbing houses. And you can bet that by dawn, that ore pile of ours will be down to nothing, bunch of burglars floating around here."

"You're the one to know," MayBelle said.

"What do I do? I rescue MayBelle's holdings by feeding the wolves carrion, and you complain," the colonel said, sipping hard. "Were it not for my quick wit and native ability, we might have nothing at all."

"That's exactly what we got, nothing at all. I shoulda got some red sticks primed, and waved a few around at that bunch. They don't understand words, but they sure understand a red stick with a spitting fuse."

"I am the recipient of a vote of no confidence," the colonel said gravely. He rose, with vast dignity, refilled his tumbler with corn whiskey, and proceeded out the door and into the night. His partners just didn't appreciate his talents or his strategy. He stood on the veranda, eying the stars. The old town was not silent tonight. He spotted cook fires, pedestrians, gaggles of shadowy men standing on street corners.

They had dreams, every one of them, and they were his to exploit if only MayBelle and Cracker would quit worrying about that fool mine and see where the real wealth lay. They could make their pile without a lick of work.

He knew more argonauts were arriving every hour, even in the darkness. But they were orderly enough, and most of them simply drifted through Pearlygates, staring at pale, moonlit buildings and the old gallows frames of the dead mines above, ghostly in the white night. At the first hint of dawn they would all stir, lay claim to everything in sight, and grouse if anyone suggested it was owned, deeded, private land. He would deal with it. If his partners would let him.

He heard motion behind him, and found Safe Cracker standing beside him on MayBelle's porch.

"I didn't mean that," Cracker said. "I just was talking through my hat."

That astonished the colonel, who had never before heard any word resembling penance or retraction from the wiry safe robber.

"MayBelle says come on in and get some chow she's fixing," Cracker added.

"Why, I believe I will."

The colonel was oddly pleased. Only moments before he had considered packing his kit and walking out, leaving this burg to his perfidious partners, letting them suffer in their lust for gold, and miss the big chance, the one nobody was thinking about.

He felt something wash through him akin to tenderness, though he would scarcely admit to such maudlin sentiments. Instead, he wheeled through the four-panel door behind the mad dynamiter, and soon found himself bathed in the lamplight of MayBelle's kitchen, and felt somehow pleased.

They were a threesome. Three lonely outcasts. Three raucous, quarreling independents, trying to outdo each other in sheer badness. Three loners, somehow welded together by fate and circumstance, each with a unique talent that could help their enterprise.

It surprised him to be thinking such things. He eyed MayBelle, who was setting a table for them, discovering strength, and what's more, a bonding with her two guests. The colonel didn't have another person in the world; MayBelle was alone too, and Safe Cracker had made no mention of a family, or wife, or children, much less cousins, brothers and sisters, or parents.

"You alone in the world, Cracker?" he asked

"No, I got a pet giraffe for company," Cracker said.

"You alone in the world, MayBelle?"

"I've got a few friends," she said, and left it at that.

She served them flapjacks and some stewed tomatoes. There wasn't much else to be had in Pearlygates. They ate silently.

"I'll wash those dishes, MayBelle," the colonel said.

She stared, so astonished she nearly dropped a bowl. "No, I'd rather you let me do it. I don't think I could get used to it."

Relieved, he produced a cigarillo, scratched a match, and sucked in some smoke. "It's time to do some planning," he said.

"I gotta go guard the mine," Cracker said.

"Not for a little while."

"If I don't get up there, our ore pile will vanish overnight."

"That's not all bad, you know," the colonel said.

"Not bad! Losing a fortune to a bunch of jackals?"

The colonel sighed, sucked smoke, and exhaled grandly. "You have a dreadful passion for backbreaking toil," he said.

"I'm glad somebody does," MayBelle shot at him.

The colonel sucked, until the end of his cigarillo glowed orange in the night. "We are sitting in the middle of a town owned by MayBelle. By my calculation, upon examining the plat map on the wall of the office, there are over three hundred residences, thirty-eight commercial establishments, a dozen defunct mines, minus those we raffled off, and fifty-odd mining claims. At a price of one hundred dollars for a lot, two hundred for a house and lot, three hundred for a commercial building and lot, five hundred for defunct mines, and a thousand for undeveloped mining claims held by MayBelle's land company, we are in the midst of a fortune, one that can be gotten with no more physical exercise than the scribble of a pen. By my calculation, the two hundred vacant lots are worth twenty thousand, unless they get bid higher in a frenzy. The three hundred residences are worth sixty thousand or more. The thirty-eight commercial buildings are worth almost twelve thousand. The nine remaining defunct mines are worth forty-five hundred; and the fifty or so mining claims are worth fifty thousand. And you want to sweat away in foul air, in a hole in the ground."

Cracker glowered. "The gold's real; your figures are all just thin air."

"But is the gold real? How do you know? You might be six inches away from the end. The land and buildings, Cracker, are real; that pile of gold up there is our advertisement, the cheese in the mousetrap. All we need do is let that pile of quartz melt away, and we'll make a merry living with the scrape of a pen."

"I don't like it. Gold's gold, and we've a gold mine."

"I can't educate the uneducable," the colonel said.

"We don't even have proof of ownership anymore," MayBelle said, as she wiped a dish hard, removing what the dishwater failed to remove.

"My dear, my little cockatoo, trust in Colonel Raines."

"All right, I will. Dry the dishes."

Raines was so astonished that he did not object. He drilled the glowing cigarillo into a plate, stood, and astonished himself by picking up a dish towel and setting to work. It was loathsome and beneath him, but it would show her his bona fides. Never before had he stooped so low as to wipe a dish, but this evening had yielded something special. They were bonded now, a trio of badgers rooting up a fortune.

"Jaysas, I never thought I'd live to see it," Cracker said.

"It is only for a short duration, by which I will demonstrate the folly of labor by performing it. I could, right now, be in our office, preparing for tomorrow's land riot. The trouble, Cracker, is that you lack a good eye for opportunity. You have a single-minded itch to sweat, blast, shovel, tote, and grind yourself down. There rests in the bosom of the land office assorted blank pads: sales agreements, titles, promissory notes, receipts, and so on. There are two bottles of good black ink, and a dozen nib pens. The total effort expended to get ourselves three hundred or five hundred dollars cash wouldn't weary my pinky finger."

"You sure got a mouth."

"My dear colleague, my bosom companion on the road to wealth, I will require some labor of you on the morrow, and after that, rest easy, for naught will be required evermore. I shall request that you bring as much of that quartz to the land office as possible, broken up into fine chunks, souvenirs to whet appetites. To each who enters the office, will I bestow a fistful of real, gold-bearing quartz, and even as they turn it over in their fingers, and lick it, and grow lustful of mind and groin, so will I sell them lots, lots and lots of lots."

"See, you want some work after all. Packing that ore here and busting it's a big job! So much for your life of leisure."

The colonel rubbed and rubbed a plate. "Hire it. I'll hire it done," he said. "The world brims with people with strong backs and weak minds."

"No, I'll do it," Safe Cracker said. "Hire it done, and half the gold wouldn't get here."

"Then you make my point for me, friend. Your blasting and mucking days are over."

Chapter 22

Safe Cracker bestirred himself just before dawn. The colonel had given him a mission, and even if the colonel was a crackpot, there was something to it. Some samples of quartz gold floating around wouldn't hurt the sale of town lots.

Not that he had any faith in the idea of selling town lots. Gold was the only thing; he and MayBelle and the crazy confidence man had a real mine, a bonanza, and nothing on earth would dislodge him from it.

He collected his sweet old Agnes, rubbed her jaw, examined her teeth, loaded a packsaddle onto her, and headed through town. The place astonished him; men lounged everywhere, even in this twilight hour before sunrise. The noise! And lamps in store windows. And a crowd in front of a false-fronted building. He walked up Nevada Street, suddenly aware that a hundred more had arrived in the night. Maybe two hundred. There were men everywhere, waiting for the day.

In one lamplit mercantile building, he discovered a saloon. He could scarcely credit his eyes or accept what he was seeing. But there, within, were two gents in bartender aprons, an array of bottles, a keg of beer with a spout, and a mob of burly roughs and prospectors crowded against the counter and clamoring for drink. At six in the morning.

The colonel had not sold this saloon outfit the lot or the building. Cracker frowned. That was the flaw in the colonel's scheme. He could offer lots and buildings for sale, and no one would buy them.

Gold! There was only gold, and Raines be damned.

"How long's this been open?" he asked a lounging miner.

"I reckon one hour. Brought a whole saloon in on a wagon last night, and set up right smart, two bits a drink, which is robbery, since a drink is a bit in Storyville, but for the moment they got themselves a corner on the market."

Safe Cracker had a terrible itch to repair to the oasis and imbibe.

"It won't last," Cracker said. "Get a rush going, and there'll be a new saloon opening once a day."

"Yeah, but these boys will clean up meanwhiles," the miner said. "You know where to hunt for gold?"

"It's an old mining town, and all I can think is to pick up a few old claims from the land office and go deeper. It ain't like some new diggings, where everybody's scrambling to stake a claim, you know."

"Yeah, there's hard-rock reality in that," the gent said. "Me, I'm not buying some old claim. I'm going to study on that new find, and see if I can find the same formation outside of town some, two, three miles away, where there's nobody yet looked."

"Not a bad idea, but for insurance, you oughta buy a few claims and a few town lots too," Cracker said. "Git in on the ground floor. Town's gonna bust pretty soon, more coming every hour."

"Haw!" The prospector dug into his pockets and pulled them out. They contained not so much as a dime.

Cracker nodded, and headed up Nevada Street toward the mine, privately laughing at the colonel's notions of what could be gotten for lots and buildings in a ghost town. There was only gold.

The sky had blued some and the surrounding cliffs had become distinct. Ahead loomed the steep grade to the ruins of the mansion and the mine head. He started upward, leading his mule toward the mine. That's when a tough bearded fellow whirled out of the darkness and leveled a shotgun.

"Far as you go," he said.

"Far as I go? What's all this?"

"Turn around and vamoose."

"Vamoose! That's my mine up there!"

"Was," the hard case said. "Was."

Cracker knew suddenly and sickly that he and MayBelle and the colonel no longer controlled the Wine Cellar Mine, and that things had changed in the night. Claim jumpers had taken over.

"You gonna take me up there and let me talk? We got legal claims filed, and we got 'em in that cairn there too."

The hard case grinned. "Did, maybe. Names in that cairn been changed too."

"Yeah? And who stole it?"

"Whitebreads, them that got blown out of here last time. Only this time we got us a little syndicate with shares. And no one with a stick of powder can even get close."

The rough turned slightly. "Look at that cliff. See the man standing above the mine? See the one over to the right? Those aren't broomsticks they're carrying."

Cracker saw heavily armed men above the mine and patrolling the plateau. No one but an army could pierce to the mine.

"What you say your name is?" the rough asked.

"Cracker."

"Ah, I thought so. The powder man. Godfrey, he wants

to see you. Yeah, you're the one he wants. He's gonna send you a little message or two." He jerked a thumb. "March. I'll be right behind."

Cracker walked slowly forward, feeling, if not seeing, the black bore of the shotgun at his back, and knowing that his captor would not hesitate to blow a load of double-ought buckshot straight through him. He had felt this way before, when coppers nabbed him.

"I guess old Clyde and Godfrey, they'll be pleased to see you again," the man said. "Maybe they'll put you to work."

Cracker didn't reply. He was looking for a way out, but the road uphill offered no cover, and in any case, several small figures above, on the plateau where the mansion had once lorded over Pearlygates, were watching his progress.

He realized at once that the heap of good quartz ore had not diminished in the night; it stood beside the mine head, well guarded. He remembered every chunk of it, lifted out of that mine with his bare hands.

On the plateau he discovered an entire bivouac: a cook tent, sleeping tents, and a dozen men, of whom the Whiteheads were two. They were waiting for him. Godfrey had a heavy plaster wrapped around his knee, while Clyde sported a white bandage around his skull.

"Ah, the old Cracker," said Clyde. "We've sort of expected you."

Cracker nodded. About half this outfit wore side arms or carried shotguns; the other half looked about ready to muck and blast.

"Thanks for the ore, Cracker. We figure there's maybe ten thousand dollars in it."

"What do you want?" Cracker asked.

Godfrey stepped close, until he was wall to wall, chest to chest. "Your life," he said. "That's what. Maybe we'll wrap a few sticks around you, fuse 'em, and watch."

Cracker's pulse quickened.

"But maybe all those crumbs down below wouldn't like that. So we'll settle for a warning. You mess with us, you fool around here, you try to get this back, and you're dead. You and that dame and that blowhard mountebank down there. You hear me?"

Cracker nodded.

"If you got any sense, you'll pack up and get out. You and your cronies. You need killing, all three. I just happened to get aholt of those lawmen's dodgers in that sheaf hanging in the post office, and I took me a long look. You're a wanted man, Cracker. You're wanted in three places. That Raines, he's not welcome in a dozen. He can't even go back to Storyville! His specialty's bilking widows. And that woman, she's lived more horizontal than vertical, I imagine. That's how she ended up in Pearlygates, married for her special talents. You know what that adds up to? You mess with us, we kill you, and nobody on earth's gonna care."

"That it?"

"No, that's not it. We're taking every claim along this here cliff. We've already put our names on a claim in each cairn. The ore, it apexed here and we'll just follow it in both directions, all according to the mining law, and you tell that bunco artist down there, he messes with these claims, or tries to sell them, he's going to be stuffed into a stamp mill and amalgamated into bullion."

Cracker studied the armed men gathered round, and knew they were nail-hard and quick on the trigger, except the two that looked consumptive. His gaze swept the mining crew. That was harder to gauge. They looked like first-rate miners, and were probably getting good wages, or maybe even a cut. Maybe they were lured away from the Amalgamated Climax Mine. And they were busily turning the flat overlooking Pearlygates into a company camp.

He spotted half a dozen crates of DuPont's dynamite, in which he took a professional interest. Dynamite was something he knew much about, along with black powder and nitroglycerin. Nearby was a wooden case filled with blasting caps. Yes, most interesting. A stray bullet could have an amazing effect. But surely they knew that. What counted was what this outfit did with all the pyrotechnics.

"You mind if I take a few souvenirs?" he asked.

"Souvenirs?"

"Yeah, a couple of bags full of samples, just to take with me down the trail. That's why I brought old Agnes here; load her up with a few samples. That quartz is real pretty."

"No," Clyde said.

"You worried about losing three dollars of ore, are you?"

"If anything, Cracker, you owe us about thirty dollars in doctor bills."

"Well, you mind if I get my stuff? My tools and all that? I've got some of my stuff here."

"That's ours, Cracker. You're just plain out of luck, aren't you?"

"You want to hire a good powder man?"

"You?" asked Godfrey.

"I'm the best there is. I can blow a steel door off a safe and never stir up the banknotes. I can knock that drift back faster than any man alive, so long as you got some good muckers and timbermen to back me. I can get your gold out of there better than anyone alive."

The Whitebreads looked at each other.

"We'll let you know, Cracker," said Godfrey. "Now you get out of here and tell your cronies what we told you to say."

Cracker figured that was pretty good news. If he could just get to drilling with this outfit, he'd soon enough crack another safe.

Chapter 23

MayBelle fumed. A horizontal living! That's what Cracker was saying. What a way to start a morning, having her reputation besmirched by the Whitebreads. She had never gone beyond a semihorizontal living.

It was all bad news. The Whitebreads had returned with reinforcements and now her mine was as good as gone forever. Cracker had returned from the mine early in the morning with nothing on his mule's back but an empty packsaddle, and nothing but bad news.

Only the colonel seemed unperturbed.

"More flapjacks, MayBelle," he said.

"Cook your own."

He stared benevolently at her. "I offered to wipe the dishes last night and was most indignantly refused."

"You didn't lose a gold mine last night; I did."

The colonel set down his fork and leaned into his chair. "My little goldfinch, it's all the very best fortune we could ask for. Men are blinded and maddened by gold, so let them have it and devote their every waking minute trying to get it. We have . . . a town lot company."

"Yeah, and I didn't get any bait," Cracker said.

"We shall do without. And don't forget we have a jar

full of wire gold, extracted from the quartz. It will suffice quite nicely. We'll just set it on the counter and let it do our selling for us."

"Maybe they'll hire me as a powder man, and then I'll blow away the whole outfit," Cracker said, sipping Java. "I'll paste the Whitebreads to the ceiling. I'll turn those lookouts into hamburger. I'll blow the miners out of the hole."

"You are entertaining violent thoughts," said the colonel, "and worse, you are proposing to work for a living."

"And what's wrong with that?"

"Safe Cracker, my old friend, you have yet to learn how to let others toil for you. Now, this fine day, as more argonauts drift into town from all points of the compass, they need to be excited, heated you might say, seduced, dazzled, until they are concupiscent."

"What's that?"

"Lustful."

"That's my department," said MayBelle. "What do you want me to do?"

"Dress up, get your parasol, and parade up and down Nevada Street. You are the sole representative of your sex in Pearlygates, unless certain sorts arrived last night and set up shop. We shall take advantage."

"You're mad, Raines," Cracker said.

The colonel ignored him, polished off the last flapjack, and sipped his coffee.

"It just so happens, Cracker, that I have a mission for you. Put a little gold in your pockets. Repair to that new saloon you told us about. Talk. Show the gold. Mention the land office. Lots, buildings, claims, getting in on the ground floor."

Cracker spat. "I blow safes."

"Ah, but you must expand to new turf. I'll man the land office, and both of you will bunco the trade to our door."

MayBelle had heard enough. "How'm I supposed to do that? Start peeling gloves and undoing buttons?"

The colonel eyed her suavely. "Not a bad start, MayBelle, but once you start undoing, smile."

"You really want me to do it."

"Nightingale, nothing is beyond you."

"I'm a respectable grass widow."

"Was, MayBelle, was."

She wondered if he meant it. He sipped benignly, and then stood. "I'm going to open shop," he said. "Today, we lost a mine and gained a fortune."

"Bunco steering," Safe Cracker said. "I never thought I'd come to this."

She watched the colonel rise, brush crumbs from his somewhat grubby black broadcloth suit, don his silk top hat, and vanish into the morning sun like a stately galleon. She marveled that he could be so content. All she could think of was her Wine Cellar Mine, and the thugs occupying it.

"What does he know about blowing safes?" Cracker asked.

But MayBelle was already thinking about the dresses rescued from the mansion, wondering which one to wear while she swished up and down Nevada Street. As she cleaned up the remains of the breakfast, she decided on her lavender silk. It would match her sole remaining parasol. She lacked the right slippers—most of her footwear had perished when the mansion did—but who'd know?

She brushed a shine into her hair, donned her silken dress, which would be a bit skimpy this chill day, and sashayed out upon the world. The old ghost town fairly bulged with males, and she did not go unnoticed. When she reached Nevada Street she discovered a busy artery peopled with bushy-bearded prospectors tugging on mules, gents in carriages, clerks carrying their worldly goods in a wheelbarrow, horsemen, broad-shouldered miners, and foreigners in exotic dress and odd caps, fresh off the boats, here to make a quick killing.

Two hundred yesterday, maybe five hundred today, prowling the old ghost town. She approached one knot of men, who gaped at her, amazed.

"Say, fellows, do you know where the land office is?" she asked.

"What land office?" asked a dapper young one with a storekeeper look about him.

"The one that sells the lots and houses and claims."

"Lady, nobody owns nothing here."

"Somebody owns it all! I'm going to buy some houses. Gold comes and goes but real estate lasts forever."

"Ma'am, maybe in some places lots would get you something, but this is just another boom and bust. They find a little gold; six months from now it's a ghost town again. Here's what you do; set up shop . . ." He eyed her contemplatively. "Ah, whatever you do, anyway, and just move into one of these empty piles of lumber."

She laughed. "You'll be my first customer, sonny."

The gents guffawed.

"But meanwhile, I'm buying land," she said. "Ten lots around here's worth more than a gold mine. That's what my mommy always said."

"For two weeks, sweetheart," the dapper one said, growing bolder.

She grinned. "Then the lots'll be cheap. Maybe you'll buy me a dozen."

He smiled, which slowly leaked into a smirk. "You want some lots? Maybe I will, just for you. Then what?"

"That's for you to find out, sonny."

She made her way a few steps, when she heard a shout. "Hey, stick around. I'll buy you some lots. How many you want?"

"The more you buy me, the happier we'll be," she said.

"I gotta see this," said another gent.

She watched half a dozen trot down the street to the town lot company. Now they were the colonel's meat.

She felt gazes directed her way, and felt the heat in them.

She sashayed toward the booming saloon, peered in, and found Safe Cracker hard at work, waving his threads of gold. A dozen men were listening.

Bunco steering sure beat hard work. She'd damn well hire a maid and a laundress as soon as she had some cash.

Most of these men weren't sticking to Nevada Street for long. They were eyeing the cliffs, the old glory holes, the dead mines, studying the rock and preparing to lay claim to it. But there were others who were examining every false-front structure on the street, and these were the ones she hoped to steer.

She headed toward a majestic two-story frame structure that once housed Baker's Hardware below, and Dr. Phineas Partridge above. Dr. Partridge was a practitioner of homeopathic medicine until Pearlygates could no longer be dosed. Now the structure lay silent and forlorn. It still exuded a rank odor, but maybe that was nothing more than the smell of pack rats. Dust lay thick, and shards of glass scattered across the begrimed floor. She had memories of this place in happier days, when it bustled with men wanting nails and bolts and sheet metal and glass and rope and kingpins.

She was not alone. There, pacing around the building, was an oily-haired man in pince-nez and a white shirt, quite a perfect specimen, she thought.

She ignored him and proceeded inside. The place had been ransacked, and its shelves torn loose for firewood by vagrants.

But she patrolled the ruins, knowing that White-shirt would soon follow her in.

"Ah, madam, I saw you here . . ."

She smiled. "It'd make a nice saloon, and those rooms upstairs, yes, just right for my trade."

"Ah, I was thinking of employing this myself."

She smiled. "Maybe we have a conflict."

"I was here first, you know."

She smiled broadly. "It's quite simple. Whoever buys it, gets it."

"But these buildings are abandoned."

"Owned, is the word, sir. Owned. This will do quite nicely. I can have the bar operating in two days, and the ladies in a week."

"Not if I buy it first!"

"There's lots of buildings, sir. Maybe you'd prefer another one."

"No, this is just the one. I'll live above and operate the mortuary here."

"You can come visit me anytime, stranger." And she sashayed past his sore eyes. "If I get it first, it's mine."

He gaped at her, huffed, and beelined for the land office. She watched him disappear into the colonel's lair, where he would be swiftly rendered for any lard he possessed. Three hundred dollars would buy him this building: fifty down, the rest on credit, 5 percent a month.

This beat blasting and mucking. It also beat semi-horizontal occupations. Maybe the colonel had a point, she thought.

Chapter 24

Colonel Raines studied the sharp-edged businessman across the counter, knowing it would be a hard sell. This one wasn't going to fork out money without some careful checking. Behind him, a dozen other gents waited.

"A splendid choice," Raines said. "It'll be the perfect site for a dry goods store. I do believe that was the very way that building was employed back in the town's salad days."

"How much?"

"Three hundred, sir, easy terms if needed, only five percent a month interest."

"Is the title clouded?"

"Clouded! The town lot company developed and surveyed this entire tract, filed it with the authorities, sold lots, and retrieved them when the town fell on hard times. Rock-solid pedigree."

The man surveyed Raines, as if discovering faults in him. "Let's see the conveyances. What I especially want is the paper conveying this building back to your company when it was abandoned."

"Why, sir, those are all in safekeeping. All the town lot papers are kept in fireproof storage. It's not possible for a single document to burn, sir. You could pour coal oil over the whole trove, and not a sheet would perish. It's like heaven, sir, which is proof against the devil. I will absolutely guarantee that the town lot documents are beyond the terror of fire. No match, no holocaust, no tipped-over lantern will ever harm the company documents."

The man sighed. "Where are they?"

"They are nearby, sir. For fear of foul play, I cannot tell you precisely, but every document can be found at a location within sight."

The stringy fellow paused pregnantly. "I think I'll rent."

"My friend, a most wise decision, but of course you won't get in on the ground floor. Pearlygates is rising from its ashes."

"And likely to fall back into them in two weeks. But I make hay whilst the sun shines."

The colonel leaned forward. "If you believe it, then you're doing the right thing. But mind you, a string of ten business structures, rented at a thousand percent a year, would get you a handsome purse if this bonanza lasts only three months. Three thousand, ten businesses, and you'll walk out with twenty thousand."

"What's rented so far?"

"Sir, that's confidential. We respect the privacy of our buyers."

The gent smiled. "I'll think about it."

The colonel lifted his heavy glass jar and rattled the gold. "Don't think too long. Gold like this, ribbons and wires and gobs of it in quartz, stirs a passion in the bosom of many a man. I expect to sell out every commercial structure before sundown."

But the dry goods man was working his way through the silent mob and out the door. Raines straightened his suit coat. He may have lost one customer, but everything he said had funneled into listening ears, and for every skeptic, he would sign up twenty believers.

Next in line was a hollow-chested miner wanting a cottage. The colonel pointed at the plat map on the wall. "There, my friend, on C Street, is an entire block of fine, sturdy, tight houses, where any man can be king. I recommend this one, right here. You'll discover that some have lilac bushes and roses about; others have a new and well-limed outhouse. There, friend, is the place to build a life; bring your bride, if you have one, enjoy the rejuvenating Nevada air . . ."

"Yeah, but I just want a roof for me and my pals. A roof and some bunks."

"Why, friend, these comfortable homes will warm you all when the winter winds blow, keep you shaded in summertime . . ."

"You take credit?"

"Just fill out this form, my friend. You won't be disappointed. Ten dollars down, thirty a month, plus a little interest if we carry your house on our books. You can scribble your John Henry there, and walk out of here knowing that you'll be snug no matter what ill winds blow, and no town-lot jumper can push you out."

"Here goes nothing," the miner said, and signed.

Moments later, the fellow walked out with papers entitling him to the dwelling at 219 South C Street, for which he had duly forked over an eagle. The colonel bit the eagle, nodded, and tossed it into the iron box under the counter.

The pile of banknotes and gold in the colonel's strongbox was expanding all too slowly. Most of the miners wanted all the credit they could get. Some wanted to rent. And he understood why: they didn't want to get stung if the whole boom collapsed in a few weeks.

One walleyed entrepreneur did buy five houses but put down only fifty dollars on the whole lot. "When I pay these off, what sort of deed will I get?" he asked.

"You'll own them free and clear, friend, each a castle that cannot be breached by the minions of the law.

There'll be no mortgage at all burdening this wise and farsighted investment. And the title to each will reside in the county clerk's office."

Even in the midst of a gold rush these gents did not slap down money recklessly, and there were few who crowded to the counter ready to buy. But Raines had not been a bunco steerer for nothing, and with effusions of compliments and admiration, he softened each mark and made his sale, and sometimes made an additional sale.

"A second lot, sir, an investment. A gamble? Of course! I pity the timid wretch who holds his cards so close that he fears to play the aces!"

The crowds outside were not exactly thronging in. During slack moments, when he gazed out the window, the colonel swore that another five hundred hardy miners had flooded into Pearlygates, clogging Nevada Street with buggies, wagons, saddle horses, and even an occasional elegant black carriage drawn by trotters. The Whitebreads may have stolen a mine, but they had also started a rush. Plainly, that fabulous quartz gold they were showing around Storyville had triggered it.

Both MayBelle and Safe Cracker steered clear of the land office, and he was pleased by their good sense. The colonel didn't see them the entire day. Several times, a customer said he had been referred by a lady in lavender; some others talked about a stringy fellow showing ribbons of gold in the saloon, who proclaimed he knew where he could get tons more of it.

Late that day, a rainbow-load of bawds arrived in a victoria driven by a black coachman in livery, along with a madam in a phaeton drawn by coal-black trotters. Such a hoot and howl arose on Nevada Street that the colonel rushed to the front window to examine this apparition. There they were, six fair ladies in gaudy and scanty attire, showing various amounts of black-stockinged leg, some missing teeth, and amazing amounts of wrinkled cleavage. These were not the freshest flowers ever to be plucked.

The barrel-shaped mistress of this female pleasure factory alighted from the phaeton, which creaked as she lowered her corpulent body to earth, and proceeded directly to the land office. She burst in with a rush of Asiatic perfume.

"Gimme a building," she said.

"Madam, there are twenty-four commercial establishments remaining. I shall be happy to oblige."

"I want the biggest one left with a mess of rooms in it."

"That would be the former Clawson Sisters Boardinghouse, where thirty miners took breakfast and supper and played whist in the downstairs parlor."

"What's whist?"

"A polite card game."

"All card games are polite." She smiled, and peeled off a hundred dollars from a huge green roll in her pocket. "You satisfied?"

"Ah, no, the price is a tad higher. Three hundred."

She peeled off ten tens. "High as I go. For all I care, my gals can do business in the street. I'll charge for the peep show."

"Three hundred."

"Two hundred, and you get fifty visits, pick of the litter for your starved pecker."

"Ah, fifty visits, pick of the litter, and a free bar tab."

"Write it up, sweetheart; we're opening in ten minutes."

"A woman after my own loin," he said, scratching out a sale. "And what's the name?"

She stared at him dead-eyed. "Sally Strumpet."

He nodded and filled in the blanks. It annoyed him that his pen would not write properly, and he puddled ink and was forced to blot every few words. "Here is a deed from the Pearlygates Town Lot Company, conveying parcel thirty-nine on Nevada Street, to Madam Sally Strumpet."

She barely glanced at it. "Thanks, hon. You want your first one now? I'm always willin' and eager."

He smiled wolfishly.

"Where's this building?"

He pointed north. "Next block. It still says Clawson on the front. It lacks a little glass."

"We're in business." She eyed him sharply, measuring him with a glance. "Anyone tries to put us outa there, anyone troubles me about this deed, anyone gives me legal trouble, land-office trouble, owner trouble, and I'll be in here with my nine-barrel pepperbox, and you won't like the racket when I pull the triggers, which will be the last thing you'll hear."

The colonel smiled bravely.

She departed and boarded her wagon, and the black driver whipped the draft horses to life.

"Open in five minutes," she yelled. "Soon as I get the merchandise laid out."

A dozen miners howled.

Chapter 25

They stared glumly at the small wad of money on the kitchen table.

"Some bonanza," Safe Cracker muttered.

"Two hundred seventy isn't bad," the colonel said. "Twenty-seven sold. Ten down, lots more coming."

"Yeah, and maybe six hundred people in town. You know what they're doing: moving into any house they feel like."

"Then we'll sell the house out from under them."

"And who's going to evict the squatters?"

"The people we sell the title to."

"We'll get dragged into every fight."

The colonel could see the melancholia seeping from his cohorts, and resolved to brighten their spirits. "It is an improvement on blasting and mucking," he said.

"Improvement! I'd rather be blowing safes any day. I'd rather be in a mine sweating by candlelight. This thing, this bunco stuff, it's harder than blowing safes."

"Pshaw, you don't even dirty your hands steering people my way."

"I'm not good at this. I'm good at cracking anything: safes, rock, bedrooms, you name it, I'll crack it. I'm the best powder man in the world. I can blow a sheet of paper out from under a fly and not hurt the fly. I can blow a five hundred pound steel door off its hinges and not harm the diamonds. But this . . ."

Cracker's voice trailed off so desolately that the colonel knew he had come to a great crisis.

"What choice have we? The mine got itself stolen."

"Well, I'm gonna steal it back! I'm gonna blow that bunch out of there."

"How?"

The seconds ticked by and Cracker made no reply.

"Put the law on them?" the colonel asked.

Cracker glared.

"The law's forgotten Pearlygates," MayBelle said. "And not likely to help even if you asked."

"Lawsuit?" said the colonel, delicately, steepling his hands into a little church.

Safe Cracker laughed sardonically. "What law? What courts? What lawyers?"

"I think, then, we should make use of what we have, namely a lot of houses and lots. Ah, my friends, dream a little. What is it you desire most, Cracker? Maybe you'll have it."

"You'd like to know, wouldn't you? Sure you would. It's my business what I want."

"I know exactly what you want: to leave this country behind, with enough boodle to keep you happy the rest of your life. Ah, let's see now, where would a wanted safe cracker go? Argentina maybe. The Argentine ladies are willowy and eager."

"Yeah, eager for Argentine millionaires."

"Cracker, the raven-haired beauties are eager to tango."

"Yeah, tango," Cracker said, his voice wistful. The colonel had suddenly struck home.

"Let's persevere, my friends, and you can tango your life away. You'll have a sweetheart on each arm."

But Cracker was gazing into space, as if the vision of life in Buenos Aires were a window upon heaven.

"And you, turtledove, I can see your dreams in your eyes. An orange grove in California; a fine and noble house with Doric pillars, gardens, and a climate that is perpetually mild; grapes, wine, an attending and affectionate swain who is neither too attached nor too unattached, but available to you at the beck of a little finger. Ah, for all that you've suffered for two years, held this dwindling asset in a death grip, hoping for this very moment. And now, my little sparrow, the moment is upon us!"

"You want to wipe dishes again?"

"MayBelle, your response only tells me how deeply I touched upon something within you, something that craves to be released. I will play the genie, and if you rub my lamp the right way, I will grant you your wishes."

She elbowed him. "That's all men think of."

The colonel sighed, letting his woundedness fill his face. He turned his head so his best profile fell into her view, and frowned gently. "I have only your interests at heart. What have I gotten from this? I toil night and day, my fevered mind at work even while I sleep, so that we might all, and especially you, escape the sorry estate that has befallen us."

"Jaysas," said Cracker.

MayBelle rose suddenly, dishes in hand. "Claudius, if you had wandered the streets of Pearlygates today instead of hiding in your land office, you'd know that hundreds of men have taken over whatever buildings suit their fancy. And we won't get a dime out of them. And we've no way to evict them."

"Yeah, and some are armed," Cracker added. "Your housing stock's vanishing. In a week, there won't be a building left, and what'll we get out of it?"

"Why, the claims. We've dozens of claims, collected by MayBelle's unlamented former mate."

Cracker laughed. "They're crawling the slopes above us, Colonel. They're claiming anything that looks like mineralized rock. They're toting cases of powder. They're whacking rock with pickaxes and hammers. They're following mineralized strata right up the mountainsides. And they're not going to buy MayBelle's old glory holes. And we ain't gonna sue them, not *you and me.*"

The colonel pondered this, and spoke with particular gentleness. "You don't understand my game."

"What do ya mean? Your game is to sell off this ghost town to suckers."

"No, no, my game is to sell dreams. All one has to do is sell dreams to get filthy rich. Now, Arnold," and he used Safe's real name for the first time in days, "Arnold, my old friend, what you truly lust for is a raven-haired beauty in Argentina who adores you and says, *'Sí, sí'* whenever you wink? Am I not right?"

"You want me to leave the room while you boys dream?" MayBelle asked.

The colonel turned sideways so she could admire his profile, especially his long patrician nose. "No, MayBelle, my little hummingbird, you'll find no cause for closeting yourself while in my company. My proposition is that it doesn't matter if there is nothing to sell; a true magnifico, on the order of P.T. Barnum, needs nothing more than an understanding of the things we all crave, and a few wits."

MayBelle yawned. "It's been a hard day, all this lewd winking and smiling. My lips are tired from smiles. My eyelids are tired. I'm going to bed."

"You could invite us to join you," Safe Cracker said.

"Just go down to Nevada Street," she replied.

"I have some credit with Sally Strumpet," the colonel said. "You're welcome to it, Arnold."

"No, I'm going to look at the Wine Cellar Mine in the moonlight. I'm going to find out where the guards are and how many. I'm going to plant a stick under each one some day soon, and I'm going to fuse them so carefully that they all go through the pearly gates together, and we'll have our mine back."

"It's safer to sell dreams, Arnold."

"My dream is to blow up everything and everyone. When I am done around here, this place will be *flat.*"

The colonel had the sense that Cracker meant it. MayBelle hung up her dish towel, and Cracker slipped into the night to begin his reconnaissance.

Colonel Raines found himself alone in MayBelle's kitchen but he didn't mind. He did his best thinking right after people told him his cause was hopeless. He sat back in the wooden chair, gazed out the window, and was not surprised to see lights glowing here and there around Pearlygates.

He considered himself part of an elite. The most valuable people on the planet were the storytellers and dream peddlers, for without them the world would perish. He included actors and whores and novelists and ballad singers and poets among those he admired, people like himself who spun little frauds and awakened hungers and articulated dreams. Yes indeed, they were all bunco steerers like himself, people who turned nothing into something, who fed upon the yearnings of the needful.

Of these, novelists were closest to his heart, for novelists turned delirious fantasies into cash, exciting lusts and passions in their poor victims, always for money, and they weren't a bit shy about demanding it, either. Yes, Claudius P. Raines knew he was at heart a novelist. Scribbling fiction was surely one of the world's most despicable trades, and compared to writing fiction, bunco steering was a saintly pursuit. If all else failed, he would lower himself and become a novelist, and thereby get rich, for what trade was lower than selling fantasies, and more lucrative?

But now he had a monumental task, for the hope of

turning Pearlygates into a heap of cash was swiftly diminishing. The stark reality was that he and his colleagues had no way to keep anyone from commandeering anything in Pearlygates. If they could not protect real property, then the only recourse was to sell something else: dreams.

He ached to come up with something, anything, that would inflame the passions of this multitude. What did they really want? And how could he supply it? Diamonds? Sapphires? Rubies? Health? Ah, there was a thought. The cure-all. The elixir, the panacea. Maybe he could do a little something with that, bottle up something so miraculous, so astounding, that people flocked to buy it. Pearlygates Possum Tonic. A little opium, a little alcohol, a little mint for flavor . . . Yes, there was something to it: give them a Nevada mountain medicine so sublime that people clamored for more and more and more, the highest, mightiest, noblest invention of occult science.

He sighed. It would take some doing to get a bottling works going; probably more than the two or three hundred dollars his little syndicate had for capital.

He would think of something. He always did. Claudius P. Raines knew he had the most fertile mind this side of Mesopotamia.

Chapter 26

The first person to walk into the Pearlygates Town Lot Company offices the next morning was Godfrey Whitebread. Colonel Raines took one look at him and knew that no good would come of this meeting.

Whitebread exuded dark joy, the sort of cheery malice that springs out of revenge and contempt. He still wore a bandage around his head, and another braced his knee, but he sported banker pinstripes now. He surveyed Raines, eyed the office, studied the plat map on the wall, and smiled.

"We're taking over F Street," he said. "The mine is. You got any objections?"

"I do. I've sold three houses on F Street."

"Sold." Whitebread's mirth spilled out.

"The houses will cost you two hundred each," Raines said, bravely. "Cash in advance. No credit. There are, let's see here, thirty-three houses remaining on F Street. That will come to six thousand six hundred."

Whitebread laughed. "We're putting our miners in, and our guards. You will support our peace plan. We will do what we do, and you will agree to it, and there will be peace in the world between us and you."

"I, ah, get your point."

"It's the American way," he said, "the genius of this country. Each man does exactly what he wants. Property is protected. When property is safe, then commerce is safe, and when commerce is safe, we all prosper.

"When bunco steerers, bandits, and mountebanks are kept at bay, the world is a happier place. We can mine gold peacefully, sell our gold, purchase those things we need in perfect harmony, all men in America guided by the principle of free trade and voluntary contract and the sanctity of property. If there is no government at all, that is highly desirable.

"Think of what would happen to you if the law arrived in Pearlygates. Think of what would happen to your little swindler game if the law snatched Arnold Cracker and hauled him away. Think of what would happen to poor MayBelle. She would become a working girl, and at her age, too."

"You are a philosopher," Raines said.

"No, I leave philosophy to wretches in musty warrens on dreary campuses who love abstractions and bone-picking logic. I am out in the real world, where one bullet is worth more than all the philosophy tomes ever written. I can win any argument with the logic of cold steel and black powder."

Raines nodded. No point in provoking the man. "Then you are a poet," he said.

"No, not a poet."

"Then what are you?"

"I am God," he said. "When you want anything, pray to me. And do not provoke me, because I cast sinners into hell."

Raines nodded.

Whitebread smiled, catlike, and departed with a feline grace. A deep silence pervaded the office, as if a great tumult had just ceased, like Niagara Falls suddenly halting, though Whitebread spoke so quietly the colonel had trouble hearing him.

It was the beginning of another expulsion. The Whitebreads would soon commandeer the rest of Pearlygates just as they had commandeered the mine. The colonel gazed at the plat map, sensing that bits and pieces and chunks of the city were vanishing from his grasp.

The Wine Cellar Mine was rattling windows. The colonel had heard a distant roar all morning as Whitebread men mucked rock and dumped it into the tailings pile. Late this afternoon the whole town would hear the thump of dynamite exploding, the noise blowing out of the mine head and trembling the very earth. And all for the gold that once was MayBelle's.

He peered out his window and saw a parade of newcomers breasting the ridge where the road wound into town; dozens more gold-seekers rushing to Pearlygates on the news of a bonanza. But no one entered his office, and he knew, somehow, that few would.

He watched MayBelle sashay down Nevada Street once again, this time in bottle-green velvet. She made a point of talking to every teamster, mule skinner, prospector, and businessman wandering through the reviving ghost town. She was not shy about it, and he could see her gesturing toward the land office now and then. She focused on the businessmen, who were a little more cautious—and vulnerable—and wanted some sort of title to the buildings they were about to occupy. Maybe she would fetch a few dollars more. The thought plunged the colonel into melancholia.

He espied MayBelle engaged in lively conversation with a carriage-load of deacons. At least they all looked like deacons, in black suits, boiled white shirts, and string ties. Their hair was well greased. On closer examination, the colonel decided they were not deacons. They wore pinky rings, and headlight diamonds on their cravats.

Sure enough, she steered them to the land office, and the driver eased the ebony barouche to his hitching post.

The colonel studied his plat map, and knew just the building to offer these gents, a former saloon with a large rear room.

The deacons descended, wiped their patent leather black shoes free of dust, and made haste to the shade of Raines's emporium.

"Brethren, you've come to pray," Raines said.

"You could spell it that way," replied one, withdrawing a pencil-thin cigarillo. "Do you tempt fate?"

"No, I seduce it," Raines said.

"We're miners," said another of these gents. "We extract gold."

"Welcome to Pearlygates, the doorway to heaven," Raines said. "You can purchase an establishment for three hundred dollars in advance. I have just the one for you; a former saloon with a sporting salon at the rear. It would require a little dusting, and some window glass when you get around to it. And of course a chandelier. You will have to import some chairs and tables, though. What furniture was left behind in the old Pearlygates became firewood for vagrants. Even so, if you're enterprising, you can be open for business by evening. Just sign here."

"Or we can just move in."

"If you do, you won't have title."

The gent stroked his beard. "Title, what's that?"

The others wheezed happily, baring gold teeth and blue gums.

The colonel got an idea. "I will flip a coin. Heads, you pay me and receive a deed; tails, you move in for free."

They laughed. "We don't like the odds," said one.

"How about a ten percent cut?"

"How about a gold brick?"

The colonel sighed. "Take your pick, gents."

"We intend to."

"Do you want a silent partner who knows the ropes around here?"

"We need a bartender."

The colonel saw how it would go, and waved them off.

The foursome removed themselves from the premises, which lightened up considerably once those four black suits vanished.

A second vehicle had arrived, this one jammed with roulette wheels, green baize tables, chairs, and other paraphernalia of the sporting set. There would be, in that freight wagon, a few hundred decks of cards, some with shaved edges and odd wavy designs on the back.

The rest of the day was devoted to undertakers. Two more arrived, one with a wagon load of coffins. Wherever miners gather, undertakers are sure to follow, and a mining town of five hundred needed at least three. The day was redeemed when the colonel sold a three-hundred-dollar building, formerly an ice and coal dealership, to the Render Brothers Mortuary for 10 percent down. Within the hour they had put up their board sign, saying in dignified gilded letters:

RENDER BROTHERS
Render yourself unto God
And Render your Remains to Us

And in smaller black letters:

We purchase deceased livestock
Dogfood, Grease, and Hides for Sale

It occurred to the colonel to start a cemetery. There was nothing quite so profitable as a good boneyard, twenty dollars a hole. Pearlygates had an old one, but the stones had fallen and vagrants had burned the wooden markers for firewood. It would be no good to dig a grave there, only to discover the premises were occupied. Plainly, a new one was needed. Yes, he could sell cemetery lots: every man wanted a place to look at the mountains for eternity.

Excited, he studied his plat map for extensive areas that would be suitable, and noted several. It would be something to discuss with his partners. Safe Cracker could probably blow open the earth faster than a dozen demented grave diggers could chop out a hole, and maybe Cracker could improvise a whole new labor-saving technology of mortuary science.

Anything that saved labor pleased the colonel.

By that evening, the colonel noted two new assay offices, a butcher shop, a tonsorial parlor with two bathtubs, a blacksmith, a wagon yard, a livery barn, and a bevy of new saloons. All of which galled him because none except the undertaker had laid down so much as a dime for their premises, and there was little he could do about it.

Late in the day he discovered two Ursuline nuns, Sister Marcella and Sister Suzanne, at his door. They intended to start an infirmary and wanted a building donated for that purpose. The colonel wanted to charge them double because an infirmary would save lives, which would reduce the mortuary trade, which meant that the undertakers would be less inclined to pay off their mortgages on the buildings he had sold them.

But the colonel swallowed back common sense and sold the sisters a dilapidated rooming house for a 15 percent discount, one hundred seventy dollars in all, payable in three installments.

He hadn't added much to the kitty, and that grim night the partners counted out only one hundred seventy additional dollars. Worse, the town was half full. There was a land boom, all right, but the colonel and his colleagues weren't riding it.

"What'll you do now, Raines?" Safe Cracker asked.

"I will think of something," the colonel replied. "Trust me."

Chapter 27

MayBelle's dreams were falling to pieces. The miners flooding into Pearlygates simply commandeered houses and cottages, without a by-your-leave. She worked the three better saloons, trying to drum up some trade for the colonel, but she may as well have been talking to deaf men. The empty houses were there; miners occupied them, and if someone claimed them later, who cared?

Cracker was having no more luck. The whole scheme was coming to nothing. Worse, the Whitebreads had opened up their own land office, The Whitebread Mining and Land Office, and were brokering mining claims right and left and peddling an occasional town lot. One night the plat map vanished from the colonel's office and reappeared on the wall of the Whitebread company's office, and from then on, the Whitebreads began moving newcomers into buildings the colonel had sold—usually evicting the current tenant at the point of a gun.

The crack of gunfire became commonplace, but so far no one had been planted in the boneyard. A shot or two fired into a ceiling had all the potency of an eviction notice.

And now the few who had bought lots or houses from the colonel were demanding their money back, which grieved the colonel. He loudly proclaimed he had never seen these gents before in all his life. He did fork over to one glowering miner who drew a six-gun and threatened to dispatch the colonel on the spot if he didn't get his ten dollars back.

The town soon acquired two assayers, a blacksmith, a harness maker, two livery barns, a freighting company, a Wells Fargo coach connection with nearby Nevada towns, a post office located in a grocery, a billiard parlor, a French restaurant, three boardinghouses, a second bordello, two more gambling emporiums, an opium den run by ten smiling Cantonese, and a milliner.

All this MayBelle and her colleagues watched glumly, helpless to cash in on any of it. MayBelle cursed the day she had met the colonel and listened to his grandiose schemes. They all feared the Whitebreads, who now were the sole armed force in Pearlygates, and making their own rules. No regular officer of the law, such as a sheriff's deputy, had yet to show up, nor any justice of the peace. There was not even a lawyer in town, and by the time any showed up it would be too late.

All that was bad enough, but late in the week, worse fell upon them.

Clyde Whitebread knocked on MayBelle's door, along with a fat stranger.

"I just sold this house, so git out," he said.

"Sold! This is my house!"

"Was, you mean, so git."

"You'll have to carry me out, because I'm staying."

He grinned darkly. "Just might oblige you," he said. "This here's Judge Amos Grassley, and he just bought this place fair and square, and don't take partially to squatters."

MayBelle slammed the door.

She peered about wildly. Everything she had salvaged from the manse lay within: clothing, furniture, kitchen things, linens, bric-a-brac.

She refused to acknowledge the rapping on her door, which soon turned to thunder. Then she heard only silence. And then the kitchen door burst open, and there was Whitebread and the fat man.

He didn't waste words. He grabbed her arm with a steely grip, and dragged her out the kitchen door.

She struggled furiously, and finally bit him in the neck.

"Ow!" he yelled, and pitched her to the clay of the yard.

"You're trespassing," she said. "I'm going to the county courthouse. I'm getting the sheriff."

He laughed.

The judge grinned wolfishly.

"We booted your crony in crime out of his palace," Whitebread added. "And out of that office. And if I knew where the powder man lived, I'd boot him out too."

She clambered to her feet, dusted off her dress.

"You mind if I get my stuff out?"

"Ten minutes."

"Ten minutes! That's as good a way to steal as any."

He laughed.

She slapped him. "You'll harness my buggy and help me load."

"I forgot about the horse. You just sold it to us."

"You're stealing it."

"Naw, just restoring loot to lawful citizens like me and the judge here."

"You watch out," she said. "You watch out."

"You can go hire out at the whorehouses," he replied.

He dragged her to the street and left her there, and then led the judge, if that's what he really was, inside. In the space of a few minutes the Whitebreads had cleaned her out of her last possessions and put her destitute on the streets of Pearlygates. The Whitebreads were the law, there was no other, and they enforced it with a dozen well-armed toughs.

She walked, dazed, into town, past cottages, through neighborhoods suddenly alien, onto Nevada Street, where every building had once been her own.

The ghost town was suddenly booming. Glaziers were repairing windows. New signs announced new businesses at every hand. She heard the clamor of a piano in a saloon. Overnight, almost, Pearlygates had sprung to life. Crowds drifted down the street. She noticed a few women, miners' wives, and even some children. And here she was, without even a dime for a lunch, and no future unless she chose a profession she had always avoided.

She remembered that the colonel was keeping their meager cash, something over three hundred dollars derived from the sale of a few lots and buildings, so she started hunting for him. She wanted it all; this had been her town once.

She scarcely knew where to look, because their land office was now being converted into a cigar store. She hiked to his house on B Street, and discovered that he too had been evicted by the Whitebreads; two strange men sat on the porch.

She prowled Nevada Street, systematically looking in each saloon and gambling parlor and restaurant, and found him at last in the new Bucket of Gold Saloon, sitting at a card game with a meager dozen blue chips before him.

In horror, she realized he was trying to win something out of the remains of their cash, and had lost all but a dozen chips.

"Colonel," she said, and motioned him to quit.

But he sat stubbornly, pushed his last chips out onto the green baize, watched them vanish, and stood up slowly. This was the lair of those gents who looked like deacons, and now they had cleaned him out. He steered her into the busy street, and the bright afternoon sun.

"Ah, my little grouse, we seem to have come to the bottom of the well," he said.

"You and your miserable schemes," she snapped. "I suppose you've shot what little we had."

He eyed her soulfully. "What recourse was left?"

"You could have divided it up before you threw it away to those sharpers. At least I would have a hundred."

"I don't suppose you could spare me a meal?"

"I was ejected from my own house by force and violence. I have nothing but the clothes on my back."

"It is a fearsome thing to die of want."

"I never should have listened to you! I never should have let you walk into Pearlygates! I never want to see you again."

He sighed. They had lost a gold mine and a city.

"Where's Cracker?" she asked.

"I haven't seen him."

"Let's go to his cabin. Maybe they missed it, over there in the gulch beyond the mines."

"Why?" he asked.

"Beans. He's a bean-farting fool."

That settled it. Dolefully, they hiked clear through the town they once called their own, traced their way down a steep path to the gulch, ascended the gulch until it rounded a slight bend, and then climbed up a narrow footpath to the snug log cabin perched on a small flat, a toolshed invisible from town. An autumnal chill lay on the air. They studied the place, looking for signs of eviction, and found none. Cracker probably still resided there.

"Arnold?" MayBelle yelled.

A shutter creaked, and then snapped shut.

"Arnold?"

Safe Cracker materialized silently in the doorway. "You're disturbing my labors," he said. "Don't come here."

"Arnold, we're hungry."

The safecracker grunted. "You can wait," he said.

"We've been pushed out."

"I know. I watched it."

"Can we come in?"

"No, you'll get blown to bits. I'm arming a few sticks."

"What are you going to do?" she asked.

"Get it back."

"Arnold, if you blow up anything of the Whiteheads, they'll know who to go after."

"They don't even know I'm here." He stared at the colonel. "Where's my third?"

"My friend, I made a strenuous effort at cards to double our largesse, and instead—"

"I knew it," Cracker said. "We ain't got a thing to our name but a case or two of giant powder."

He shrugged, and stepped aside to let them in.

She entered nervously. Six waxy red sticks of dynamite lay about, three armed with primers and fuses, and one cut open to receive the fulminate cap.

"Nobody's cooking a flapjack, not now," he warned.

"What're you going to do?" she asked.

"None of your business. Anyway, you'll know soon enough."

"Don't hurt anybody, Arnold."

"I'm going to kill as many Whitebreads as possible."

"What have I gotten in with?" she cried. She stared at the wiry safecracker, now at work pushing a copper cap into a stick of high explosive. "A safe robber, and a lazy bum who lives by skinning suckers."

"MayBelle—" the colonel said.

"Don't you MayBelle me. I don't want to see you again. Neither of you. I despise you both. You've wrecked my life. You've destroyed my chances. You've left me without a penny."

"But, my dear little woodpecker—"

"Shut up!" she yelled, and stalked out, slamming the door behind her.

For some reason, the slamming door didn't blow them all to bits, and she tromped back into town, hating what she might have to do to keep from starving to death.

Chapter 28

Arnold Cracker knew exactly what he would do. He would show those Whitebreads a thing or two and then cut loose of Pearlygates. He'd gotten in with a hysterical woman and a lazy confidence man and now he was going to get his dear old mule, get out, and never look back.

But first, a little revenge. That gold mine was his. He found the gold, blew open the rock, and revealed it to the world. He couldn't snatch it back from the Whitebreads but he could make them suffer for it.

He hustled the colonel out of his cabin and told him never to show up at his door again. The old fraud had even gambled away what few dollars the partners had squeezed out of the rush to Pearlygates, and now they were all starving. Which was their tough luck.

With the lowering of full darkness, Cracker gently loaded three armed and fused sticks of dynamite in a canvas carrier and drifted silently into the night. He was dressed in dark clothing, including a navy watch cap, and had rubbed earth into his face to obscure it. He wore his revolver, but wished he hadn't buckled it on.

For several days he had quietly surveyed the mine up

on the plateau. The Whitebreads had actually made much progress toward a large-scale working mine. They had erected a hoist works, salvaged rails from the dead mines, imported a small steam engine, and a drum and cable to bring the ore cars up a shallow grade to the mine head. Now they were engaged in following the drift and running laterals to either side.

Good quartz ore heaped in a mound near the mine head, while the pile of tailings tumbled down the slope. They had fed the shattered boards and beams of the manse into the steam engine's firebox, thus cleaning off the flat around the mine head. The tent city had vanished as miners moved into town and took up residences there.

Their powder magazine was located in the same little glory hole, a dozen feet into the cliff where Cracker had kept his explosives, but now it was stacked with cases of dynamite.

All this was guarded by two skilled and well-armed watchmen at all hours of the day and night. This was what concerned Cracker. He had dealt with watchmen all his life and these did not particularly worry him. One patrolled, while the other was stationed on the road from town that led up the steep slope to the mine.

He didn't particularly need reasons to do what he was about to do. The Whitebreads had stolen his mine and that was reason enough. Neither did he give thought to the consequences. He'd blow what he could to smithereens and head into the Nevada desert with his mule, and that would be the last anyone in Pearlygates would see of him.

If he paralyzed the mine, fine; the crooks deserved it. If he killed anyone, fine; they deserved killing, having stolen the Wine Cellar Mine from him. If the Whitebreads revenged themselves on that confidence man and his dotty woman he'd hooked up with, too bad for them. If he blew the mine to pieces and the boom turned into a bust, so what?

He circled wide, wary of any guard on the cliff above the mine with better night vision than his own. But there was no one this chill night. He approached from the north, the direction opposite from Pearlygates, walking a few feet at a time, studying the cliff, the distant works ahead, the rhythms of the night. He didn't see the patrolling guard, and that worried him a little.

But he was in no rush. He advanced a few yards at a time, moving from cover to cover. He felt the charged sticks move in their canvas sling he carried. If they blew him up, that was fine, too. It beat lying sick or starved in some desert hideaway.

He didn't know when the moon rose, and that was the wild card. But he'd broken into many a bank with full moonlight shining on him and had never gotten caught at it, so he didn't worry about it. There had been no trouble for many days; the guards would not be alert.

He worked close to the cliff, freezing into it now and then, until he reached the magazine. There, he found cases of explosive stacked neatly in the low hole. Oh, this would be entertaining. He would wake up Pearlygates, and the town would not soon go back to sleep.

It didn't much matter where he put the charged and fused sticks he had brought with him. He slid one into a crack between the cases, and the other farther back and less visible. Both of these had a two-minute Bickford fuse crimped to them.

He peered out of the hole and discovered one of the night guards busily high-grading at the ore pile, sliding pieces of quartz into his pocket in the light of a sliver of moon. That suited Cracker just fine. The man had set down a shotgun to perform his nightly ritual of augmenting his pay.

The next would be harder. Cracker wanted to blow the hoist works to bits, but that was on open ground and situated right in front of the mine head, and next to the ore pile. There was nothing to do but wait.

The guard was in no hurry, settling down on the ore heap to watch the world. Down below, the last lamps of Pearlygates dimmed out and the old ghost town slumbered. Cracker waited. Down on the road to the mine, the other guard was stationed, and sooner or later, the two would get together.

It seemed a long time, and the night's cold pierced his black sweater. At last the guard at the ore pile lit a cheroot, the match-light blinding him for a moment, and drifted away.

Cracker wasted not a moment. He slid ahead, a black wraith, and reached the hoist works. Expertly, he set one stick under the boiler, choosing a hidden place that would not reveal the spitting fuse, and another under the big drum and pulley that fed the cable into the mine, also shielded from sight by tinplate.

He pulled out his pocketknife and sawed the fuse off at two feet, or one minute.

He took his time. He studied his escape route, looking for anything that might trip him. He would light these fuses at the mine head, retreat toward the magazine, light those fuses, and fade away from the mine. If his matches, lit candle, or the sparks from the fuses caught the eye of the guards, he might be in trouble.

But he had learned over the years in his curious trade how to shield a flaring match from other eyes by employing his body, and now he placed his wiry frame between the fuses in the hoist works and the road below. With any kind of luck, he would ignite the fuses and beat it out of there without being discovered.

He pulled the stub of a candle from his pocket, lit it, pressed the flame to the first fuse until it spat, and then slid a few feet to the second fuse, and lit it. He heard nothing behind him. He doused the candle, hastened toward the magazine, which was twenty seconds away, scratched a lucifer, lit his candle, and soon ignited both of those fuses as well.

He heard no shouts, felt no rush of movement in the quiet night. He drifted north along the face of the cliff, ignoring cover now, wanting distance . . .

The hoist works blew first, two violent cracks that lifted the boiler and engine, toppled the frame, and shattered the night's peace. But that was only a prelude. A moment later, an earsplitting crack rent the night. It was a boom that shivered the very earth, an explosion that shot fire and violence out of that magazine for a city block in all directions. The percussion knocked Cracker flat and battered him twice more, knocking his head back and almost breaking his neck. He could not hear, because the noise had stopped his ears.

Cracker had never known such violence. It awed him. He peered into a night sky that was raining rock. He wanted to move, to retreat, but could not. He lay paralyzed by the violence, witless and addled. At last, by sheer will, he pulled himself to his feet, trembled, slid away, circled widely, and crept into town.

Half-dressed people were astir, some of them wandering the streets in a daze, others talking excitedly.

"Magazine blew, up to the mine!" yelled one.

"Not a pane of glass left in town!"

"Did you ever!"

"My Gawd!"

"Never saw the like!"

"Sabotage!"

"Never saw the like since Gettysburg!" yelled an old man.

"I thought the earth was splitting open and letting the devil out!"

"Someone did it!"

"Naw, those Whitebreads were careless is all. Who'd blow up a gold mine?"

Shadowy men appeared with rifles and drawn revolvers. Possibly Whitebread guards, Cracker thought. More and more, such armed men had patrolled the old ghost town, becoming law where there had been none. And now they were out on the dark streets.

Cracker ignored all that, clung to shadows, worked darkly through the town, whose gaze was fixed on the mine, and reached his own cabin unobserved. He heard distant shots, and wondered who was shooting at what. Probably a lot of powder was being expended on shadows.

The hoist works was burning, casting a sickly and wavering light over Pearlygates.

"Haw!" he exclaimed, feeling at last a certain pride of achievement.

He had hitched his mule to a post in front of the cabin, but now it was gone; probably that awesome blast had terrified it into bolting.

"Where are you, Agnes, damn it?" he yelled.

But his old mule had beat a retreat into the blackness.

He hunted down the dark gulch and up it, but found nothing. He called softly, checked the banks of the rivulet in the gulch, whistled, and finally gave up.

Well, he'd leave at first light, just as soon as he could corral that nasty, long-eared, willful, ornery beast, and then he'd put Pearlygates behind him, along with the Whiteheads, and that miserable pair he had partnered with for a while. He had gotten even, but he was just as broke as ever. He returned to his obscure cabin near the mines and waited for dawn, chortling and chuckling now and then, as tides of amusement swept through him.

Chapter 29

Claudius P. Raines bellied up to the bar of the Four Deuces Club, a new drink and gambling emporium on Nevada Street, surveying the crowd. He clutched a tumbler half-filled with a rowdy red-eye, which he had commandeered when its owner headed for the outhouse. That licensed him to stand among the patrons without being harried by the white-aproned bartenders.

He spotted a hawk-nosed silver-haired gent in a costly suit as a likely mark, and struck up a conversation.

"Lots of opportunity in a place like this," he opined.

The man looked him up and down, and nodded.

"My own instinct is that this is mineralized terrain; and it will yield far more than precious metals when it is thoroughly plumbed," Raines said. "There's more to mining than silver and gold."

"You a geologist?"

"No, a capitalist."

"I didn't catch your name."

"Raines, sir. Colonel C.P. Raines. I do have some specialized experience in mineral exploration. I was struck the other day by a formation I saw below town, sir, not above; not high up those cliffs, but down in the gulch draining Pearlygates. It was a type of rock that forms the matrix for sapphires. I've seen it in Montana Territory. Interesting idea, sapphires here in Nevada. I've always been partial to those blue gems. They match my eyes. And blue's the color of liberty."

"Sapphires? I doubt it."

"I doubt it too, but that decaying vein of crumbling clay stays in mind. I saw it while taking the air. And your name is?"

"Stanford Altgeld."

"Mr. Altgeld, let me buy you a libation."

Altgeld nodded.

"At any rate, the minerals here have scarcely been tapped. I suspect, from personal observation, that there might be that most precious of metals, aluminum."

"Never heard of it."

"A marvelous metal, sir, lighter than any known except magnesium, and so rare that only a few pounds of it exist in pure form, and these mostly devoted to tableware of the very rich. It's a king's novelty, you see, to eat with it. It's smelted by a galvanic method, and gotten from a mineral called cryolite and another called bauxite. Rather common in nature, but desperately difficult to reduce. It's a metal I'm keeping my eye on, and I devour everything written about it in the journals. . . . I think it's here, in this mineral belt, and not a man in this mob knows it."

Altgeld drained his glass and pushed it out on the bar, expecting a refill, but the colonel seemed not to be aware of it.

"My plan, now that I've looked the district over, is to bring in a certain geologist in my employ, and set him to work. He's no mere assayer, believe me, but a man so versed in earth science that I lap up his every word."

"Ah, I know a few; that's my field too. Who is he?"

"Why, Mr. Altgeld, I dare not reveal his name, because I fear someone would steal him away from me. He's made me rich. He's uncovered mines, not the usual sort of mines, but little holes in the ground that cough up gems and rare metals like platinum. I have a little nickel mine too, in Canada. A dandy little metal, and I've never wanted a market for it.

"It's not a matter of money; it's a matter of keeping the best man in the world on my payroll. He's just as happy in the field, with a tent and a portable lab, as he is in our works with his little furnaces and retorts. Well, it's time for me to sup," Raines said, knocking back the red-eye and settling the glass on the plank bar.

"You want company, sir?"

"I do believe that would make a most pleasant evening of it, Mr. Altgeld. Have you a restaurant in mind?"

"Be my guest for dinner, sir. I'm interested in your proposition."

Food at last. Raines had felt the growing cavern in his belly all evening, and had worked a dozen dodges to get himself fed, and now the vision of beefsteak and potatoes danced before his eyes.

He was walking the precipice, and the smallest failure would send him into the abyss. The thought of swamping a saloon for a meal and a flop on a billiard table sent tremors through him.

"The restaurant right here is first-rate," Altgeld said. "I had good veal last night."

"Then let's have at it," the colonel said.

Suddenly, the room lit up. The town was rocked by a violent blast, followed by a huge boom a moment later, which seemed to lift Pearlygates right off its foundations and let it crash to earth. In the wake of that awesome explosion, the remnants of windows clattered to earth, fragmented by a giant fist that shivered the saloon and punched its inhabitants.

"What the hell?" yelled someone.

"It's the magazine. The mine blew!"

They could see now, at the Wine Cellar Mine far above, a ball of fire where the hoist once stood.

"Did you see it? A ton of dynamite! It's a miracle the town still stands!"

"Watch out for fire! That blast could knock over every coal oil lamp in town!"

Altgeld clutched a rail. "Amazing," he said.

Raines peered into the night, descrying the carnage at the mine and knowing at once its cause. He peered about hastily, fearing that armed Whitebread guards would clamp their mitts on him and haul him into the street. There had been more and more armed Whitebread men in town acting as if they were the law. They kept a sort of peace in an unruly burg, but it wasn't an official peace. Whitebread justice was a mockery.

The mob in the saloon rushed through its batwing doors into the street, the better to observe this holocaust, and Altgeld soon followed.

"I'll be waiting, sir," Raines said, and as soon as the dining room had cleared he settled comfortably in a chair and polished off half a loaf of bread, a veal cutlet, a glass of port, and a baked potato.

That would serve for the moment. He spotted a glass of white wine at the next table, and downed it too, before a few people drifted back.

In time, Altgeld himself appeared, and Raines met him at the door.

"Mr. Altgeld, I take it this explosion's damaged the town. I've some properties here I'd better examine," he said. "Twenty-odd buildings."

"That's wise, sir."

"Where are you staying? I'll look you up. Perhaps we can find some mutually beneficial interests."

"At Hutton's, Mr. Raines."

"Hutton's, then. I'll be in touch."

The colonel excused himself and headed into the

night, where men milled and shouted as the fire boiled through the hoist works at the mine.

The Whiteheads would come hunting. That miserable Cracker had gone too far this time and Raines feared for his life. He had no place to hide, and those armed thugs would do with him whatever they felt like doing.

Raines felt a clutch of fear in his belly.

If there was no place to hide, a crowd would do best. He retreated to the Miner's Exchange Club, a gambling parlor and saloon. He snatched a full glass of beer from the bar, where it had been abandoned. With that in hand he quieted his spirit, looked for easy marks, and waited for the excited crowd outside to drift back in.

What a fix. He grieved the betrayal by his partners. He had put MayBelle's town on the map again. He'd steered Cracker straight to gold; won them wealth. He had been a loyal friend and succored them, but at the first sign of trouble they had ditched him, as if he meant nothing to them. He had taught them everything he knew about living. He had inspired them to avoid stoop labor or other silly, absurd pursuits. Cracker hadn't absorbed the lesson entirely, but at least he saw that there was a better way to extract wealth than sweat and humble toil.

He sorrowed. They would have to look a long time for so faithful a friend as Colonel C.P. Raines. He sipped, sighed, and wished them well. He had always had a fancy for MayBelle, and even Cracker occupied a tender spot in his bosom. Some day, in their dotage, they would remember the colonel and how he inspired them to greatness.

But trouble didn't come. The crowds drifted back to their saloons and gaming halls, and the Whitebreads' terriers didn't slash through crowds looking for those to blame.

Then, indeed, Clyde Whitebread himself strode in, carrying some quartz.

Men crowded around him.

"It blew," Whitebread said. "Twelve cases of Hercules."

"What's the story, Clyde?" asked one.

"Story? Biggest story in days. Our magazine blew, and when we got in there, we found gold. That's the story."

Colonel C.P. Raines felt dizzy. He clutched the bar. That little hole in the cliff where the Wine Cellar Mine stored its explosives was fifty yards from the old manse, on the edge of MayBelle's backyard.

"Let's see the quartz," yelled one fellow.

"Look at this!" Clyde said. "Best quartz gold yet. Gents, we're sitting on another bonanza!"

Chapter 30

MayBelle sat at a table in the Four Deuces, surveying the crowd. She had a glass of red wine before her, but no means to pay for it. She had switched her ring, the sole remnant of her erstwhile marriage, from her right hand to her left because in these circumstances it was convenient to be a married woman once again.

The Four Deuces had emerged overnight as the best club in Pearlygates, after two freight wagons loaded with saloon and restaurant equipment had arrived. Now it sported the only crystal chandelier in Pearlygates, which shed brilliant light from six coal oil lamps.

MayBelle had no place to lay her head that night, having been ruthlessly expelled from her house by the Whitebreads. But that didn't worry her. A girl could make do. She had spent most of her life surviving with no visible means of support, and would resume her old ways if she had to. It wasn't the sort of life she wanted. Oddly, her soul these days pined for something so sweet and innocent that it resembled the yearnings of a young girl, not a woman in her circumstance. A cottage surrounded by lilacs, a life as fragrant as roses, a man to cook for.

Earlier, she had spotted the colonel working on a mark or two at the bar, but except for a single glance they had not acknowledged each other. She preferred it that way. His was the harder course. He, too, had been evicted, penniless, from his quarters. But he didn't have her assets, and was likely to spend a frosty night under the stars unless he could conjure some cash out of nothing but his wits.

She pitied him a little, but not much. If he would lift a finger now and then he might be worth some pity.

She sipped quietly, watching the entirely male crowd, knowing which of the patrons of this club were surreptitiously watching her, and waited. She wished she could have arranged her toilet, but a lady without a vanity, mirror, or wardrobe could do little but comb her hair with her fingers, freshen her face, and hope for the best. She took pains to button her silk dress right to the top in order to present the gentlemen in this rough café with the image of perfect propriety, so far as a single woman in a pleasure resort could manage it.

The ring on her left hand and the way she wore her attire would discourage all but trespassers, but it was a trespasser she wanted; a trespasser would likely be much easier to bend to her needs. Hard men, like gamblers, were trouble; however, trespassers of all sorts were easy marks.

In time, a silver-haired patrician gent did circle around, eye her, and finally approach. He simply sat at the table next to hers with a drink in hand.

"Here you are in a crowded saloon and all alone," he said.

She nodded and said nothing.

"What brought you to Pearlygates?"

"I live here and look after my husband's properties. He owned the mines and the town lot company, and I've been here for many years. It was never totally abandoned, you know."

"I see. And where is he?"

"He's out of town."

"Then perhaps you would enjoy some quiet company."

Hooked. She nodded.

He moved himself to her table without further invitation. "Armand Esterhazy," he said. "And you?"

"MayBelle Harbinger, Mrs. Harbinger."

"A charming name. Harbinger, meaning portent, one that foreshadows what is to come. I think good things are coming, don't you?"

She smiled. What was to come was already in the air.

"And how does a lovely lady look after her husband's business affairs in his absence?"

"We're selling off properties. I sell for whatever I can get and ward off trespassers."

"Ah. And what is the price of, say, an exhausted mine?"

"More than you can afford."

He laughed. "A dead mine is nothing but an empty hole."

"Yes, and what I really sell is dreams. There are those who believe that just a foot farther, they will strike a bonanza and end up in paradise. And so they pay an amazing price for a dead mine, dreaming of riches and heaven on earth."

"Ah, you understand human nature. And what of the town lots? I thought the Whitebread interests controlled them all."

She smiled again. "Ask them for a deed, for a conveyance, for a title, and you'll discover the truth of it."

"And you have the titles?"

"Mr. Esterhazy, the Whitebreads barged into my land office, carted every title to every property in town into Nevada Street, and burnt the entire pile with a generous infusion of coal oil to make sure the deed was done."

"So . . . how are you, and, ah, your husband, dealing with this?"

"We do have a county courthouse, even if it seems halfway across Nevada."

"I see. And that is where he is, at present?"

She shrugged.

"I'm an opportunist," he said. "Always looking for the main chance. I love wild cards, the ace, the deuce, the joker that tumbles a fortune into my lap. I think this is a most fortunate acquaintance."

She nodded.

"May I replenish your wine?"

"I prefer a man's drink. Such as whiskey. The wine is a cheat, if you want to know."

She spotted the colonel staring at her from the bar and nodded slightly. Maybe, if her luck held, she could help him. The thought startled her and she wondered why she would want to help the old dear. But she did, and she found herself wishing she knew how.

"Consider it done," he said. He could find no waiter to summon and eventually repaired to the bar to order drinks from the slick-haired bartender in his dirty white apron.

Esterhazy was fashionably dressed, but so was the impoverished colonel. And for that matter, so was she, and without a cent to her name. But Esterhazy was also richly dressed, and wore his black suit with a flair. He had means, and that was as good a recommendation as any.

The evening proceeded according to classic design. They discussed many things, including the strange explosion that had rent Pearlygates and shattered glass a few hours earlier. She probed but got no hint of his vocation, and ended up supposing he had come into some money by easy means. Yet the man was educated and used elegant words, not all of which she fathomed. But what did it matter?

Esterhazy gently probed into her marriage, or what

he presumed was a marriage, and MayBelle let him think what he would.

"He's been gone so long," she said. "That's why I just had to find some society tonight."

A faint blaze ignited in his eyes.

He plied her with more drink, and then dinner, such as it was, because food was at best a haphazard business in Pearlygates. The boomtown lacked regular supplies of nearly everything, though that was changing fast as word of the bonanza spread through Nevada.

The place managed some spinach and dandelion greens from the Carson Valley, moose steaks, breast of ptarmigan, wild onions, and flan. Not bad for an establishment that had barely opened its doors in a ghost town, MayBelle thought.

This very evening a young sheriff's deputy had arrived, the steel star glinting off his pin-striped vest: the first tendril of the vine of law and order to reach the wild town. The lawman seemed quiet enough, doing little more than wandering from club to club, letting his presence be known. At least he was not a Whitebread man. She thought to warn Cracker, then wondered why she cared. Let Cracker take care of himself. He had dodged the law long enough to know when trouble was brewing. Odd that she thought to warn him. All the man did was blow up everything she owned.

Esterhazy offered her a chocolate-brown cigarillo along with a green liqueur, and she accepted. The moment of truth was fast approaching, and she was enjoying herself.

"You are a woman of extraordinary virtue," he said. "I envy your most fortunate husband."

"He gives me more than compliments," she said.

"I have a fine room on the second floor of the new hotel, the Grande, with a breathtaking view of Pearlygates from my window. I thought you might wish to see the city spread before you, its lamps lit and twinkling in the dark."

"You mean, I might wish to observe the ceiling spread above me."

He laughed softly. "You are a woman of quick wit and discernment."

"It'll take more than compliments to seduce me," she said. "Words fall so easily from your tongue."

"Ah," he said. "You inspire me."

"That's not all I do to you."

"That, too," he said.

"I don't seduce easily. I am a woman who sets a high standard."

"Ah, MayBelle, if I may call you that, you may have whatever your heart desires."

"That's quite beyond your means, Armand. I am insatiable. And it's best that you contain your fevers for now; who knows when my husband will return?"

He sucked and exhaled smoke. "That only makes you all the more . . . fascinating."

"I imagine," she said, toying with her ring.

The quiet vanished when several argonauts burst through the doors with news. "The Whiteheads hit gold! The blast opened a new seam. Richest gold yet! Clyde Whitebread's showing quartz with thick ribbons running through it."

"Amazing," said Armand. "The town's a phoenix."

The clamor at the bar ruined the moment for MayBelle. That miserable Cracker; not only had he gotten them into trouble, he had just opened up a new bonanza in her backyard.

"The place is filled with gold, it seems," Armand said. "It's a wonder it was all missed the first time around."

"It's in my backyard," she said.

"Your backyard?"

"My house stood where the Whitebreads are mining. Their mine was my wine cellar. That's the one place no one mined in the old days. We didn't want anyone digging holes twenty feet from our bedroom."

"Amazing. Your land? Mineral rights and all? You, ah, have title to challenge them?"

"Just you wait and see," she snapped.

"It so happens, MayBelle, that I'm an attorney and my speciality is mining law."

She laughed. "They'll have all the gold out of it before you'd get my, ah, our property back."

"No, I have resources. Trust me."

"You mean tryst me."

"That's my fee, MayBelle, my modest little fee."

"No," she said.

"But, MayBelle—"

"I am worth much more than the sum of my parts."

He laughed. She laughed. The night was young.

Chapter 31

Colonel Claudius P. Raines grieved. There, across a crowded saloon, sat his true love MayBelle, skillfully emptying the purse of a stranger. He sighed. He thought maybe MayBelle would take up with him and settle in the orange groves of California. But there she was, employing her wiles on a well-dressed gent, and soon she would have bed and board for herself. A comely woman had all the luck.

Things had gone badly for him. He felt his stomach protest at the hollowness within. Except for a quarter of a veal cutlet and a few odds and ends snatched from tables, he had not succored himself. But try as he might, he could not fashion a true meal out of that evening. Nor had he wet his whistle for two or three hours. He had kept a sharp eye for half-filled glasses abandoned by departing customers, but had found only one, and that a miserable inch of sour beer. He lacked the ordinary tools of his trade, such as a deck of cards, or three walnut shells and a dried pea.

But that didn't entirely faze him because his tongue was the best of all tools of his trade. He was a man of a thousand propositions, and if he had nothing to bet, he could still peddle dreams. There, in that sweaty saloon, eighty or a hundred lustful miners dreamed of bonanzas and eldorados, pink parlors and lace curtains, and that was all a man of the colonel's skill needed to make some headway.

The days were shortening swiftly, and it was not possible to sleep comfortably under the stars now, which only added to the colonel's anxiety. He had no place to shelter his weary flesh this night, and that was a matter of mounting concern. He had not so much as a ratty blanket, having lost all of his possessions to the Whitebreads.

Late in the evening a hood-eyed gent with a combed and glossy blue beard slid in beside him, a mining man, surely.

"Ah, friend, how have you fared?" asked the colonel.

"Just got here."

"Looking for the main chance, I imagine."

"Indeed, a thimble full of success."

"Maybe it's just around the corner. The trouble with most prospectors is that they're blind. When they're hunting gold, they miss the nickel ore. When they're tracking down silver, they miss the sapphires. When they're looking for coal they miss the tin." He eyed the man shrewdly. "Actually, it's all there for the taking, to a man with an eye for it. Why just today, while strolling an area not visited by all these miners hereabouts, I saw something that caught my attention."

The colonel edged his nearly empty tumbler outward, hoping for a refill, but the man just stared blandly.

"Yes," the colonel continued. "They all head upslope, these prospectors, as if gold climbed mountains. But me, I stroll along on the level, and my entire lifetime of experience in the mining field equips me to see the unseen."

"Yes, and what?"

"Sapphires, sir. I spotted a dike, a foot thick, a dike of

disintegrated blue clay. I've seen a hundred of those around the world, most recently in Borneo and Madagascar, and a few in Ceylon, and I know what's usually in them. Not always, of course, but usually. Sapphires, sir. Blue gems. The most beautiful of all gemstones. There is nothing like a glowing, cornflower-blue ten-karat sapphire to put an end to melancholia. Some are no good, of course, miserable discolored stones. But I suspect this little seam will yield fine blue gems, gems so pure and brilliant that even Tiffany's will go mad for them."

"Where's that?"

The colonel chuckled. "You're a wily one."

He edged his glass outward again but the fellow didn't summon the jowly pug behind the bar.

"At any rate, that's been my experience in the mining field. Look for gold and find iron. Look for iron and find emeralds. Look for emeralds and find tin. Look for tin and find diamonds. Tomorrow I'll probe a little further, and not a soul in this gold-crazed burg will have the slightest idea what I'm about. . . . Does that interest you?"

"Nope, I'm a tailor. I wouldn't know a glory hole from a spittoon."

"A tailor. I wouldn't have guessed. Well, you think about it. I always take on a partner or two, and in every case, without fail, we've all profited. In fact, partners are good luck for me; I strike out only when I don't have a couple of partners."

Blue-beard smiled, baring small yellow teeth. "Sure, my sapphire friend, and when you do, I'll sew you a new suit. That one's been around the bend, I imagine. But that's how it is in a gold rush. I can put a fine broadcloth suit on your back for only twenty-nine dollars, and a second vest for two more, and a second pair of pants for three more. You'll not find a better man with the needle, and I can outfit you from stem to stern in less than a week."

"Ah, thank you. Fieldwork does wear out my duds."

The colonel sighed. Another ten minutes wasted.

The hour was late. The night was growing icy. The crowds in the saloon were swiftly disappearing. MayBelle and her well-manicured gent had vanished.

"You want a drink?" asked the barman. "Last call. We're closing."

"Ah, no . . ."

With every flap of the batwing doors a chill gust of air swept the heat out of him.

He studied the remaining few and found them unfit company. Some were lost in a boozy haze. Others stared mournfully into their beer. There wasn't a one who had more than two bits in his jeans.

The colonel steeled himself against the cold, plucked up his silk hat, and headed into the icy night. He stared at bright stars in a black sky, examined the few remaining lamplit windows, and then knew where he would go, though the very idea of it amounted to defeat.

He set foot quietly through slumbering Pearlygates, resolutely walking toward the dead mines and the great dark gulch that separated the two parts of the town. Wood smoke hung in the air, along with a wintry breeze eddying off the peaks. There, near the bend in the gulch, he found the path that would lead to Cracker's obscure cabin clinging to the slope, which he hoped still had escaped the greedy cyclops eye of the Whitebreads.

He had resolved never to have a thing to do with that cur of a powder man, but that was before necessity intervened. Ten minutes later he was at the threshold, where the cabin looked dark, cold, and forbidding. If he tried to enter unannounced, he would probably end up with steel through his ribs, so he knocked gently.

"Cracker, it's the colonel."

Nothing stirred.

"Cracker? Colonel Raines here. I've come to help you out."

The night lay heavy. The colonel was starting to shake with cold.

Then, suddenly, he felt cold steel jab him in the back.

"Sneaking around here, are you? Think you could pull a fast one, did you?"

The colonel startled. "Gad, man, how did you get around me?"

"What do you want?"

"Just to chat a bit, old friend. Food, warmth for a little while. I've a little proposition to put to you. I think I have discovered the big one, the chance we've been waiting for—you, MayBelle, and your humble servant."

Cracker laughed nastily. "I'll blow you up, too."

"Yes, quite a display! You rattled every window in town."

"Beat it."

"But, Cracker . . . don't you know?"

"What're you talking about?"

"That blast opened up a new bonanza. Clyde Whitebread's been all over town showing off his quartz. It's got threads of pure gold running through it. And there it was, a seam of gold-bearing quartz just a foot from the back wall of that little cubbyhole where they'd stored their powder, right in MayBelle's backyard."

Safe Cracker began cursing with such fluency and skill that Colonel Raines thought maybe the man had taken his doctoral degree in the field.

"I'm cold and hungry, and I have a proposition," he said gently.

A ticking silence ensued, and then the colonel no longer felt the pressure of a revolver barrel in his kidney.

"All right, come in. I'm leaving before dawn anyway. Soon as I find my damned mule."

"Ah! You are a saint."

Cracker wheezed at that. He steered the colonel into the snug log cabin, which exuded certain acrid odors, such as those of burnt gunpowder. In a moment a light flared, half blinding the colonel. The safecracker lit a candle lamp and stuffed the glass chimney over it against draft. The cabin was almost naked, save for a packsaddle and two panniers loaded with Cracker's worldly possessions.

"Can you put some food in my belly, Cracker? I just happen to have found the biggest bonanza of all and if you'll modestly succor me, I'll share it with you."

Cracker cackled. "Help yourself. Beans in the pot."

The colonel found no spoon or ladle, but indeed there were some dried-up beans lying dead cold in a Dutch oven. Gingerly, the colonel fingered a mess of beans into his mouth, masticated, and repeated this mannerly process until he felt comforted by a leaden mass of cold beans in his belly.

"Much obliged," the colonel said, wiping his bean-smeared hand upon the log wall for lack of any other towel. "Now, then, on to my end of the bargain."

The safecracker settled wolfishly on the floor and waited.

"Sapphires," said the colonel. "Sapphires. We're going to stake claims, you and Maybelle and I, along a certain ledge where a certain green rock extrudes."

"Raines, there's not a sapphire within five hundred miles of here."

"Cracker, your cranium is packed with solid wood. What I need you to do is to build some rock cairns to hold our claims and blow a small hole in a rock cliff face, say three feet deep, to establish our bona fides."

"Our claims? What are we claiming?"

"Whatever fevers the brow of speculators," the colonel said sagely.

"Ah," said Safe Cracker. "Another of your schemes."

"Exactly," said the colonel.

"Count me out."

"But I need you. Out of long and faithful companionship, I will file claims for you and MayBelle as well as myself."

"How generous," Safe Cracker said. "What you really want is my labor, as usual, you lazy bum."

The colonel smiled benevolently. "You are a true friend," he said. "Spend another day or two and it will get you to Argentina."

Chapter 32

Dawn found the colonel in an empty cabin.

He peered about from his bunk, discovered Cracker's packsaddle lying just where it had been the previous night, and sighed. He had not been abandoned. There would be more cold beans for breakfast.

The place exuded strange odors but so did Safe Cracker, who always smelled as if he had emerged from a laboratory with chemicals eating through his white smock.

The man would return; his worldly goods remained.

Happily, the colonel greeted the day, did his toilet, licked beans off his fingers, and waited. By the time the sky had brightened into a true blue, the nefarious Cracker had returned cussing.

"Someone stole Agnes," he said.

"Cracker, that blast last night drove your mule into the next county."

"Someone stole her. She takes kindly to blasts."

"Well, now you're stuck here," the colonel said hopefully.

"Not for long. Just long enough to steal another one."

"Well, before you do, you'll help me set up some

claims. That's all you need to concern your skinny carcass about. Just a few moments of work."

Cracker laughed. "Measuring claims, building cairns, and blowing a hole, all in a few moments."

The colonel smiled blandly. "Rich will be your rewards in the kingdom of heaven, when you do finally pass through the pearly gates. Have you some paper and a writing instrument?"

The safecracker muttered, dug into his pack, and produced a pad and a pencil. "I don't know what I'm doing this for."

"For the Glory of God, Cracker. You are laying the foundation of a cathedral."

The colonel took the paper and stubby pencil. "Dictate to me the exact terminology, Cracker."

Something came to life in Cracker and he waxed almost poetic. "We, the undersigned, claim three claims of three hundred feet each upon this gold-bearing ledge."

"Not gold, Cracker. Think up something else."

"Around here? Copper."

"A base metal?"

Cracker shrugged. "Good copper ore often is laced with gold and silver."

"Ah, then we shall say so: gold and silver and copper-bearing ledge." The colonel scribbled.

"—extending north and south from this notice, along with all its dips and spurs and angles and variations and sinuosities together with fifty feet of ground on either side for working the same."

The colonel transcribed all that. "That's it?"

"Well, you gotta place that in the middle in a secure way, build cairns on the boundaries, write up duplicates for each of us, file it with the government or the mining district ledger, and prove it up."

"Then we'll do it."

"You mean, I'll do it."

"Of course you will, and leave the rest to me."

"I am a beast of burden. I am like my Agnes, a creature you wish to drive along, carrying tools and powder; a beast who will knock holes in rock, heap up cairns, measure large chunks of land."

"Cracker, old sport, I am about to make you rich. Get that in your head, absorb that in the sawdust between your ears. I'll convert your slight and easy toil into a bonanza so fat and glowing, so high and mighty, so endless and deep, so sweet and heavenly, that you will never have to crack a safe the rest of your days, and you will die a sated and respectable old sage."

"You take all the fun out of life," Cracker said. "And what're you gonna do to earn yourself this bonanza?"

"I am an alchemist, Cracker. I turn lead into silver, tin into gold. Trust me."

"About as much as I trust the Whitebreads."

The colonel wanted no further argument from his bosom friend and admired colleague, and hastened Cracker into collecting some tools: pick and shovel.

"Where we going?" the burdened prospector asked.

"Follow along now and avoid company, steer clear of others, and hasten through town before the whole of Pearlygates falls out of its bunks. We shall proceed invisibly to my discovery."

"Discovery." Cracker whickered nastily.

Nonetheless, the colonel plunged into the chill morning air as if no cold would suffice to drive him indoors. He strolled amiably down the gulch alongside the creek dividing Pearlygates, through a great hush.

In time, they proceeded downslope until they were well below Pearlygates, and not far from the base of the mountain range, where foothills and debris splayed out onto an arid plain five hundred feet lower than the town. But still the colonel plodded on, his silk hat embracing his cranium even though a chill breeze blew.

"Where the hell are you going? I'm getting tired of carrying this stuff."

"Peace, my friend, I am going along that narrow path to the pearly gates of heaven."

"We're going into a desert is what, and there's not a drop of water in sight."

"Cracker, friend, we're not a mile from Pearlygates."

At a certain point the colonel turned sharp right and proceeded along a course parallel to the mountains. Here was evidence of a bit of moisture; saltbush crowded the base of a low cliff, and midway up its face was a thick seam of green-tinted rock, half hidden by the brush.

The colonel could see the town above, perched as it was on the side of the mountain. They had come a roundabout route from Cracker's cabin, but were now only half a mile from town as the crow flies. And yet they were standing in an utterly desolate gulch, a gulch carved by the rare rains of Nevada, the sand laced with the tracks of small animals and birds.

"Behold," the colonel said.

"Behold what?"

"Behold our fortune."

"It's just rock."

"No, it's green rock. It is the only green rock I've discovered in the area."

"So what's that supposed to mean?"

"It means that it will excite the imagination of miners. We will stake our claim and walk away with a modest fortune."

Cracker set down his tools and eyed the place skeptically. The ledge rose maybe fifty feet, and the streak of green ran two or three feet thick. Above, the slopes covered with scree stretched clear to Pearlygates. A great deal of the green stuff had weathered loose and lay heaped in the gulch. Its basic color was a lustrous gray, but it was streaked with a mineral that ranged from lime to turquoise and gave the rock a greenish cast.

Cracker plucked up pieces, licked them, rubbed them,

and laughed. "This stuff isn't worth laying a claim to," he said. "This is some sort of schist around here."

"You have sawdust in your head."

"You can bet that when Pearlygates was going full blast, this was clawed over a hundred times, colonel. We can practically shout and be heard in town."

The colonel only chuckled. "We shall build a claim cairn here in the middle, and measure nine hundred feet in all."

"You mean I'll build a cairn here and you'll sit on a rock and watch."

"You're a discerning fellow. Better you than some lout who doesn't deserve a fortune."

"This is some type of country rock."

"Get to work, Cracker."

The skinny prospector sighed, pulled a hundred-foot tape out of his pocket, and began measuring along the base of the gulch, scaring up some sort of small animal in the process.

"Watch for snakes," the colonel said. The cold was biting at his flesh but what did it matter?

Eventually the rising sun reached the shaded gulch and almost at once warmed the country. The colonel hummed, felt the rays burrow into his black suit and heat it, and watched Arnold Cracker fuss around angrily. Cracker was an industrious sort and soon had a nine-hundred-foot claim laid out along the ledge.

Then he returned to the colonel. "Build your own damned cairns. I'm done. I stuck a stake, some ironwood, in each corner. I'm going to find Agnes or a facsimile of her and git a hundred miles from Pearlygates."

"Cracker, if you leave, how will you know whether your name is on the claim? How do you know I am a man of great probity?"

Cracker stood and stared at the colonel, spat, and muttered.

In a few moments, the skinny gent was heaping rocks into the discovery cairn. In twenty minutes a distinct pyramid of rocks rose at the foot of the green-laced cliff.

"All right, put her in there," Cracker said.

The colonel signed the claim for himself, MayBelle, and Cracker, while Cracker watched, stuffed the claim into a snuff can, and pushed it into the cairn. Cracker added a few rocks to the heap.

"Now gimme' a copy," Cracker said. The colonel had long since written out one for each claimant, and handed a copy to the safe robber.

"You can build up the other markers yourself," Cracker said. "I'm quitting."

"But, Cracker, when I sell this, how'll I get in touch with you?"

Cracker laughed. "Sell this? I figure I'm a fool to think I'll get a nickel out of any game of yours."

The colonel saw there would be no stopping the man. Cracker plucked up his tools and hiked off, leaving Colonel Claudius P. Raines sitting on a rock beside a half-completed claim. He stared at his soft hands, at the blue sky, at the loose scree lying all over. The colonel knew what he had to do, and there was no escape from it.

Chapter 33

The colonel stared aghast as Arnold Cracker walked away. The man had no faith. Just another hour or two of toil would have given the colonel what he needed, three properly marked claims to sell.

Claudius P. Raines grimly considered the options and found there were none. He might persuade some rummy in Pearlygates to stack up rock for him but that was too risky. He might find MayBelle if he was extremely lucky, and persuade her to build the cairns. But he knew what the odds were.

There was nothing to do but heap up rock himself. The very thought horrified him. He would dirty his smooth, clean, white hands, chip his fingernails, reveal his low estate to the world. That violated every canon by which he ordered his life. A confidence man needed spotless hands, the hands of the privileged and the rich.

He had always found suckers eager and willing to sweat, tote, drag, lift, scoop, and dig. He could not bring himself to lift rocks, as if he were a convict in a work gang.

He sat down and grieved mightily. Maybe if he sat long enough some cheery yeoman would wander by, and maybe the fellow might be persuaded to build those cairns. But the more he sat, as the sun rose and warmed him, the less he believed he would be rescued by a stroke of good fortune. No, it was up to him.

He waited awhile longer just in case Arnold Cracker decided to return, but with the sun well up in the heavens Colonel Raines knew that Cracker was gone.

Claudius P. Raines would have to lift rock. He wondered how much stone he would need to mark the boundaries, but he hadn't a clue. He eyed the discovery cairn, which rose two or three feet. Sorrowfully, he stood, resolved to endure this affront to everything he believed in. The colonel hiked along the green-streaked ledge until he came to a stake, then hiked the other direction until he came to another stake. And another. Three claims of three hundred feet along the ledge.

With a sigh, he shed his black suit coat and set down his black silk topper. He kicked at a rock. It didn't come loose. He leaned over, feeling the unaccustomed bending of his back, and lifted it. He carried the rock to the stake, and then another, and another. He rested. There was plenty of loose rock around, and he wouldn't need to pry it up.

If only MayBelle and Cracker could see him now, sacrificing everything for the sake of three claims. If only they knew the nature of the sacrificial gift he was giving them. Sorrily, he saw himself as a much-abused rescuer of his friends and colleagues, who were, of course, unable to grasp the future.

Slowly, painfully, Colonel Raines erected a small cairn marking the northernmost boundary of their claims on the ledge. He found it necessary to rest between every stone, but eventually he had a small marker in place. He studied this monument, found it almost handsome.

By noon he had erected the other cairn on the south side of the ledge. An hour later he completed two small heaps dividing the nine hundred feet into thirds. He sat on a rock, admiring his handiwork. Never in his entire life had he invested so much physical labor in anything. He was weary and hungry. Finding another meal would be a problem, but he was ready to capitalize on this bonanza.

As a last measure, he pocketed a few egg-sized chips of the green-streaked rock and labored his way to Cracker's cabin to wash up and maybe find a meal, if the renowned powder man had not absquatulated.

No one was about, but Cracker's packsaddle rested on the floor right where it had been that morning. The man was still trying to find Agnes, which the colonel deemed a stroke of good fortune. The beans had been scraped out of the Dutch oven and the colonel could find not a scrap of food to nurture his broken and abused body.

There was much to be done but he had no time at all. His stomach was howling. As best he could, he sponged his battered and grimy suit and hat. The stubble of a beard decorated his jowls, and his fingernails showed evidence of menial labor. He scrubbed the dirt off his hands, but his bruised and battered digits would never be the same. Oh, for a shave, a bath, a set of duds!

He would need a real or concocted assay report to peddle that green rock, so he headed toward one of the new assay offices that had sprung up on Nevada Street. He settled on one near the end of the street, closest to the Whitebread mine, operated by one Rubin Picotte. A good French name. Raines had always supposed the French were the most excitable and therefore the easiest to gull.

His entry jangled a door chime, and in time a small, bug-eyed black-haired gnome in an apron emerged from a back room, where heat radiated from a refractory oven.

"What is it that it is that I may do for you?" asked the diminutive gent, turning French into English.

"I'm looking for an assay and don't know how to go about it, my good man."

"Well, show me the sample."

"I'm not so sure I want to."

"Then don't bother me. You can see I am busy."

"Ah, I was a bit hasty. I have some ore; I just don't know how all this is done."

"And where is this magnificent specimen that is so secret you won't show it?"

"How do you prepare a report?"

"I reduce the rock, bake it in that oven back there, subject it to numerous tests known only to those in my profession, and scientifically prepare a report."

"And what's in the report?"

"Why, the metals, if any, rendered in various proportions, such as troy ounces to the ton, or sometimes percentages per ton, which is common when I assay base metals."

"Is this written on a form?"

"Yes, a standard form." He held out his hand. "This marvelous bonanza of yours, if you please."

"I'd like to see the form. Just to educate myself, my friend. This is all a bit new to me."

"So it seems. You're not a prospector, I take it?"

"No, but I am allied with a man of such skill that he can find minerals that elude everyone else. He obligated me to select the finest assayer in the district and I have little doubt that you're the one. All the information in my possession leads me to you, sir."

"Ah! So it is that you are cautious. I am cautious as well. Well, I will show you."

He beckoned Raines, who proceeded into the laboratory, where he beheld an array of mortars and pestles, a small furnace, ceramic containers, test tubes, grinders, and assorted chemicals in bottles.

"Right now, in the furnace, I am reducing a sample from a certain gold mine for a certain client. When I am done we will know all there is to know. This operation will probably yield a mixture of gold and a little silver and maybe other metals. After I complete this phase, I must separate the silver and other metals from the gold. It's a process that takes many steps, some delicate, some with chemicals or reagents, some with heat."

"May I see a typical report, Mr. Picotte?"

"They're confidential, sir."

"I suppose that's the final task; you fill out a form, and give it to your customer."

The colonel decided he could fake a report if he could filch a few of the blank forms that were lying in pad form on the assayer's desk in front.

"Well, now, my good friend, I just think I might go ahead. I should like you to keep the results totally confidential, of course. We think we're on to something and don't want a word to leak out."

Picotte drew himself up. "Sir, to question my integrity is to invite yourself out of my offices."

"Good. We see eye to eye." The colonel rummaged in his pockets and withdrew a handful of small samples. "Is this enough? I can get much more."

He dropped the creamy rocks, striated with green, into the assayer's hands.

The man peered at the largest rock, plucked up a huge magnifying glass and hummed, licked his lips, spat and wiped saliva over the rock, and sighed.

"You just have yourself a good look, and I'll be back," Raines said.

The gnome was turning the rocks over and over, sometimes licking them or rubbing them with his grimy thumb.

"When shall I call?"

"Tomorrow," said Picotte. "And what is the name, sir?"

"Colonel Raines, Claudius P. Raines."

"I haven't seen any like this," Picotte said. "Very interesting. Yes, perhaps there is something. Nothing I've ever seen before. Most unusual. You will tax my skills."

Raines nodded, but the little fellow was absorbed. The colonel eased into the front room, slid over to the pad of assay forms lying on the cramped desk, plucked up a few sheets, and jangled his way onto Nevada Street. Swiftly, he folded the blank forms and jammed them into his breast pocket. Good!

His next stop was the Nevada Queen Hotel, where he hovered about the small lobby waiting for the clerk to busy himself elsewhere. When the coast was clear the colonel made off with the nib pen and ink bottle on the counter, and vanished into the cold sunny day.

But he still needed to see an assay report. He could scarcely draft a few fakes without knowing what the real ones looked like, and for this he would rely on Arnold Cracker. He hurried back to the cabin with his pen and inkpot and blank assay reports, but Cracker was nowhere in sight. He left the pen and ink there, and headed into town again, this time straight toward the Pearlygates Land Office, where he had once reigned supreme.

If the Whitebreads had some factotum at the counter it would go well. If not . . . he would have to come up with some other scheme.

Again he was in luck. The man at the counter was a young stranger.

"My good man, I'm interested in mining prospects, ready to examine properties. I've had a most difficult trip, attacked by Paiute Indians, dragged a hundred yards behind a war pony, but here I am, ready to plunge in. Show me, sir, your absolutely finest claims and the assay reports, and I'll consider investing in them."

"Got a bunch of those," the man said. "You looking to lay out some real money or just nibble at the edges a bit?"

"I won't buy a thing without several assays, young fellow. And I'll probably have one or two done independently before I sink a nickel into any property. So bring out the reports."

The clerk soon produced an array of them, and the colonel proved to be a good student, asking learned questions and noting the things that excited the clerk.

Then he was ready.

Chapter 34

Yes indeed, yes indeed. The colonel studied assays for various properties, so much gold per ton, so much silver, so much copper, so much tellurium. The rare metals were expressed in ounces per ton of ore; the base metals as percentages.

Raines hummed his way through reports as the clerk shuffled papers.

"This here's a good claim," the young fellow said. "That's bonanza-grade ore, sixty ounces of gold per ton, most of it in quartz for free milling. But the owner's asking a stiff price."

"Sixty ounces, you don't say. I should take a look. Where is it?"

"Adjacent the Whitebreads' Wine Cellar Mine."

"Ah! No wonder they want twenty thousand."

The colonel studied assay reports until he had mastered their style as well as content and finally pushed all the paper away.

"I suppose I'll just go take a look," he said.

"Better hurry; properties like this don't languish in this office," the young man said.

Raines nodded, settled his begrimed silk hat on his

gray locks, and retreated. Ounces and percentages whirled through his mind as he made his way back to Cracker's cabin. But he was certain he could manufacture a fine forgery and sign Picotte's name to it.

He found no one in the cabin, but Cracker's packsaddle still rested in the little room so the safe robber hadn't yet fled town. The colonel uncorked the ink bottle and spread a blank assay form before him. The temptation was to load it with bonanza figures but something stayed him. He would be more likely to unload the claim if he kept his figures modest. Sensational numbers would only excite investigation.

So, dipping his nib pen into the black ink, he began on the report for MayBelle's claim: of copper, 2 percent per ton, primarily as chalcocite with malachite striation; of gold, six ounces to the ton; of silver, ten ounces to the ton; and of lead, half a percent; traces of other metals. He blew gently on the form, drying it, and then signed Picotte's name with a flourish. It was certainly satisfactory.

He completed assay reports for his own claim, increasing the values slightly, and for Cracker's claim, lowering the values slightly. And Picotte's signature appeared on all the claims. Then he added an additional assay report on MayBelle's property, noticeably higher in ounces of gold per ton, and signed it with a name of his own invention, Augustus Barony. He sighed, done at last, and stoppered the ink. How generous he was, looking after the wastrel Cracker, who had deserted him, and the mysterious MayBelle, who hadn't been seen since she disappeared with that swain.

Hunger ransacked him. He toured the cabin looking for chow, but nothing could be dredged up. Well, he thought, this very night he would eat, and well. He would surrender his claim only reluctantly, and only to the right party, a modestly greedy prospector with cash in his britches. Then he would manufacture a few more of these little cream puffs at some other local cliff. He set his inkwell and pen on a high and dusty shelf, ready for further action.

He was sorely tempted to probe the gear in Cracker's pack, with the hope of finding something that could be swiftly converted to food or drink. But rectitude intervened, or perhaps a fear that Cracker would retaliate, or perhaps an odd spirit of affection for the scoundrel. He puffed himself up: they might desert him after all he had done for them, but he would not desert them. Had he not prepared bonanzas for each, which now rested comfortably upon his bosom? And so, with hands that pined to untie Cracker's bundle and relieve it of something of value, the colonel edged out the door and into the late afternoon. He felt utterly virtuous, but ascribed it to hunger. No one thought clearly on half rations.

What next? The matter would be difficult. But he had fathomed that the Four Deuces would be the proper place to peddle a claim to speculators. Within its confines were sharpers, crooks, cheats, gamblers, confidence men, tarts, out-of-luck easterners, and jailbirds. He would have a much easier chance among these sorts than among the more virtuous, who would fret and agonize at the thought of investing in anything.

He examined himself as best he could, given that he lacked a looking glass. His begrimed suit offered no assurance to the keen eye, and neither did the stubble on his cheeks. Ah, for a trip to the barber; a bath, a shave, a new suit.

He eased into the Four Deuces and found it crowded as usual, with a haze of blue smoke layering the dark room. Three of the chandelier's six coal oil lamps flickered in smoky chimneys. Afternoon sun slanted through a single window, turning the air into white haze there.

He was assaulted by the usual wave of sour body odor,

cigar smoke, kerosene smoke, perfume, stale beer, and sawdust. Plenty of marks lining the bar. Now, if he could just liberate a drink. But he saw no half glasses, not one abandoned drop of spirits.

Off in a dark corner he spotted a veiled woman, and closer examination revealed MayBelle, hiding her face behind a swath of gauze. Ah! Salvation! For the moment, at least, she was alone, and her paramour was off somewhere.

"Ah! So it's my dear MayBelle," he said, eyeing her drink lustfully.

She turned away from him.

"MayBelle, it's the old colonel."

"Leave me be," she said slowly.

He peered closely at her with eyes that were at last piercing the gloom, and saw that beneath the veil half her face was purple, red and livid, blotched and swollen.

"MayBelle, that cad!"

She didn't reply.

"MayBelle, could you spare a dime for a sandwich?"

"I don't have one. I don't have anything."

"May I ask what happened?"

"Why ask? Isn't it obvious?"

"That cad . . . Might I have a little sip?"

She shoved her tumbler in his direction. He downed a slug of raw whiskey, coughed, and felt his throat and belly heat nicely.

"Ah! I needed that."

"Now go," she said. "You're keeping men away."

He leaned close, until his words would carry no more than a foot or so. "MayBelle, I've prepared our salvation. Before this evening is done you will be well fixed." He patted his breast pocket. "Here are three claims, one in your name, one in Cracker's, and one in mine, complete with assay reports promising the buyers a modest little bonanza."

She sighed. "You and your schemes," she said.

"Look!" He slid the claims out of his pocket and showed her the one in her name, and the assay.

She refused to read it. "You and your swindles. Leave me alone. I've got more to sell than you do, if you'd just get out of here."

"In your name. I got you a claim. You own a claim," he said. "I've been looking after you. That's more than, ah, anyone else can say."

She sipped and turned away from him.

He sighed. She had become a stranger. But any woman who had suffered the obvious abuse she had suffered would be a stranger to any man. That handsome swine had hurt MayBelle, and that handsome swine would suffer if the colonel could manage it.

"Where is he?" the colonel asked.

"The farther from here the better," she said. "Now beat it."

Raines spotted an abandoned tumbler with an inch of amber fluid in it, and hastened to recover it before some serving wench or barkeep caught hold of it. He swirled it about, found it was a tired lager, and sipped. It would do.

It was time to do some spadework. He slid over to the bar and pressed into the brass rail next to a likely prospect.

"Great little town," he said. "Hardly ever heard of a ghost town rising out of its ashes."

The prospect, well dressed in business attire and wearing a pince-nez, looked Raines over closely, his steely gaze missing none of the shambles of his suit, nor did it miss the stubbled face and grime.

The man nodded.

"Mining properties, that's what it's about," the Raines said. "I buy and sell them, myself."

"I doubt, sir, you've sold a thing . . . at least not one that any speculator would consider."

Raines ignored the insult. "I have some good prospects. You never know."

"Your prospects wouldn't sell for a cent on the dollar, I'm afraid. And they probably smell as much as you do."

Raines ignored the man; that was all he could do. "Look at this," he said, sliding his claims and assays from his vest pocket.

The mark laughed shortly. "I don't even want to touch them." He downed his Nevada red-eye, set the glass on the bar, and started to leave.

"You just missed the opportunity that knocks once in a lifetime. You just missed the chance to get rich, stay rich, and enjoy the rest of your days at ease and in comfort."

The man laughed shortly, but paused.

"I'm game," he said. "Show me."

The colonel handed the man one of the assay reports and one of the claims.

"Picotte's a good assayer. I'll question him about this," the gent said. "Where are these located?"

"Scarcely half a mile from Pearlygates."

The man laughed. "Everything within ten miles of this little burg has been pawed over and prospected a hundred times. Sorry, my friend, your little confidence game won't wash. And do take a bath."

Claudius P. Raines retrieved his papers, downed his leftover beer, and hunted for a new mark.

Chapter 35

MayBelle watched the colonel's pathetic efforts to peddle some sort of fake mine, and her heart went out to him. There he was with a smile pasted on his face, his jaw shadowed with stubble, trying to peddle a financial document. His brow was smeared, his hands grimy, and his once handsome suit hung in tatters with mud-stains. The poor wretch could not even afford a glass of beer. He clutched an empty glass, hoping for a refill. She doubted that he had eaten in the past few days.

MayBelle wasn't in much better shape. Something about her tonight was keeping men at bay. Maybe it was the veil she wore from her hat, which hid the purple and red bruise across her cheek and nose. Maybe it was simply her posture. Or maybe it was the glare she directed at all males; she was sick of men this night.

She was as hungry as the colonel surely was, and as homeless, and desperate. So she nursed the drink a hopeful gent at the bar had sent her way, waiting for things to happen.

They weren't happening. She would faint if she didn't eat soon, and she didn't know where or how she would spend the night. These evenings, the high northern Nevada mountains were turning frosty.

The lawyer gentleman had mistaken her for a slut who would perform various acts upon him for the price of a meal. She had furiously resisted. She might have had a few lovers; she might have been kept for several years in San Francisco by a man she cared about, but she had never stooped to whoring. She didn't care how hungry she was; there were things she would not do.

Swiftly, her suave new friend's demeanor had changed. When she was about to abandon him, he grabbed her, pinned her down, and took her, even as she fought and scratched and bit. Her resistance had only loosed a cruel fist, then two fists, and a few kicks for good measure. When he was done, he abandoned her in the room and stormed out the door. She had not seen him again. At least she had a warm room for that night, which she clung to until the innkeeper evicted her.

She was hungry, and she despised men. She wasn't very pleased with herself; She radiated anger. She wondered, bitterly, whether she would end up a two-dollar slut tonight, so she might put food in her mouth and sleep warmly.

She watched the colonel try another mark, and another, but these men laughed him off. She had to give him credit: he didn't quit. He plastered a smile on his face, carried his battered silk hat to another corner of the saloon, and tried again.

She pitied him; she scarcely knew why. But he had been there with her, fought the Whitebreads beside her, and dreamed up his grand schemes to enrich them both. Indeed, for a little while, in that old manse on the hill, he had shared her bed. She shouldn't be brushing him off. They still needed each other.

She saw him fail again, and this time he slumped a moment, hanging on to a table. Hunger was beginning to weaken him. It soon would weaken her, too. He sat down at last, waiting for yet another mark to walk through the swinging saloon doors, waiting for salvation, for succor, and finding only a cold and hard world.

She couldn't stand it. She arose and headed for a consumptive gambler who was coughing behind his faro layout. He had been eyeing her curiously.

"Stake me to a dollar," she said.

He grinned.

"You'll get your reward, but not now."

He slid his hand into a cash box, and handed her a dollar.

"I remember debts," he said.

She nodded coldly.

She found the colonel slumped over a chair.

"I got a dollar. That's a miner's dinner for each of us."

"MayBelle . . ."

He arose slowly, clinging to the chair. That shocked her.

"Can you make it to the café?"

He nodded.

She herded him out of the Four Deuces and into a sharp night, with an ill wind blowing down from the mountains. He clung to her, and somehow it touched her. She was stronger than he. She would work; he had never worked in his life and had come to ruin trying to dodge ordinary labor.

The Blue Café catered to miners, and the four-bit plate came loaded with potatoes and a bowl of stew. She ate quietly, taking her time; he wolfed down the potatoes and then began spooning the stew, which had an occasional chunk of gray meat in it, along with a few vegetables. But it tasted like nectar. She couldn't eat all of hers, so she shoved the half-emptied bowl in his direction. He devoured that, too.

When he had finished, he dabbed tears from his

eyes. She reached across the raw plank table to him and clasped his hand.

"What happened to your face?" he asked.

"The gentleman wasn't."

"Where are you going to spend the night?"

"I don't know."

"It's cold."

"I could find a warm bed if I had to."

"Please . . . MayBelle, there's Cracker's little cabin. You were there once."

She remembered it. "That sounds like heaven."

"Maybe he's gone. He's been hunting his mule. Someone probably stole it. He needs it for his gear."

"Can he prove he owns it?"

Raines smiled. She had seen him smile in the saloon while he was starving, but this was a different smile. "I doubt that Cracker can prove he owns anything. And the Whitebreads know it."

"You think they got the mule?"

"They're running mule trains of quartz to the mill."

He stood suddenly. "We can get out of the cold there."

She stood too and eyed the sorry and bedraggled man she was with. "Let me run back to the Four Deuces a minute."

They walked along Nevada Street, which was humming now with the thousand people who had flooded into the old ghost town.

At the saloon, she turned to him. "Just wait here. I don't want you to go in there now."

She hurried in, headed straight to the faro dealer, and waited until he had completed a turn. "I need to borrow a razor and a mug and a bar of shaving soap," she said.

"And?"

"You'll have it before you start work tomorrow."

He smiled suddenly, and coughed delicately. "Back stairs, two rooms above, mine is on the left."

She found the gloomy stairs and climbed into a narrow loft above the saloon. Feeling her way down a crabbed hall, she found the door on the left, and entered. She had no light, but slowly discerned a dry sink with a basin and pitcher on it. Some objects lay on top. She felt, rather than saw, the razor, and found the mug, discovering some soap and a brush in it.

She felt her way out, down the stairs, and nodded to the gambler.

He nodded.

MayBelle found the colonel standing in the gallery before the saloon. Together they hiked through the busy town, past the last houses, and into a sort of wasteland near the mines. He led her down a steep trail into the gulch. There, the gulch curved, shutting out the glimmering lanterns of the city and the dead mines with their black head frames poking into the dusky sky.

The air nipped at her.

She recognized the strange little flat carved into the side of the gulch and the snug dark cabin that rested there.

The colonel halted, and held her back.

"Cracker, are you there?"

There was only silence.

"It's the colonel and MayBelle."

Nothing.

He eased toward the door, opened it, and they entered.

The cabin exuded cold. He fumbled around, found the lamp and a lucifer, and lit it. The light blinded her for a moment. He slipped the smoky glass chimney back in place.

"Gone," he said. "He's left. The packsaddle. It was lying here while he was scouting his mule. Now it's gone."

She sorrowed. "I'll miss him. He helped us, worked hard, tried to help me."

"I was going to sell a claim for him," he said. "Now I'll have to forge his signature."

She laughed suddenly, surprised at her own humor.

He was waiting for her to build a fire. When she didn't, he reluctantly began crumpling old papers and stuffing them into the firebox of the range.

"Good. I'm cold to the bones," she said, but she let him do the work. "Start some water heating, and you can shave and bathe."

He seemed downright industrious, laying kindling into the firebox, dipping water from the pail, and pouring it into the stove reservoir.

"How'd you get so filthy?" she asked.

"Building cairns."

"You? Building cairns? Lifting rock?"

"Do not ever mention it again. I don't want to hear about it."

She laughed. Together, as they waited for water to heat, they helped him out of his duds. She started sponging his suit coat and black silk topper while he worked up a lather in the shaving mug and began brushing his jowls and throat. It would take some doing, but ere the eve had passed, he would be presentable, not only to the world, but to her.

She had grown fond of him: a confidence man he might be, a lazy bounder, but he had treated her kindly, even affectionately, and generously too, with good humor all the while. That was more than she could say about that respectable gent whose beating she still remembered in every pore of her body.

This night she would welcome the colonel and hug him tight.

Chapter 36

Cracker fumed. The Whitebreads had made off with his beloved Agnes, his hinny, friend, adviser, and companion. They had robbed him and his partners of a bonanza mine. They prowled Pearlygates, running the town as they chose. And just to add to Cracker's misery, when he struck back by blowing the Whitebreads' powder magazine, the blast blew open another bonanza.

He didn't know where Agnes had gone, but he knew that the Whitebreads were packing rich quartz ore in mule trains to the mill at the Amalgamated Climax Mine. It was not far away, and the hinny had probably been recruited for service. He had watched these trains depart, a string of twenty mules, each carrying two hundred pounds of bonanza ore. They were guarded by two armed mule skinners, fore and aft. He watched these comings and goings for days but couldn't get close enough to know whether poor old Agnes was hauling the ore.

Before he left the country, he was going to get Agnes back and fix the Whitebreads' wagon, no matter that they had surrounded their operations with armed toughs. Cracker would deal with all this his own way, consulting no one: alone, solitary, and effective—unlike certain partners with whom he had been temporarily allied.

Thus, he prowled the arid slopes and valleys, looking for ways to settle some old scores. He ghosted along obscure paths and studied the precipitous trail to the Amalgamated Climax Mine and mill, looking for the best places to conduct an ambush. With a little luck, he would recover Agnes and capture two tons of rich ore. He didn't think he could hang on to nineteen additional mules, whose hoofprints in the dust would lead followers to them. But he would spirit away his own and sole friend, Agnes, who had been his prospecting companion for years. Those crooks who stole the Wine Cellar Mine from MayBelle, the colonel, and himself had no right to her company.

Just how to do all this he wasn't sure, but he had devoted a lifetime to cracking safes without the help of confederates. He would crack this mule train at a place of his choosing. It would take giant powder, but he had most of a case of it, along with fuse and primers. Dynamite solved all problems, from poverty to hunger.

At last he chose a place of great silence and solitude, where the road clung to an umber cliff side. On the right the rock rose steeply; on the left was a long talus slope that dropped an awesome thousand feet into a dry canyon that was well vegetated with brush and an occasional tree, drawing sustenance from the seasonal watercourse. Down in that gulch he could stow the ore for a while—if he could get it there. Two tons of ore would yield many thousands of dollars. He meant to keep it all, even though something about that nagged him.

He hated to hurt a mule; he regarded mules as the most splendid creatures ever fashioned. He didn't much care about horses; they were stupid. About the two mule skinners employed by the Whitebreads to haul gold ore, he was indifferent. His indifference helped firm his resolve. They were toughs employed by a rapacious outfit, so he had no qualms about what he would do. Those thugs knew exactly the sort of company they worked for and the risks they took. They had put themselves in harm's way, for a price, so he would supply a little harm.

Having settled on a plan, Cracker spent some quiet hours at his cabin one evening collecting giant powder, caps, fuses, and candles. He then set out on foot, carrying his equipment in a gunnysack. It was heavy, and he had to rest frequently. He would set up his ambush and return for more gear. It might take a day or two before a mule train showed up, so he needed a blanket, ground cloth, and some chow.

He hiked carefully, not wanting to jar his cargo, walking in solitary peace through a silent wilderness of arid and mysterious slopes, dun rabbit brush, naked gray rock, and occasional dusty green streaks where vegetation fattened on a watercourse. He saw no one, and that suited him. He had never partnered with anyone until he met MayBelle and the colonel, and intended never to do it again. Agnes was the only partner he ever wanted.

He reached his destination after half a day of hiking through a chill and autumnal morning. The cliff-side trail was laden with dung, but none of it very fresh. Days had passed since the last transit. A mule train could arrive at any moment. He slipped downslope to the floor of the canyon. There, in pale sunlight, he armed a stick of dynamite and attached a long fuse to it. The trick would be to light it at just the right moment, so it would explode closest to the front horseman.

With a little luck, the entire mule train would plunge down the slope, leaving the mule skinners to wrestle with their blast-crazed saddle horses on the trail. Horses are excitable; mules stay collected. There was a hidey-hole halfway down the slope where talus had collected.

It was invisible from above. He would light the fuse and race down to that before the train rounded the bend.

Then he would get Agnes back.

He had his doubts. Anything and everything could go wrong. But he wasn't in a position to command fate. He would deal his cards and see how the hand played out.

He clambered up the steep slope carrying his charged dynamite, and by the time he reached the trail his heart was hammering. He selected the place where he intended to lift the lead horseman off his nag, and settled the red stick in a crack in the rock. The charge would blow outward across the rough trail and spray rock in several directions. He chose a place where the trail turned slightly, thus concealing the spitting fuse until too late.

He studied the approach, walking the trail at what he thought would be mule-train speed, a pretty fast clip actually, so that he would know exactly when to light the fuse. He needed a full minute to skid down the steep grade and duck into his hidey-hole. Add another thirty seconds to light the perfidious fuse; so he needed a minute and a half of fuse, or three feet. He cut the fuse to that length, then figured the exact point where the lead horseman should be when he lit the fuse, working out all the details.

He would show those Whitebreads that they had better not fool around with Cracker, ace powder man.

Then he hunkered down and waited. It might be a long, slow afternoon. He might have to curl up in a blanket overnight at his camp down in the bottom of the gulch. All that was beyond his control. With a little luck he would recover Agnes, and the thought of rubbing the muzzle of his old hinny cheered him. Agnes was an improvement on any wife because she never nagged.

He whiled away an hour on a lofty ridge above the

trail, bored but alert, and then he heard a jingle. There, in the distance, trotted the mule train, making its usual good speed. A gent with a peaked sombrero rode a dun horse ahead of the train. A rifle was sheathed upon his saddle. One by one, the laden mules rounded the bend, each of them burdened with heavy gray canvas ore sacks tied over a packsaddle. Twenty mules. A slouching rider followed up.

They weren't expecting trouble.

Cracker slid and scrambled downslope, stationed himself where he could watch unobserved, and waited for the lead rider to reach a certain prominent outcrop that resembled an upraised loaf of bread. Cracker took this as a good omen. When the rider reached that crucial spot, Cracker scratched a lucifer into flame, lit the candle in his hand, and held the steady flame to the notched fuse. Just when Cracker started to worry, it finally sputtered and hissed.

He scuttled and crabbed downslope, hurrying along before the outfit rounded the bend and spotted him. He reached his hidey-hole in the nick of time. The train was moving faster than he had thought possible, racing along at a reckless pace.

He peered around a slab to watch: a thin trail of smoke lifted from the rock, and just around the bend, the pack train raced like an express passenger train.

The lead man rounded the bend. He saw the smoke spitting from a niche in the rock ahead, saw he could not slow down twenty mules trotting behind him, and spurred his horse savagely, yanking the mules forward. He plunged past the dynamite, dragging mules with him, howling at his partner behind: one mule, two, three, five, nine passed before an orange whump blossomed above, the shock wave slapping Cracker an instant later.

He watched mules lift into the sky, flying in each direction. He saw both riders cling to their bucking horses while gray canvas flew open, scattering quartz every which way. One gray mule rolled down the cliff toward him, tumbling slowly, legs akimbo. The beast's neck snapped, coming to rest only twenty yards above him. Two other mules sprayed quartz as they tumbled. He saw the train split in two, the rear mules retreating while the mules that had passed the detonation plunged forward, butting into the pitching horse and rider.

After a few wild moments, the rear man quieted his mules, and the front man reined his skittery horse forward to stop several mules from bolting up the trail. Three mules were down, one not far from Cracker. Those above bleated piteously. The mule that had rolled closest to him didn't utter a sound. It was soaked in blood, its ore bags burst open and depleted, and its packsaddle askew, hugging its belly.

It was Agnes.

Cracker stared, unbelieving, at his lifeless hinny, his old friend, his savior, his desert companion. He sank into a free fall, his spirit tumbling down and down, as if it had leapt off a cliff. He peered out, unsure. Maybe it was a mule that looked like Agnes. Not Agnes. It couldn't be Agnes. This wasn't supposed to be.

But it was Agnes. He recognized some dun chevrons on her flanks, the humped cut of her nose, and the odd notches in her ears. He had unwittingly doomed his old friend.

He pushed back a sob. Why did everything go wrong? Why had life treated him so badly? Why was he cursed? Above, the rear man had dismounted and was staring sharply about. He mostly looked upslope, supposing that ambushers would want to descend a precarious slope to steal ore, not ascend it.

Cracker watched the lead man dismount and limp back to the detonation site where dust still whirled. He studied it, kicking at loose quartz that lay scattered over a fifty-yard circle. Checking the two downed and blood-soaked mules still at the trail, he finally shot both. The hard, cruel cracks from his revolver shot chills through Cracker. He didn't doubt that soon they would be shooting at a safecracker too, trapped as he was behind a heap of rubble on that naked slope. There was no place to hide.

Chapter 37

Cracker watched the two mule skinners study the surrounding country, rifles at the ready. The mules were milling, itching to escape that perilous place, and the horses were on the brink of panic. At last, one of the men began picking up loose quartz ore and distributing it among the various mules, while the other stood guard, rifle ready.

But recovering the ore proved to be a feckless task because the animals wouldn't stand still. The lead man was determined not to leave a thousand dollars of ore scattered over the trail, and worked at collecting the quartz. Every time he approached one of the mules to add some quartz to its load, the mule shied away. Colorful expletives, the stock-in-trade of any mule skinner, drifted to Cracker's ears, and he studied on it, mastering new cuss words. The mule skinners did not descend the talus slope as he had feared, and it looked like he might yet escape.

At last, the two skinners gave up and mounted their jittery horses. They drove the mule team, reduced by three animals, toward the mill. Cracker waited until they were far gone, and even then he waited, not wanting the rear man to come back and surprise him. At last, there was only a melancholy silence.

He slipped out of his hidey-hole in the talus and fell to his knees where Agnes lay, still warm, her eyes lifeless. He lifted her heavy head into his lap. Stroking her nose, he ran a tender hand along her neck and mane, grieving the loss of his one friend, his only friend, his companion in the desert all these years. Several times she had saved his life by leading him to water. Once she had alerted him to Paiutes lurking in the area, and he had slipped to safety.

But mostly she had listened to him: he told her about life in the penitentiary; about the art of safecracking, of which he was the world's foremost master; of growing up in a motherless home with a hard father who didn't scruple to short customers, supplying eleven bolts where twelve had been ordered, and less than a pound of tenpenny nails when a pound had been requested.

Cracker had simply carried the chiseling one step further: what lay in safes and strongboxes was his if he knew how to reach it, and he did. But his was a lonely and bitter life because he couldn't trust a soul with his secrets, and had no friends except Agnes.

And now Agnes's head lay in his lap, lifeless, by his own doing.

At last he stood, a solitary man under an empty heaven, and clambered up to the trail, where gold-shot quartz lay about. The mule skinners had scarcely loaded any of it. He saw it glint in the cold sun, a fortune for the plucking. He saw the wealth and ease in it, but what good was wealth to a man who had lost everything?

Cracker sighed, abandoning the gold-veined quartz, and carefully slid down the talus slope to his camp at the base, so as not to break a leg in his descent. Loading his gear into the gunnysack, he drifted away. He had no place to go and no friend to carry him or his gear, and so he wandered back to Pearlygates in the setting sun.

He was oblivious of the sharp, sweet beauty of the wilds as the dying sun lit arid cliffs, throwing purple shadows across canyons, gilding tawny bluffs, and promising sweet sleep.

It was full dark, and cold by the time he reached the cabin perched on the side of the gulch at the edge of Pearlygates. He supposed the colonel had commandeered it; the old fool had run out of luck, just as he deserved. But oddly, Cracker didn't mind. Even the colonel would provide some sort of company to a lonely man.

Still, a man ought to be cautious. He slid his gunnysack, loaded with pyrotechnic devices, into the little magazine he had fashioned nearby, and padded silently to the cabin.

"Raines, are you in there?" he asked.

Silence replied.

"Raines, it's Cracker."

This time the plank door crept open. "Cracker? Ah, my good man, you've returned."

A match flared, and soon a lamp threw light. Cracker discovered not only the colonel in his grimy white drawers, but MayBelle in a chemise and petticoat, a condition of dishabille that didn't disturb her in the slightest. They beckoned him in.

"We thought we'd lost you," Raines said, affably.

"I tried to get Agnes back. They stole her. I found her in a mule string hauling ore to the mill. I tried to get her . . . and she's dead."

"Oh, Cracker," MayBelle said. "Oh, that's terrible."

She swept over to him, clasped him to her bosom, and held him tight. He had never known a woman to hug him. Not a real hug, from a woman who wasn't for sale. He marveled at this, and was in no hurry to free himself.

"Tell us," she said.

The three settled around the rude table, the lamp between them, and Cracker told his story, not sparing himself for destroying the only living thing he had ever loved.

MayBelle held his hand the whole while. No woman had ever held his hand before. Cracker hardly knew what to think or do, and suddenly turned shy. He didn't want these people to pry inside him. He didn't want friends at all, yet he now had some. Here they were there at the table, sharing his loss.

They told him of their desperation: they had barely kept food in their mouths, and only because MayBelle had borrowed a dollar from a tinhorn. The colonel told about visiting an assayer, swiping some assay forms while the man looked over that worthless rock, and how he was now primed to sell three valid claims to any mark who would bite. He had studied a few assay reports and fashioned three for the green-rock claims, keeping them modest so that they might be believed.

"You'll never sell wild cards like those, take it from an old prospector," Cracker said. "Anyone with brains'll head to that cliff, take a gander, see not the slightest exploration work, and laugh in your face."

"But the assay reports . . ."

"Your doctored assay reports will persuade only the worst of fools. Anyone laying out real money will run his own assays, and he'll want to do it from an exploratory shaft, not some surface outcrop. What'd you say the values were in your assays?"

Raines coughed. "I don't remember. A little gold, a little silver, a little copper."

Cracker grunted. "What you need is a hole blown in one of those claims. Then we can salt the mine, find some marks, and sell."

They stared at him.

"All right," he said. "I'll knock a hole a few feet in. You fool around in the saloons and bring the suckers down for a little peek. At least they'll see a glory hole, a ledge being worked. You better have a silver tongue, because no one in his right mind would lay a nickel on a proposition like that. What did the real assay report say?"

"Oh, that? I wouldn't know," the colonel said. "I don't have a dime to pay the man. It doesn't matter. I got a dozen sheets off Picotte's pad, and we'll just manufacture our own reports."

"Can't we go out on the trail and pick up the quartz?" MayBelle asked.

"We could, but we couldn't spend it or trade it. That's hot ore, easily identified from the Wine Cellar, and the Whitebreads blanket this burg. Show a piece of that in a saloon, and they'll know who tried to rob their mule train. We'd be strung to the nearest cross beam without benefit of a trial."

MayBelle nodded. "Maybe we could hide the quartz for now."

"Best leave it alone," Cracker said gently. He had a soft spot in him for her. She was almost like Agnes, and a lot prettier, too.

"I hate them. I own that property. That was my mine. You are my partners. They took it away, just like that, and now they're getting rich while we're sitting in a cold cabin without a cent."

"There's no justice," Cracker said. "It's a rotten world."

The colonel shook his head. "Don't waste your time thinking like that, my friends. Whether the world is just or not doesn't concern us. Whether life is good or not doesn't matter. The race goes to the swift; we will be the swiftest. From this moment on, we'll focus on one thing: selling those claims for the biggest pot of boodle we can get."

"They're not even claims; not until we get cairns up and corners marked," Cracker said.

"I did that."

Cracker didn't believe him. "You mean you got some sucker to do it."

"I did it."

"Not you."

"Me."

"You lifted rock?"

The colonel nodded.

"I'll be damned."

"I'm not proud of it. On the ledger of my life, this is accounted as pure shame. But it couldn't be helped. You vamoosed, and there was no one to do it."

"Have you ever done a lick of manual labor?"

Raines sighed. "Ask me if I've ever prostituted myself."

Cracker laughed happily. The world's most work-averse man had hauled rock and built a few little piles of it. "That's something. If this don't pay off, Raines, you'll have suffered for nothing."

"I'm glad you understand," the colonel said, mustering dignity. "But now, we have a task before us. We are bonded together by a common enterprise. We will share equally in the bonanza: I will sell, you will dig, and May-Belle will find ways and means to keep us afloat."

"Ways and means: seducing males is what you imply," she said, "and making off with anything they offer."

"We all have to stoop to succeed," Raines said. "But once we're set up, once we have something to show the marks floating around Pearlygates, once I can bend wills and loosen purse strings, watch out! We'll all retire to Cuba and sip rum!"

Chapter 38

Not a thing for breakfast. Not a scrap of bread. Not a spoonful of oats. No coffee, no marmalade, no eggs, no scones, no jam, no fruit.

The three stared at each other. MayBelle knew she could eat if she wanted. All she had to do was walk into town and up some stairs into a bawdy house, and she would immediately receive all the food she could stuff down her throat. But she hated the thought of it. There would be a price.

They had arisen silently, putting off the day as long as possible, knowing it would be a hard one. The previous evening, Cracker had curled up in a corner. MayBelle had taken the bunk, and the colonel had found a spot on the floor. But his groaning and honking and sniffing were too much, and she had finally invited him to share the bunk: she didn't care how public it was.

The moment he eased his dirty long johns onto the bunk, his restlessness evaporated, and two minutes later he was asleep. Only she didn't sleep. Being in a room with two males was one male too many.

Now they were awake and expectant, as if each had imagined the other would fetch a meal somehow.

"I can usually hit up a tinhorn, but not for a while. I can't do anything until the saloons open," she said.

"Some clubs stay open around the clock," the colonel replied.

"The tinhorns are asleep," she said. "It's the tinhorns, they're the ones I can get something out of. But not when they're alone at the table. When they've got some players around, that's when they spring. That's when to ask them. It's good for business."

"No barkeep?"

"I can try. Who knows?"

Cracker silently pulled his shirt off and commenced scrubbing himself with a rag and a bucket of cold water. He was far more meticulous about his toilet than she had imagined; he not only scrubbed his body, but washed his flowing dark beard as well. He was lean and fit, his muscles well formed from hard work. Something about Cracker quickened her interest.

"I'll get something," he said quietly. "I know how."

"Well, how?" the colonel asked, testily.

"Steal from a horse," Cracker said. "And don't think I like it."

That mystified MayBelle, but she knew she would discover what was afoot soon enough. Cracker pulled his shirt on, got into his jumper, and slipped outside. She saw his breath steam. It was cold.

MayBelle and the colonel attended to their toilets as well as they could in such straits. She knew that only her wiles would save them from starving, but seduction was a night game, and this was dawn; they were hungry. The colonel, for all his special skills as a confidence man, couldn't beg a bun from a baker or steal a soup bone from a dog.

She examined herself closely, looking for signs of decrepitude and finding them. Crow's-feet at her eyes, soft sags around the lips, sandpapery elbows, ropes of flesh hanging from her arms, and her bosom sagged.

Oh, well . . . give a man the bold eye, and he wouldn't notice, at least not in a woman-starved bonanza town like this.

Cracker blew in suddenly, having been gone only a few minutes, and carefully emptied his pockets on the battered table. Oats mounded there: hard little tan seeds, as appetizing as gravel.

"Waited for the livery man to walk out to the back pen, slid into a stall, and copped some chow," he said. "Poor old black stud, he won't miss it anyhow."

"Ah, how are we going to eat these?" the colonel asked.

Cracker grimaced at such ignorance, pulling out his six-pound hammer as if to answer the question. "Build a fire and start some water boiling," he said.

MayBelle found some kindling and crumpled the last issue of the Pearlygates *Trumpet*, the long-gone weekly that had thrived when there were people to subscribe and businesses to advertise.

Cracker pulled out his Dutch oven and poured his oats into it. Then he patiently mashed oats with his mining hammer, an improvised mortar and pestle, pulverizing them until they would boil into a gruel that would nourish them this sharp clear day.

He poured the whole mess into MayBelle's steaming water while she added some salt, thinking how absolutely luxurious oat gruel would be resting comfortably in her stomach. She laughed suddenly. Not long ago, up in the mansion, she would have scorned such a dismal meal.

Her frame of mind amazed her. For the surcease of her hunger she would do almost anything: eat anything, compromise any principle she ever had, violate any morals she possessed, and connive at any scheme that might yield some comfort. She knew she was doing all of those things, or was about to, and it startled her. She had never crossed certain lines before.

The partially mashed oats were slow to soften in the

churning water, and the colonel paced the cabin irritably, as if the steady thump of his boots would hasten the cooking. Cracker just sat quietly, staring at the steaming Dutch oven, more disciplined than the others.

MayBelle opened the firebox door impatiently, stuffing in kindling that wasn't needed. She wanted heat, fire, boiling water to soften that sludge of oats into something they all could eat.

In time she beheld the gruel: soft, pasty, gray, and plenty of it, too. Cracker had blown another sort of safe, a horse's feed bag, and made off with precious loot.

"All right," she said. "Don't burn yourself."

She spooned the gruel onto Cracker's tin mess plate. He was the only one with an outfit, and it was an outfit for just one. Well, let Cracker eat first; he copped the food.

The colonel glared, pursed his lips, and paced.

Cracker dipped his sole spoon into the gruel, licked, found it much too hot, and waited.

The colonel paced. MayBelle clenched her hands. Cracker ate gingerly, sucking and blowing air, but in time he downed his portion.

He handed his empty plate to her and she dished up the colonel's breakfast. The colonel washed the spoon and waited. He slid the steaming gruel into his mouth, yelled, spat it out, and squirmed restlessly. He rose suddenly, plunging outside with his gruel. He waved it about, danced with it, gyrated it until the cold air had cooled it down, then slipped inside and wolfed his meal.

"Ah . . ." he said. "Delmonico's couldn't do better."

MayBelle followed the colonel's tactics, cooling her plate out of doors, and ate, feeling the pasty oat gruel slide down her throat. It tasted odd, as if Cracker's hammer had pounded unwanted flavors into the oats. But what did it matter? This was food! She swiftly felt the comfort of hot gruel in her belly, and knew that for a moment, at least, their ordeal was over.

But there were no more meals in sight.

Silently, Cracker loaded a gunnysack with the gear he would need: the hammer, drills, some fuse, a candle, and a small pick. They watched him edge into the bright morning to collect from his cache five waxy, red sticks of dynamite and some copper blasting caps. He slid these gingerly into the pocket of his jumper, and trudged away. Sometime before nightfall, if Cracker succeeded, he would shoot the first load of rock out of the odd-colored ledge.

"He's changed," Raines said.

"It's Agnes. Losing his only friend."

"It's something more," he said. "Remember when he first showed up? All push and shove? Wanting eighty percent, and then everything? Now look at him. He's all for equal shares."

"We're the first friends he's ever had," she said.

"He's no friend of mine!"

She stared at him. "Cracker is my friend, and you're my friend. We're in this together."

"That's a stupid thing to think," Raines said. "I pick on widows and orphans. I'd loot my own grandmother. He cracks safes."

She smiled, and he turned away sharply.

"We've all changed," she said. "You hauled rock and built a cairn. You soiled your hands, and no one forced you to. I . . . I would stoop to conquer. I'll soil my heart."

She turned her face away so he could not see it. She had principles. She might not be welcome at church socials, as she had a past, but there was a line she had never crossed—a line that meant everything to her. It was the line she would now probably breach, entirely for her new friends.

"You know, this is all your show now," she said. "This game you'll play with some odd green rock, talking some fool into buying a dog of a mine. Not just one fool, but three fools. Are you up to it? It's not Cracker's game. It's not mine. It's yours, and we'll sink or swim, all of us, on your talents. I'm your handmaiden. Cracker's your beast of burden. But it's yours to win or lose, with your fake assay reports, your pieces of stone, and a ledge of green and pearly rock."

He nodded. "I don't have much faith in it," he said.

The confession amazed her. She had never before heard him utter a word of doubt. Maybe Raines had changed most of all.

The prospects were slim.

She would go to town soon and try to borrow two dollars from a tinhorn. Or maybe she would try to sell her singing act, if one could call it that, to a saloon. There were seven or eight saloons now; Pearlygates had spawned them even faster than eateries and bordellos. The Four Deuces catered to speculators, men in black suits. The Exchange catered to prospectors, men with grimy hands. The Nevada was the place for cheap games and decrepit tarts and hustlers and pickpockets. The others . . . she didn't know about. They mushroomed up, a new one every few days. This was her town, but she scarcely knew it anymore.

Two dollars from a tinhorn. For some reason they often forked over. Especially when asked by a woman. But there might be a price.

She wrapped a tattered blanket around her rumpled dress and headed into the sharp morning chill. It wasn't the time of day to approach anyone in the saloon business, but they had to eat, and she would get them something, somehow.

Chapter 39

Cracker trudged his way down the steep slope below Pearlygates, covering anonymous land that grew only a little sagebrush and saltbush. Far below, a gulch wound its way toward a distant playa, or dry lake. Cracker wondered what had inspired the colonel to hike in this vicinity; the mountains and gulches above town were far more absorbing.

In ten minutes he reached the floor of the gulch, where saltbush grew thicker, and some brown grass clustered in low areas. He supposed the gulch ran water only when distant storms in the mountains sent runoff cascading this way. There were naught but the tracks of small animals and birds pocking the sandy wastes.

Yet this was where the colonel, in his meandering, had struck some odd-looking rock, a two-foot-thick stratum streaked with muted green, a rock so different from anything around it that it had caught his eye.

Cracker found the place easily enough. The stratum was nearly horizontal, but rose gradually from the gulch at its north end. He found the colonel's discovery cairn intact, and marker cairns along the ledge, demarcating the three-hundred-foot claims. The colonel had done it right; goodly cairns on the ledge. It must have been an ordeal for such a soft man to carry loose rocks, one at a time, to build those cairns. The man had changed.

Cracker set down his pack, unloaded the dangerous blasting caps some safe distance away, and studied the bogus bonanza, wondering how to make it look more authentic. Some evidence of mining would help: a heap of rubble, a hole of some sort burrowed into the cliff. He would trample down the saltbush in the vicinity of the works and maybe saw a few limbs off the stunted willows that populated the dry watercourse.

But before he started all that, he needed to satisfy his curiosity. He was a prospector, after all, and here was a hitherto undetected stratum of odd rock that bore unmistakable signs of copper, which weathered blue or green, often brightly. But copper was a perfidious mineral; the smallest amount of it could weather into bright color, exciting prospectors only to deflate their dreams.

Carefully, Cracker withdrew a small wooden case from his gunnysack, and unlatched it. Within, snugged into small cloth-lined compartments, were several handy chemicals and devices with which to perform field tests. Among these was a charcoal block that had been hollowed out in the middle, glass flasks of nitric and hydrochloric acid, ammonia, an iron wire, a blowpipe, horn spoon, a beaker, matrass, or test tube, and various other equipment.

Using the blowpipe he could turn that little block of charcoal into a tiny furnace, and he could employ the various acids as reductive agents and end up with at least a crude knowledge of the value of that rock, if any value existed. He doubted that it did. The hint of copper in the green wasn't enough to whet any experienced prospector's appetites.

He studied the float that had fallen from the stratum, and selected an egg-sized chunk that was typically pearl-colored and green-streaked. This he patiently reduced, using his six-pound hammer, until he was satisfied that he had the teaspoon of fine powder he needed.

All metals but gold would combine with the nitric acid to form nitrates, and if he added salt they would form chlorides. He loaded the matrass with nitric acid, added the powdered rock, lit his candle, and heated the tube for a while, watching.

A white milky cloud in the glass tube, which swiftly turned purplish, indicated some silver chloride. That was interesting. He studied the tube to see if any white precipitate remained, a sign of lead, but saw none. Next he poked a clean iron wire into the mixture and waited awhile. When he withdrew it, and held it up in the bright sun, he marveled. It was thickly coated with copper, as bright as a new penny. He tried one more test, pouring ammonia into the tube, and was rewarded. The mixture turned bright blue, a sure sign of copper.

He didn't know how much, but he knew copper laced this stratum, and some silver was present. Maybe there would be enough copper to make a real claim of it, with real assays, instead of the colonel's bunco. But copper was a base metal and not important. The silver was what would interest speculators. Maybe the genial confidence man, bent on fraud, had stumbled on to something real for once in his checkered life. Maybe it was time to pay off Picotte, the assayer, and have a look at that genuine assay of rock taken from this very spot.

Maybe the three of them would make a square living. Maybe he would pocket a few thousand dollars, head for Buenos Aires, and learn the tango. Maybe old Raines, the quack colonel, would end up eating oranges and hiccuping in the California sun. Maybe that fine old broad MayBelle would see her long vigil in Pearlygates turn into something. Maybe, if the Whitebreads didn't steal this one too, they'd clear a few grand.

He squinted at the silent landscape, so arid it scarcely could hide a hare from his view, and saw no one. If a

Whitebread snooped around here, that Whitebread would likely end up under six feet of clay, with a few saltbushes growing on top of him.

He hooted softly as he gently packed away his gear and closed the pine box. He could do more tests, turn his charcoal block and blowpipe into a tiny smelter, but he saw no need. The task now was to chop a little hole in the ledge and make the whole place look like it had been industriously worked, and then let Colonel Raines gull the suckers in the saloons.

He selected a likely spot and pulled loose rock away with his prospector's pick. The saltbush jammed so close to the ledge that he could not swing a sledgehammer, so he chopped and mashed and cut it back until he had some elbow room.

He moved his sack of equipment well back. He didn't want flying objects to detonate his dynamite or caps or knock his delicate field-testing equipment about. By the time he had done all this, the sun was nearing its zenith, and he had yet to drill a single hole for blasting. He was hungry, too; that oat gruel hadn't sufficed.

He selected the shortest of his good sharp steels, and began tapping it rhythmically, twisting it between each tap of his hammer. It drove easily, and the rhythm of his hammer soon knocked the steel six inches into the ledge. A tiny scatter of debris collected under the hole. He stopped work, sucked at his canteen, and eyed the bold blue sky, realizing it was noon. And there would be no lunch.

He selected the next steel, longer and slightly thicker, and drove the hole another six inches. Then he switched to the third steel, seven-eighths of an inch in diameter, and finished up. Then he cleaned the hole with a tiny spoon on a wire, and set about knocking the second one into the green-striated rock. He would use only three sticks this day, and blow a nice pocket out of the cliff side.

He was nearly done with the third hole when he spotted the colonel making his way down the gulch. An odd annoyance flooded through Cracker. Why wasn't the old fool in the saloons peddling the phony claims? But a glance at the sun told him why. The man wasn't even bringing some lunch.

Cracker wiped the sweat off his brow and waited. He didn't know whether to tell Raines that the field test showed a little copper and silver. He liked his little secret. He had a prospector's instinct to keep everything to himself, and looked upon Claudius P. Raines as an unwelcome intruder.

"Ah, you're making progress, Mr. Cracker," Raines said, examining the holes.

Cracker nodded, sullenly, not wanting company.

"Is there any way I may help you?" Raines asked. The question startled Cracker.

"Yeah, stay out of the way."

The colonel retreated a few steps.

"I absconded with an apple," the colonel said, producing one from a bulging pocket. "Here."

"An apple. How'd you do that?"

"I was once in thick with a pickpocket. It's a shameful profession. If anyone picked my pocket I'd be most unhappy with the lout."

"What's the difference between that and how you get your living?" Cracker asked.

"Why, when people surrender cash to me, it is by their own free will. I am simply an orator, a persuader, a man with an educated tongue."

"And the rest of us are beneath you. We grab what we can."

Raines stared, lifted his silk topper, and settled it. "I'm sorry. I inflate myself. I use trickery to extract what I want; you use dynamite and technics, and the pickpocket uses fingers. There is no difference; only one of means. Your skills are unparalleled, and in me you have an admirer."

He handed Cracker the apple, who bit into it and masticated happily.

There was something so simple and open about this that Cracker retreated. "I did some field tests. There's some copper in this seam and a little silver. I'd have to spend a day finding out what I have, and we don't have a day."

"I thought there might be a trace of something. Odd-looking rock. Green is the copper?"

Cracker nodded. "Most copper ore's not this color at all. When it's mixed with iron it's usually warm-colored. Copper pyrite is brassy yellow. Another's bornite, reddish brown. Some copper ore shows up blue. Malachite's bright green. I don't know what this pearly stuff is." He eyed the colonel. "Do you want this assayed proper before we peddle it? Just in case?"

The colonel shook his head. "A little color, a little metal, that's all I need. I'll hold out for a thousand a claim; we'll each walk away from Pearlygates with enough for a year. Blow that hole, make it look busy around here, and I'll fob these off in no time."

"We'll see," Cracker grunted. He finished the apple and returned to his drilling, his arm swinging rhythmically, over and over, driving the steels deeper and deeper into the decayed and weathered surface rock. The colonel settled down on a boulder and watched.

Cracker finished his drilling, cleaned the holes again, gently armed the sticks of giant powder, and poked them home with a wooden rod. When he had finished there was corded Bickford fuse poking out of each hole. With mud mixed from urine and gulch grit he plugged each hole to increase the effect of the powder.

"All right, Colonel, I'm going to blow it. I don't want you anywhere in front. The blast'll blow forward, but you get far to the side and close to the cliff. And watch for snakes."

Cracker waited for the colonel to retreat fifty yards.

He lit a candle, touched the longest Bickford fuse first and waited for it to spit. Then he lit the second and the third, and then walked rapidly to the north along the wall of the gulch.

The triple blast overlapped into a boom-boom, belching rock outward, shooting a column of yellow dust and debris high into the blue sky, shaking the earth, and sending thunder up the long grade to Pearlygates.

Chapter 40

MayBelle plunged into the chill morning to hunt for food. It was that stark and simple. She needed to feed herself and two others. She might find employment as a cook, a chambermaid, or a laundress for fifty cents a day, but that wouldn't do, not even for herself.

The sweet old colonel and that shy Cracker were depending on her, and somehow that heartened her and filled her with purpose. Not long ago she would have considered it a burden and an annoyance to look after them.

She walked through a quiet morning. The peace was interrupted now and then by the rattle of tumbling ore from the Whitebreads' mine, up there on the bench where her splendid house once lorded over Pearlygates. Her bitterness toward those usurpers had not abated.

The largely male population of Pearlygates was not abroad so early in the morning, though she did see a woman or two, miners' wives, baskets tucked under their arms, doing their daily shopping. They wore bonnets against the harsh Nevada sun and tried to fashion a good life in a place they never would have chosen to live. It wasn't easy. Their destinies were controlled by the decisions of their mates who brought them here to spin out their days while their men worked underground.

MayBelle thought she might start where the food was, in the two groceries that had sprung up in Pearlygates. Neither had much stock; their shelves contained whatever the teamsters had brought in from the coast. Mostly staples. But she didn't need variety, just something to fill three stomachs.

She entered one, Ritz Bros. Groceries and Dry Goods, and found one of the proprietors, a bald man in a stained white apron, behind a plank counter. The scent of coffee and fruit filled the air. White sacks of flour, sugar, oatmeal, and pinto beans rested on the floor.

"I'd like to start an account," she said.

The fleshy Ritz brother looked her over, noting the wear and tear. "Your husband works for the mines?" he asked. "We accept accounts for mine workers."

"No. My, ah, husband is developing a very promising mine. It'll be in production shortly."

"I see. How soon?"

"Any day now."

He thrummed his pale fingers on the planks. "I wish I could help you, madam, but we just can't. I'm sure you understand. I'd be happy to fill any cash order you might have."

"Would you just lend me two pounds of flour?"

"Ah, no. It's so hard to get. My brother in Storyville had to express an order on the Reno stage, and then the order was wired to California, Sacramento to be exact, where they have grain wholesalers, who shipped it by rail over the Sierra to Reno. And then the teamster took ten days getting here, and didn't have what we wanted, which was rye, whole wheat, barley, oats, and so on."

"Do you need help? Clerking, cleaning, shelving—for two pounds of flour at the end of the day."

He smiled. "You'd find little to do, I'm afraid."

She saw how it would go, nodded, and entered into the hard and chill sunlight.

The other grocer, Casper Jarwolski, Nevada Food and Feed, was even more difficult.

"Cash, banknotes, or gold, and I pay eight dollars an ounce for dust or nuggets. No credit. Absolutely not. This is a boom town. Half the town's not got a nickel and trying to dig into the pockets of them that do."

She eyed his wares longingly. He had things the Ritz brothers lacked: shelves of tins, bottles of syrups, bins of oranges and apples, sacks of coffee beans, jugs of molasses. All for a fancy price. There weren't many sources of food in a town that had come to life barely a month earlier.

"We're hungry. We haven't any food left. Would you help?"

"Ah . . ." The grocer averted his eyes. "Come back tomorrow," he said. "Have you tried the saloons?"

It was not the right question to ask a lady.

She left, stared up and down the street, and decided it would be the saloons, even at nine in the morning. The Exchange was nearest. She entered, was smacked by the sour odor of stale beer, let her eyes adjust to the gloom, and saw the place was mostly empty. A few souses leaned against the bar rail. Some gaming tables were covered with cloth, and no tinhorns were around. No chandelier was lit.

"I don't think you want to be in here," the barkeep said.

She gathered her nerve. "I need help. I don't have a dime. I need to eat. Would you help me?"

"Depends."

"On what?"

He grinned, a faint shrug.

She walked out.

Nevada Street barely stirred. How often she had

walked this street when it was desolate, when she owned every square inch of the city, when no one but an occasional hobo lived here. She didn't miss the empty town, when she knew only boredom, anger, and desolation. But now she was a stranger, and didn't own an inch of the place. She was a beggar in the streets.

She crossed Nevada Street, lifting her skirts to keep them from sweeping through the dung heaped everywhere: ox dung, horse dung, mule dung, and maybe human dung too. No one was very particular.

The Four Deuces would be astir; it was more than a saloon. It was a resort, as people in a certain set were calling such establishments. One could eat any time of day, discover games of chance, drink at a gilded bar, do business at a green baize table, procure anything. It catered to a wealthier class. It was where Colonel Raines would soon come with a few crumbs of green rock, a fake assay or two, some real claims, and a lot of bland bonhomie.

She stepped in, waited for her eyes to accustom themselves to the darkness, discovered that at least one kerosene lamp chandelier was lit, and the place was already populated. The smell of bacon permeated the long, narrow establishment.

She discovered the consumptive tinhorn behind his faro table.

He cocked an eyebrow. "Well, paying up?" he asked.

"Not yet."

"You can settle accounts fast enough."

"Tomorrow."

"I'll hold you to it."

He coughed delicately into a stained handkerchief.

A handsomely dressed man at the bar observed all this with a faint smile. She glanced at him, taken by the cut of his clothes. He wore a black suit with a razor crease in the trousers, a dove-gray waistcoat, starched white collar, and red paisley cravat. His black hair with gray at the temples grew luxuriantly, and glowed from a recent wash. His beard was neatly trimmed.

It was Godfrey Whitebread.

"Have a little drink, sweetheart," he said. "Or some tea, if it's too early for spirits."

She paused, uncertainly, and thought that a man so finely attired might not mind sparing her some money. He had certainly prospered, and now the ensigns of his success dripped from him. She discovered a fat diamond on his pinky, another headlight diamond on a chain across his cravat, and even fingernails that showed all the gloss of a manicure.

Her wealth, her mine, her gold. The ancient rage boiled through her, the old bitterness that rose whenever she thought of how the brothers and their thugs had robbed her, and she was helpless to stop them.

She drifted his way, almost against her will.

"You're doing well with my mine, I see," she said.

"It never was yours, sweetheart. You had no more claim to it than a monkey could claim to be human. You and your dubious pals were merely usurping public property."

He said it loud enough to float around the Four Deuces.

"You are still lying, then."

"Oh, my, sweetheart, how bright your eyes look when you're mad."

"You aren't even man enough to say that you stole it from me, burnt my deeds and papers, drove me out. You aren't man enough to tell the truth here, or anywhere else, and own up to what you did."

He laughed. "You're hungry," he said.

"You told the world we were crooks."

"Well?" He arched an eyebrow.

She stared at him, her gaze locked on his, her eyes unblinking. He met her gaze just as willfully, his eyes unblinking, his smile intact.

"Maybe I can help you cure your hunger," he said, reaching into his pocket. He pulled out a shining double eagle and placed it on the mahogany bar. It glinted in the lamplight. It hadn't even a scratch on it. It had just come from the mint. She stared at it. The twenty-dollar piece had a spread-winged eagle, and the words TWENTY DOLLARS spelled out, and promises that were not spelled out. She could read the letters in the dim light, and read the proposition.

"It's yours," he said.

She reached for it, but his hand caught her arm. "At eleven tonight. Come get it."

She slapped him hard. His head jerked back. The slap reverberated through the Four Deuces.

He laughed. "I'll be here. This will be lying on the bar. Come pick it up. You'll enjoy the evening. I'm good company. Much better company than your, ah, colleagues."

She felt wave after wave of bitterness, longing, need, hatred, anger, helplessness, and fear, roiling her heart and soul. The gold piece glowed, eerily larger to the eye than it really was, glowed in the lamplight, glowed with promise. Food and comfort for a week or ten days for her and her friends.

She lifted her skirts and forced her way to the door, feeling his eyes on her as she walked into the bitter sunlight.

She stood weakly in the street, scarcely knowing where to turn. The double eagle was a temptation. Not for herself. If she were alone, she could resist well enough. She was too angry at that mine robber to think of spending a night with him.

But she had friends now, hungry friends, each in his way working for the good of all three of them.

She sensed that at eleven she would be there, at the bar of the Four Deuces.

Chapter 41

Claudius P. Raines peered into the hole in the cliff, vaguely disappointed. He saw rock, lots of it, heaped on the ground before the cliff, and an oversized dimple. The interior rock was less colorful than the surface rock.

Cracker picked up pieces and studied them. He licked one, bringing its color up. "Not much here," he said. "A little mineralization."

"I was hoping you'd blow up a seam of something. A bonanza."

Cracker shrugged. "It's all up to you, my friend. Here's your glory hole. Here's some colorful rock. You have some assays to show people."

"Right in my pocket."

"Mind if I look?"

The colonel shrugged, and handed them to Cracker, who pulled them open and studied them.

"A little gold, a little silver, a little copper. Nothing spectacular." He folded the papers. "Good. You'll do better with this than with bonanza values."

"By any chance did I guess right when I contrived these?"

"No, there's much less here. No gold that my field

tests detected. A bit of silver, not enough to excite an optimist." He lifted a few pieces of rock. "Here, fill your pockets with this stuff. It's colorful, and color is what sells mines to suckers."

"I could have it assayed. Not Picotte; I can't pay him for the assay he did, but someone else."

Cracker shrugged. "Suit yourself. I'll blow another round just so we look busy around here." He paused. "After that I'll be pretty much out of dynamite and everything else, and my steels will need sharpening. This is it, Raines. This is your game. MayBelle and I are in, but it's your play. You peddle these three claims, we get out of here with some cash; if not, we starve. I'll stick around for a day or so. If I don't hear from you, I'll steal a mule and head for the hills . . . nothing else for me to do."

"My game, then," Raines said.

"Here, let me pick the best rock to unload on suckers. Send 'em down here and I'll look busy and act like I'm annoyed by visitors."

Cracker selected egg-sized pieces, one by one, wiping them clean and licking them, and handing them to the colonel, who soon filled his suit pockets with them, making him ungainly. But what did it matter?

"All right, it's all up to you," Cracker said. The tone of his voice told the colonel he doubted that any of this would come to anything.

The colonel nodded and started up the long grade to Pearlygates, trudging across a naked wasteland of saltbush and sagebrush, the town barren and treeless on the slope far above.

It was odd how much the rocks in his pockets weighed.

And how much his spirits weighed. For the first time in his life, he doubted himself. He had never before quaked at a project: he could talk bankers into surrendering virgin daughters; prospectors into hunting oysters; speculators into buying gravel pits; gamblers into believing in sure things; deacons into atheism; temperance men into drunks; whores into carloads of rejuvenation lotions; bald men into buying a bottle of hair-restoring cream; doctors into trying mad stones.

But now he felt his confidence slither away, as if he had not spent a lifetime perfecting his scoundrel arts. He knew why: they were depending on him. All the years when he was alone, unattached to anyone, uncaring about the human race, he had no trouble robbing widows, cheating orphans, or bamboozling grandmothers. But here were two people even more desperate than he, and he called them friends. He had promised them that they would share in the bonanza if only they would help him stage the whole confidence game.

When he reached town, he scarcely knew what to do or where to go. He began with the other assayer, a fellow named Randolph, who operated a laboratory on the edge of Pearlygates. Maybe he could steal some more blanks and concoct some more reports.

A jangling bell announced his arrival. The place exuded a sharp odor, and Raines realized the man was running his refractory furnace in his lab, performing those small smelting tasks that would yield an assay report.

Raines saw no pad at all, and was about to leave when Randolph, in a smudged smock, braced him.

"Ah, some samples here. I thought you could see what's what," Raines said. He dug into his pockets and extracted three egg-sized pieces.

Randolph took them, eyed them closely, ran a thumb over them, and then wet one and studied the rock.

"Where'd you get these?"

"Some partners and I are developing a mine," Raines said.

"Ah! Secrets. Some color here."

"When can I have a report?"

"I'm backed up. Day after tomorrow at the earliest."

"I need a report now."

Randolph shook his head. "Try someone else."

"All right. I'll wait. Have you a card?"

"Nope."

"What'll it cost me?"

"Depends on how many steps I go through. The more complex the ore, the more the work. Anywhere from seven and a half to eighteen dollars."

Raines hesitated. "If I must," he said.

"I need only a couple of these." Randolph handed some rock back. "And what's your name?"

"Arnold Cracker."

"All right then, Mr. Cracker, forty-eight hours."

It didn't amount to a thing. Raines didn't find any blank assay reports to filch.

It was high noon and he was hungry.

He had to get on with it. He brushed his bedraggled suit, forced his feet to walk along Nevada Street, resisted the urge to flee clear out of the state, worried about whom he might meet or what he might say, and finally pushed his way into the Four Deuces, the one club where men of means might gather. There were few around so early in the day. And he lacked the means even to buy some whiskey at the bar. He hunted wildly for a glass, anything to fill his hand, and found nothing. A bartender with his black hair parted dead center eyed him with rattlesnake eyes.

He retreated, defeated for once in his life, and found himself blinking in harsh sunlight. Never before had he failed to find a way to make himself at home and look for marks.

He leaned against a hitch rail collecting himself. Perhaps he could practice a bit in humbler surroundings, develop the right line, the perfect pitch. The Exchange would do. It was the lair of miners and prospectors, th drinks were beer and ale, not whiskey, and the whole lot didn't have a dollar between them all. He found himself trembling while he walked, and cursed the betrayal of brain and body just when he had in his pockets the salvation of them all, a confidence game so grand that they could live like kings and queens.

He found the Exchange, pushed through batwing doors and into a crowded saloon. That it was only the middle of the day bothered no one at all. Where there was drinking to be done, miners and desert rats did their drinking. As soon as his eyes adjusted, he peered about. He was the only man in the place in a suit and silk hat, but that would be an advantage. He spotted no one he knew, and marveled that an entire town could fill up with strangers in the space of a few weeks.

He drifted casually through the crowds of unwashed males, whose rank odors offended his delicate nostrils. They were a cheerful lot, and mining was what bound them. They were less interested in shares and stocks and lawsuits than in assays, complex minerals, values, depths, flood water, ventilation, and pay.

Ah, for a beer. He looked sharply and found a full glass, its owner nowhere in sight. Better still, a brown bottle stood next to the glass of beer. Ah! He waited a moment, discovered an empty glass, boldly filled it from the brown bottle in sight of anyone who cared to look, sucked the foam off the golden brew, and drifted away with one full, cool, sweating glass of pilsner in his paw.

He sipped ecstatically. In his present hungry circumstance, a single glass would produce a pleasant aura and fortify him for the ordeal to come. Odd, how he considered it an ordeal. Before, he was so eager to skin anyone in sight that he regarded it as a great and savory game.

Beer in hand, he drifted to the bar, this one raw planks instead of mahogany, and burrowed in between a pair of prospectors, each with a waist-length beard that plainly was their pride and the insignia of their profession.

"I see you gents are the knights of the desert," he said.

"That's rich," said the older one. "Matilda would enjoy it."

"Your bride?"

"My burro. No man in his right mind would take his wife prospecting."

"No man in his right mind would have one," opined the other. I tried it. My mule, Olive, is a truer friend."

"Have you found anything?"

"I find ledges constantly, but they are perfidious little things, yielding one good drunk," he said.

"Ah, it is the universal condition. Here we are. This is one of the most mineralized corners of the world. Fortunes await. Bonanzas, eldorados, luxuries. There it is, lurking under the surface, just beyond the eye, gold, silver, platinum, maybe even rubies, diamonds, emeralds . . ."

"When I see a ruby in Nevada, I'll eat it," said the one with the longer facial mane.

"Say, do you lads consider yourselves experts? I'm not. I'm just a traveling salesman. But I was wandering along a gulch the other day, taking the air, and I saw an odd formation, streaks of green rock in pearly rock."

"Lots of that around, maybe a little copper staining it," said one.

Raines shrugged. "That's what I thought. I plucked up a piece and thought I'd put it on my mantel. It's pretty, anyway."

He slid a hand into his pocket and extracted a fine thumb-sized bit of the green stuff. "Pretty, isn't it?"

He handed it to one of the old boys, who squinted.

"You can't see a thing with them sun-buggered eyes; lemme look," said the other, snatching it from the older prospector.

The younger one stared, rubbed, licked, dipped a

finger in beer, and ran beer over the rock, held it to the light, such as it was.

"Where'd you git it?"

"Oh, on one of my little strolls."

"Near here?"

"I imagine."

"You have this assayed?"

"Oh, sure, Picotte did it."

"And what was the result?"

"Oh, me, I don't really know. Pretty poor, I think. Let's see now, yes, it's right here." He patted his breast pocket.

"What do you mean, you don't know?"

"My fine fellow, could you really read one of those things? They're all Greek to me. I wouldn't know diorite from granite if I saw it."

"Read 'em? I could write 'em, I've seen so many," the younger one said.

"Well, then, I'm in luck," proclaimed the colonel happily. "Tell me what I've found."

Chapter 42

The younger prospector studied the assay report in the faint light.

"What's he got?" asked the older one.

"Some low-grade copper, with silver and gold by-product. It's mineralized, all right, but I don't know how a man could work it with no railroad anywhere near, and a smelter so far away."

"Nothing like the free-milling quartz gold around here?" the older one asked.

"Completely different; it's not even quartz," the young one said. He turned to Raines. "You done any exploration?"

"I hired a fellow to bore in a way. He's fired his first shot."

"That's good. Sometimes the values get better. How far in is he?"

"Only three or four feet."

"Have you got a new assay from the breast of that hole? Sometimes the values change when you get in. Usually for the worse."

"I just dropped the ore off; I won't know for two days. My friends, I'm the tyro here, playing with things I don't really understand. You'll have to forgive me if I seem a little dense. But I'm learning as fast as I can."

"What's to keep us from claiming on the ledge beside you?" the older one asked.

The colonel was getting annoyed with him. "Two missionary friends of mine filed to either side of me. Not that we expect anything of it, but you know how the world is, people always trying to horn in, so two people in my Reformed Baptist prayer circle clasped hands with me, and filed claims beside mine."

"You take your second claim?"

The colonel hadn't any notion what the man was talking about. "Sir, I'm not a mining man at all. I was intending to become a minister of the gospel until I ran out of funds in the middle of divinity school and have not yet mastered the epistles. What's this about a second claim?"

"The discoverer of a lode gets himself two claims in this district. Everyone else gets one. You're entitled unless someone gets there first."

"Well, I wouldn't know about such things. I thought I was being pretty shrewd, hiring a fellow to run a test bore."

The younger one nodded, sizing up Raines. "It's for sale?"

"Well, I don't know. I've hardly thought of it. What's it worth, would you say?"

"I couldn't say unless I had me a look and we get us a couple more assays. It's purely speculative, you know. What I can't figure is how you latched on to it when this district's been crawling with prospectors and mining men for years."

"I'm a sucker for a pretty rock," Raines said. "I have a collection of bright-colored stones, which remind me of the rainbow colors in Joseph's coat, and the miraculous artistry of God. Ah, what would you offer for all three claims?"

"Nothing."

"Well, suppose the next assays support this one. Then what?"

"We'd have a look-see. It isn't just the mineral; it's access, closeness to services and manpower, transportation. Also whether the seam's growing or shrinking as you go deeper. Sometimes it's the trace elements, the gold or silver, that make the profit. Copper's hardly worth it unless there's a lot of it. But silver, that's something else again. You make your money on the silver and sell the copper as a by-product."

The older one intervened. "If it looks hunky-dory, we might go five hundred for each claim, but that's a big if. We gotta see it first."

"I, ah, am authorized by my prayer sister and prayer brother to sell for a thousand apiece. To support our ministry."

The two prospectors eyed each other, downed their beers, and nodded. "We'll think on it," said the older, "and you think about showing us the ledge, because we ain't shelling out a dime until we see what we're getting. So many confidence men around here, and half of them smooth talkers like you, that are trying to lay off some barren rock with a twenty-foot hole dug into it."

"I wouldn't know about that, sirs. I can read the Good Book, but I would need help with an assay report."

"You shown this to anyone else?"

"Not yet. I suppose I will. In truth, I could use some cash. My older brother has a mahogany plantation in Central America, and also a pineapple operation, but the profits are tied up and he can't help me just now. Those little countries are run by men with their hands out," Raines said.

"No different than around here," the older one said. "You want a beer . . . ah, I didn't fetch your name."

"Raines, sir, Colonel Claudius P. Raines, and yours?"

"Granville Burthen, and my cousin Stuart Burthen."

"Well, I'll buy a round," said the older Burthen, signaling the barkeep. "Unless your beliefs prevent it . . ."

"Not at all, friend. We are members of a more liberal sect than some."

In moments, Raines found himself sucking at a mug of foaming, fresh, but sour-tasting beer that must have been brewed by teetotalers in Salt Lake City.

"Here's to success," he said.

They drank to that.

No sooner had he sipped off the foam than he beheld an awful apparition walking into the Exchange.

Picotte, the assayer, pushed through the smoke and headed for the bar. Hastily, Raines collected his fake assays and stuffed them into his breast pocket.

"Gents, I've got to rush along," he said, downing his mug of beer. "My wife's waiting lunch in our little cottage."

But he was too late.

"Ah, Raines, it's you!" said Picotte. "I've been looking for you. Your assay has been ready for days. Very interesting."

"Oh, ah, the other one. Yes, I forgot. Well, I'll stop by and get it."

"We'll fetch it right now. I'm just two doors away."

"But, my good fellow, I don't have the cash just now. . . ."

"Cash? Don't worry about it, Raines."

"Ah, I'll get it later. I'm waiting for funds from Costa Rica." He discovered the Burthens staring closely. "This is Granville Burthen and his cousin Stuart."

"Yes, I know them. We've done business."

"Well, you gents enjoy the day," Raines said, edging away.

But the younger Burthen tagged right along, through the doors and into the street.

"Five hundred cash for each claim. I'll collect ore at

your mine and do my own assay, and if my assay agrees with yours, I'll take the risk."

"Fifteen hundred? Now?"

"Fifteen hundred payable in one week at the Bank of Pearlygates."

That was a lot of money. Not the thousand apiece he had hoped for, but the thought of five hundred dollars in his pocket made him dizzy. But he didn't want any real assays floating around, queering the deal. "Right now, not next week," Raines said.

"No, not until we have a look at the site. And we have another assay done. Our own."

Raines didn't hesitate. A bird in hand . . . Let him see the rock and whet his appetite. "All right, we'll go."

"How far?"

"A short walk."

"How can that be? This whole area's been gone over."

"We're heading down toward the gulch, not up."

The notion startled Stuart Burthen. "There's nothing down there but a sandy gulch."

Raines chuckled, and they walked down the long arid slope, over baked clay, past saltbush and lizards, until they dropped down into the dry gulch below Pearlygates.

Raines spotted Cracker packing up his gear. "Ah, here we are. There's the chap I hired, one of my brethren."

Burthen grunted and hastened toward the ledge, which was mostly concealed by brush. He paused, saw the green seam stretching in both directions, and muttered to himself, pushing brush away for a closer look.

Cracker watched them come, and looked none too friendly.

"Ah, Mr. Cracker, this gentleman is considering the purchase of our claims for five hundred each, but wishes to take his own sample and assay it first. I've told him it's cash now, but he quite properly wishes to look over the claim, our cairns and corners, and of course study the seam."

Cracker eyed the prospector, seeing a kindred spirit, and yawned. "If you ask me, it ain't worth five hundred," he said. He eyed Burthen. "I've blasted a hole in this stuff. Look at the way the surface color fades. That color is just surface bloom. Collect what you want for an assay; it's your loss. But I'm selling now or not at all."

Raines marveled. Cracker was blossoming at the confidence game.

"I'll have to talk to my cousin," Burthen said. "Maybe we can get this assayed overnight."

"No, I want my five hundred now or forget it. I'm heading for Argentina tomorrow. You got an assay from Raines here, didn't you? Isn't that enough?"

Burthen ignored him. "Which is your claim, which belongs to Raines, and who owns the other?"

"Our sister in the Lord, MayBelle, owns the other," Raines said.

Raines and Cracker showed the sucker the claims and let him walk along the ledge, studying the seam of green and pearly rock that narrowed down and petered out at a fault about where the claims ended.

Burthen returned, stuck his head in the hole Cracker had blown in the cliff, pulled out some loose ore from its breast, and pocketed it, apparently satisfied. "I'll talk to Granville," he said. "Promise me one thing: you won't sell this out from under us before the day is done."

Raines looked at Cracker. "I think we can promise it. You, in turn, will need to have a negotiable payment, gold or greenbacks, no checks or drafts."

"Greenbacks."

"Perfect. Maybe we'll do business."

They shook on it and walked up the steep grade to town.

"Suppose we meet at the Exchange at ten this evening," Burthen said. "That'll give us time."

They parted, and Burthen headed into the saloon.

Cracker slapped Raines on the back. "Haw! You did it!"

"I was hoping for more."

"He bit. He went for a little surface color and that paper you floated in his direction."

"I almost lost the deal when Picotte wandered in. I stuffed the queer assays into my pocket just before he bellied up. The Burthens never figured it out. Picotte told me to drop by and pick up my assay report, said it was interesting."

"Sure it's interesting. It'll pretty much duplicate my field testing. Some color. Some copper. A trace of silver. You did it, Colonel, you did it! Tonight we eat."

"It'll be a late meal if we don't close this until ten," Raines said. "But for five hundred simoleons in my paws, I'll be willing to starve awhile. I wonder why he set the closing hour so late."

Cracker looked worried. "Because he might talk an assayer into doing a quick run-through his furnace before then. I hope this doesn't all fall apart, Raines, and we come up with a handful of air. I'm getting tired of starvation."

Chapter 43

With rare good humor, MayBelle, Cracker, and the colonel appeared at the bar of the Exchange Saloon promptly at ten.

The Burthens were there, and greeted them with hearty handshakes.

"We'll close this transaction at Picotte's office," Granville Burthen said. "He's waiting for us. Privacy, you know. We don't want everyone in the saloon looking over our shoulders."

That made the colonel uneasy but he thought he could bluff his way through if the fake assays came to light.

"Suits me," said Cracker.

All the way into town from Cracker's cabin, the threesome rejoiced. Tonight they would feast. Tonight they would put some folding money in their pockets. Tonight they would turn some worthless rock into cash. Only MayBelle had any reservations at all: "I'm glad there's a little mineral in it," she said. "I'd feel bad if we were peddling nothing but stone."

"MayBelle, my little oriole, tomorrow we'll start living," said the colonel.

At the assay office, Picotte welcomed them, his gaze

fixed on Raines so intently that Raines suspected trouble was afoot.

A sheaf of papers lay across Picotte's desk.

"Let's get on with it," said Stuart Burthen. "Here are bills of sale. They say you surrender your claims out of your own free will and not under duress; that you own them and have a legal right to dispose of them; that the price is five hundred payable in cash for each claim; that this sale is final and all parties agree not to dispute any term; and that Picotte, here, will witness the transactions. You, in turn, will give us the copies of your claims in your possession. The bills of sale have been made out in duplicate, and you and we will each have signed copies. Is all that acceptable?"

"Why, as soon as we read these documents, sir, we shall proceed." It struck him that someone, probably an attorney, had gone to some lengths to prepare these documents, which were more elaborate than usual. The Burthens were plainly being careful.

The colonel did scan them, though he scarcely was interested in the terms. The five hundred simoleons for some dubious rock was what interested him most; that, and a late-night feast. He wondered why the Burthens were so eager to get on with it, and ascribed it to the late hour.

"It looks capital, capital," he said. "Let's be about it."

He and MayBelle and Cracker all signed; Granville and Stuart Burthen signed; Picotte added his signature as witness.

MayBelle looked dreamy. She wasn't getting much but the five hundred would stave off trouble. She pulled her claim from a small bag and handed it over, and accepted the copy of the bill of sale. Cracker and the colonel did likewise.

"All right then, the payment," said Picotte.

"These are hundreds," Burthen said, pulling out a roll. "More convenient for everyone."

He peeled off five and handed them to the colonel, five more for MayBelle, and five more for Cracker.

"Now, if you'll acknowledge receipt," Picotte said. "Just initial here."

And so it was done. Nine hundred feet of pretty-colored rock for one thousand five hundred dollars. He had done it; his skills had not deserted him.

"Gents, this has been a pleasure. I'd like to buy you all a little libation at the Exchange, by way of celebration."

"Ah, thanks, Raines, but Stuart and I have business to attend," the older Burthen said.

The man certainly looked pleased, having got himself a long chunk of slightly mineralized ledge.

"I believe that concludes our business," Picotte said. "By the way, Raines, don't you want that assay?"

"Why, I'll take it," Raines said, hoping the Burthens weren't paying attention.

"I did another this afternoon for your buyers and it confirms the first one. Very exciting prospect."

The Burthens retreated into the night, looking all too pleased, and the colonel felt the first stirrings of doubt. What was all this?

Picotte handed the assay to the colonel. "No fee, it's paid for," he said.

"Paid for?"

"The metals. I must say, Raines, that's the finest copper ore I've ever seen or heard of. Seventeen percent is a phenomenon."

"Ah, seventeen percent copper . . . in the sample I gave you?"

"Quite a find. But it was the silver that paid for the assay. Thirty ounces to the ton."

"Ah, is that high?"

"I've never seen ore like it."

Raines stared, aghast. MayBelle and Cracker looked stricken.

"Ah, perhaps we sold a little under the market?"

Picotte shrugged. "I don't know. Have you done some exploration? If it's just a pocket, five hundred would be a good price."

"Ah, suppose it's a seam two feet thick running the full three hundred feet of the claim?"

Picotte sighed. "That's for you to calculate."

He dimmed the coal oil lamp until it blued out, and showed them to the door.

It was a cold night.

Five hundred dollars. The bills didn't seem like much. The colonel's joy had fled. A bonanza. Who would have thought it?

"I'm hungry," MayBelle said.

Wordlessly, they headed for the Four Deuces, where a good meal could be had at any time. They plunged into its warmth and past the mahogany bar, where Clyde Whitebread stood, his gaze mocking, his fingers toying with a double eagle.

MayBelle drew close, caught the colonel's arm, and he sensed that she was recoiling from Whitebread. But Clyde Whitebread was not done with them.

"Five hundred dollars for fifty-thousand-dollar claims," he said, amused. "It figures."

Raines's blood went cold. Not only had he thrown away a fortune, but word was out. Picotte had been talking, or maybe the Burthens.

The evening's rejoicing had drained into despair.

They ate silently. The beans and steaks weren't very tasty. Cracker kept staring at the colonel, as if he had been betrayed. MayBelle brimmed with despair. A hundred fifty thousand was a sum so unimaginable, so high, that he couldn't even fathom how much it was, or what he might do with his third of it.

But at least they were fed and the colonel paid for the dinners, perhaps out of some sense of remorse.

"What are you going to do with yours, Cracker?" he asked.

"Outfit and go prospecting."

"No Argentina?"

Cracker grunted.

"MayBelle?"

She reached across and took his hand. "We're in this together. A thousand dollars isn't so bad. Between us we have a little, for a while. You'll get us more. Lots of people live on a thousand a year. We could get a little cottage somewhere. I just want to grow some lilacs."

That wrought the oddest feeling in him, unaccustomed warmth.

"Ah, I hadn't thought of it," he said. "Maybe some lilacs in California. We could do something for our keep."

It was late. The night was cold. They could rent warm rooms if they chose.

Something was agitating Cracker. "You up to some hard work?" he asked. "Cold, hard, mean work?"

"No, I want to sleep."

"The discoverers of a ledge in this district get to file two claims. If we wait until morning, there'll be a dozen ahead of us."

"You mean . . . stake claims now?" Raines asked, feeling stupid.

"We discovered it, didn't we?"

Galvanized, they raced to their cabin, collected the gear they would need, drafted claim notices then and there, collected the tobacco tins to put them in, and headed into the night. A white half-moon lit the way. Cracker carried his bull's-eye lantern, the sole light they would have. MayBelle carried a shovel, the colonel hefted a pick and a pike. Cracker carried a whole bag of paraphernalia, including a tape measure.

Raines reckoned it was midnight by the time they reached the bottom of the gulch. It looked eerie in the ghostly light. They headed first toward the south end of the ledge where the gulch turned and the green rock vanished. They stared at the cairn the colonel had built there. The land beyond was not promising. So they retreated to the north end, found the northern cairn marking the Burthens' property.

This was better. The green ledge ran steadily along the base of the bluff.

Cracker suddenly was in command. "Colonel, you gather rocks. You'll build a claim cairn here, about in the middle of this one, while we locate the border. MayBelle, you and me, we'll measure this and then build up a location cairn at the far side."

The colonel didn't wait. He didn't even think about his lifelong principles. He set to work prying up rock and carrying it piece by piece to the pile where the claim cairn would rise. His body rebelled at the unaccustomed labor, but he scarcely noticed. He scarcely noticed the brutal cold. He was driven by something larger, a ray of hope in the darkness.

Little by little he gathered rock and then he heaped it upward in a pyramid. Over yonder, MayBelle and Cracker were building a boundary marker. Whenever he paused to rest, he saw the pair of them, ghostly in the light of a mocking moon, toiling hard at the edge of his vision.

Two hours later they stuffed the tin bearing the claim notice into the pile of rock the colonel had built up. This claim was his.

In the deepest dark before dawn they located a second three-hundred-foot stretch of the ledge. The seam there, faint in the light of the bull's-eye lantern, was narrower and ended abruptly at a fault. This one would be Cracker's. He inserted his claim into a cigar tin and jammed it into the cairn. That left MayBelle.

The seam had run out.

Silently, the colonel returned to his new claim, pulled apart rock, opened up the tin, and extracted his claim. "Sign it, MayBelle," he said.

Cracker handed her his pencil, and she did. Then

she signed the duplicate in the colonel's possession and her own copy. There was some sort of rough equity in it. The colonel and MayBelle would share the more valuable claim, which was adjacent to the Burthens' claims. Cracker had a claim of his own, but one less promising.

They were exhausted. The moon had set and blackness had descended, so that the colonel wondered how they could navigate back to their cabin.

"Take a sample," Cracker said. He lifted his lantern and handed the prospector's pick to the colonel, who summoned the last of his energy to chip a few pieces of the ledge and drop them into his pockets. His suit was ruined. The night's toil had finished it.

Cracker took an assay sample from his claim.

They stared at each other. There was hope still, if the collected sharpers of Pearlygates didn't find some way to rob them of their property. Cracker blew out the candle and they hiked by starlight, bone-tired, up the sharp slope into silent Pearlygates, then through black streets and dim trails to their small refuge, and fell into their beds.

Chapter 44

Cracker knew better than the rest what sort of danger they were in. He arose early, weary to the bone but determined to see what could be done. He padded softly about the cabin, careful not to awaken Raines and May-Belle, who slept the sleep of exhaustion after the night's brutal toil.

He dressed and slipped into a frosty dawn, loaded up his blasting supplies, and hiked through a silent morning down the long grade from Pearlygates to the gulch. There was no one in sight. He spotted the two new claims easily enough and then studied his own. The green vein narrowed, then stopped abruptly at a fault, and disappeared. It probably would reappear above or below, depending on whether the fault was an uplift or not. Weathering had eroded the fault line and opened a crack along it, which was what Cracker wanted. It would save some drilling.

Swiftly he charged a stick of dynamite and eased it into the crack. He packed mud around it to increase its power, then lit the fuse and stepped aside. The blast shot debris out of the fault line, and opened a little pocket that would permit him to peer a couple of feet into the cliff. He approached swiftly, barely waiting for the dust to settle.

The stink of dynamite hung in the cold air. He peered in and confirmed what he had suspected, given the way the seam had been pinching. It ran only a foot or so in, and vanished into country rock. His claim was at the extreme edge of the ore body and probably was little more than a pocket mine.

That suited him just as well as if it had been solid ore. He shoveled rubble into the hole, added some mud until he had plugged the hole with smooth anonymous clay. Then he moved along the claim to its other border, close to the colonel and MayBelle's claim. He found another, smaller fault, and blew that open with a fine, authoritative whump. Here the seam did not peter out in country rock, but looked as promising as what had been claimed by the Burthens. He chipped a few samples from the back of that pocket and headed into town, stopping at a grocery to spend a few of his new dollars on foodstuffs.

He and the colonel and MayBelle would need to register the new claims in the ledger at the land office, as was the custom in the district, and when they did, the Whitebreads would soon know it. That suited him fine also. He had some unfinished business with the Whitebreads. They all did. But he had to be careful. They knew he was wanted in a couple of places, and that was a lever in their hands.

He dropped the samples off at Picotte's assay office and headed out to the cabin, pacing through a town still performing its morning ablutions.

His friends were still asleep, and he viewed their peaceful domesticity comfortably, wondering whether to awaken them. He was dreaming of other things, and with any sort of luck he would be on his way south in a day or two. If his luck went bad, he still would have five hundred dollars, enough for a new prospecting outfit.

He had been to Buenos Aires once when he had shipped as a merchant seaman to avoid the Civil War, and he wanted to go back. He didn't know Spanish but he knew the meaning of the sweet smiles on the faces of those raven-haired girls. He didn't know a waltz from a gavotte, but he knew how to tango, and the girls did too. It was a graceful, sensuous, soul-locking dance that would be banned if it ever arrived in the United States because it hinted of the beautiful things that lay between a man and a woman. He sat spellbound, squandering whole evenings on the waterfront, doing nothing but watching the handsome Argentines tango. He felt like an idiot: how could a Latin dance do that to him? But it did. Now he lived for the tango, and no one in the whole world would understand.

They brewed a good beer there, and he had found plenty in pubs along the Rio De La Plata. He would find some sweet vixens, and walk with the pair of them on his arms along the Avenida de Mayo or the Calle Florida, or maybe the Avenida de Corientes. Envious Argentine men would turn and look, and tell themselves that there went quite a fellow. Or he would sit in Palermo Park and watch the world go by. That's all he wanted; he had no desire to crack a safe again, if only he could tango.

But he did have a desire to fix the Whitebreads' wagon.

"Hate to wake you up," he said loudly. "But we got things to do."

He was greeted with muffled yawns and finally, the colonel's glare.

"I've scarcely laid my head down, and you're disturbing my beauty sleep," the colonel grumbled.

"We have things to do right now."

Cracker brewed coffee while the pair of lovebirds performed their toilet, and at last the three sat around the table sipping.

"I've been busy. I blew a couple of holes in my ledge. It peters out at the north end. I've claimed the far edge of the lode, and it isn't worth much."

MayBelle sighed and laid a hand over Cracker's arm. "I'll share mine with you," she said.

Cracker pretended not to notice her kindness. He couldn't bear it.

"So will I," said the colonel, who looked surprised that he had uttered any such thing.

"Raines, I want you to sell my claim to the Whitebreads for all you can get. Like fifty grand. Use your abilities."

"Ah . . ."

"They're greedy. They're sniffing around. A gold mine isn't enough. If there's more to snatch, they'll do it, especially from us. They've got cash and plenty of it. Fifty grand, on the barrelhead."

A beatific smile spread across the colonel's visage. "Ah!" he said, registering what this morning would be about. "Sport! Do you suppose MayBelle's and my claim would be as bad?"

"No, yours is well into the ore body, more like the Burthens' claims. Just sell mine for me. You're the man to do it."

"Where will you be?"

"First I'll record the claim, and yours too, at the land office. Then I'll be down there, looking busy when you arrive. And I'll be armed. I don't trust the Whitebreads. It'll be up to you to bring them down there and sweet-talk them into laying out cash. I need cash. I'm on my way south."

"South where?"

"As far south as I can get, where there's no coppers with warrants."

"Good!" said MayBelle.

And so it was arranged.

By the time an hour has elapsed, Cracker was poking at his claim, but he was no longer alone. The Burthens were studying the whole seam, observing the new claims, and taking more samples.

The colonel and MayBelle appeared with the Whitebreads, who were elegantly dressed, predatory, smug, and grinning.

"Cracker," said Godfrey, "here's five hundred. Sign it over."

Cracker shook his head.

"Five hundred or we'll turn you in."

Stuart Burthen laughed. "He won't let loose of it for that, Godfrey."

"Then I'll pack him off to where the view is interrupted by bars in the window."

"Maybe it's not for sale," Cracker said. "Not for less than fifty grand, anyway."

It was the Whitebreads' turn to laugh.

The colonel turned to the Burthens. "You know, gents, it would be most desirable if we formed a single corporation and took shares in it according to our holdings. There are five rich claims along this ledge; five owners of the corporation, twenty percent each. You two would own sixty percent, MayBelle and I twenty, and Mr. Cracker, here, twenty. Think what a single company could do. No conflicting claims, no boundary troubles, economies in the mining, no disputes. A big company sitting on a big body of ore could get a railroad spur. The Pearlygates Copper Company . . ."

The colonel was effectively shutting out the Whitebreads.

"I don't know. Let me run some assays and drill into your claim," the older Burthen said. "Just to make sure we're on the same footing."

"Well, fine," the colonel said, expansively. "We'll just rush an assay to Picotte and settle tomorrow. It's now or never for you and for us."

Clyde Whitebread looked grim. "Fifty thousand," he said.

Godfrey was startled. "Clyde—"

"You're always too timid," Clyde snapped. "We're watching a copper bonanza vanish before our eyes."

"Our claim, MayBelle's and mine, isn't for sale," the colonel said.

Clyde Whitebread turned to Cracker. "Well?"

"In greenbacks, today."

"I don't have that much."

"The bank does."

There was a long, pregnant pause.

"Done."

Clyde and Godfrey Whitebread stared at each other, and Godfrey nodded slightly. Cracker knew that sort of nod. This wasn't over.

"All right. You'll deliver payment at noon. We'll meet at the bank. I'll sign over my claim."

The transaction went smoothly. Before assorted witnesses at the Bank of Pearlygates, Cracker signed over his claim to the two Whitebreads and received fifty thousand in greenbacks. He counted every bill and stuffed them in a satchel.

He handed it to Joe Barnes, the banker. "Put this in your safe and give me a receipt."

"Gonna blow it open and grab your own money?" asked Godfrey.

Cracker drew himself up. "It's not everyone who pays fifty grand for a five-hundred-dollar pocket mine."

Clyde and Godfrey stared at each other, aghast. The safe clanged shut. Cracker stuffed the receipt in his shirt.

"I'm a powder man, Whitebread, and don't ever forget it. Put any notions you're entertaining clear out of your skull."

That was threat enough.

Later, at the cabin, they celebrated. He had spent the afternoon purchasing stagecoach tickets through to San Francisco, a suit of stiff black ready-mades, boiled shirt, lavender paisley cravat, bowler, new long johns, new boots, and a used suitcase since no new ones were available. He managed to slip a carnation into his lapel.

The colonel had addressed his wardrobe too, and now sported a gaudy brown and yellow checkered tweed coat, orange silk cravat, boiled white shirt, new striped trousers, puttees, deerstalker hat, and squeaky boots. He had even gotten himself a shave and bath at the tonsorial parlor, and a monocle from the oculist.

MayBelle sprang for a royal-blue wool suit with a snowy jabot, along with a wine velvet cape, kid gloves, and patent leather shoes. She looked beautiful.

The man from the weekly newspaper, along with his photographer, was collecting a story.

"How did you ever think to look for minerals down there, in that desolate sandy gulch?" the reporter asked.

"Why, God rewards the virtuous," the colonel replied. "In truth, I wasn't looking for minerals at all. I was solacing a widow who had lost everything. My mind clarifies when I hike, so I wandered along that gulch, puzzling how best to succor her from my mahogany plantation in Costa Rica, and saw some pretty stones. That's all there is to it."

"A widow?"

"Me," said MayBelle. I owned this town once, the entire town lot company, before ruffians snatched it from me and left me to perish in the desert. But now I have treasured friends, men of such tenderness that not even the most hopeless beggar ever walks away from either one of them empty-handed."

"And what do your ascribe your fortune to, sir?" he asked the colonel.

"Hard work and perseverance."

"And you?" he asked Cracker.

"I hope others would find me a man of integrity," he said. "My word is my bond. I covet no man's wealth. I prefer a simple life of poverty and chastity to a life that violates the standards my dear sainted mother taught me."

"Nobly said," the reporter opined.

They stood for a photo; the flash went off with such a snap that Cracker startled and almost yanked his revolver out. "Good, good, good," the photographer said, emerging from his black velvet tent behind the camera. And then it was over.

Chapter 45

Copper, not gold, rescued Pearlygates. Long after the gold played out, the magnificent mines belonging to the Pearlygate Copper Company continued to produce rich ore, which was shipped out on the railroad spur.

And everyone in town knew that their community owed its very existence to those three discoverers, Colonel C.P. Raines, MayBelle Haggerty, and Arnold Cracker. In time, heroic bronze likenesses of the three, drawn from some old photographs found in the files of the weekly, were cast and set on rock pedestals in Pioneers Park, just off the main street. Engraved on all four sides of the marble foundation were words from their own tongue: HARD WORK, PERSEVERANCE, INTEGRITY, TENDERNESS, HONOR.

There had been a few rumors about the three. One was that Cracker was a cousin of Jesse James. Another was that MayBelle had been a nun once. And another was that Raines had served time for stealing laundry from a Chinaman. But none of these bits of gossip had ever been proven, and the old pioneers always spoke fondly of the threesome, who, according to the best recollections, could often be seen in those early days sipping sarsaparilla in the old Four Deuces ice cream parlor, and giving pennies to shoeless boys.

As for Cracker, he successfully extracted himself and his boodle from the United States and lived in a modest precinct of Buenos Aires. He bought a part interest in a profitable brewery, spending his time exactly as he had planned, with gorgeous Argentine beauties on each arm. He became locally famous as the best tango dancer in the area. He eventually married a dancer called Estrelita, and lived in great harmony with the world.

Colonel Raines and MayBelle pursued their own dreams, living in semiwedded bliss in the midst of a profitable Valencia orange grove in Altadena, California, beneath the blue mountains. He abandoned his confidence game, no longer needing to exercise his special talents to subsist, but he enjoyed an occasional game of poker or monte at the golf club. He wasn't above exercising his considerable talents for small stakes, just in fun.

When Hard Luck Yancey found the pebble, he knew at once what it was and how it might transform his life. It was a curious pebble, dark and heavy, pocked and pitted and twisted. Its color was not far from black. He hefted it, licked it, studied it minutely, and then looked for more like it, wedged against a pink granite boulder on the slope.

It was black gold, telluride gold, but it looked nothing like gold and would have escaped the attention of an untrained eye. It was what prospectors called float, a tiny bit of mineral that had eroded from some place above, maybe miles away, some mother lode that had outcropped somewhere. Finding the source of float was probably the main task of prospectors, and a daunting one.

Yancey peered about, studying the vast and inhospitable grade, corrugated by innumerable gulches, choked with cedar and juniper, silent in the sun. Far below lay an arid sand-bottomed valley with a dry streambed. Above, the slope was capped by a naked ridge radiating out from Table Mountain. Off to the north and east the peaks of the San Juan Mountains confused the horizon.

From where he stood, the whole panorama seemed utterly devoid of human life, but in fact he was only a mile or so from a mining town huddled at the crest of this vast slope. The town was named Yancey, after him, the discoverer of a huge silver bonanza up there. He could not see the town because of a dull, anonymous stratum of pink granite that blocked the view.

He turned the nugget around, absorbing its appearance so that he might spot its kin. Then he began a sharp-eyed hunt up and down the shallow gulch, sometimes fighting his way through nettlesome brush, looking for more of the black pebbles. He found nothing. He didn't really expect to. Float was seductive and treacherous and maddening. He did not know how the gold arrived there. It might have been carried by an animal, dropped by a bird, discharged from the earth by a burrowing creature. But most float simply broke away from some outcrop somewhere, and over eons of time was transported by gravity, sun, rain, snow, wind, or even quakes, to where it now lay.

There was no guarantee that other float would lie in the same gulch, so he crawled up a shelf and dropped down into the neighboring drainage. An hour later he was convinced that no black gold existed there. He tried various other gullies, and the tiny divides between them, pausing especially at places such as the upslope side of boulders, where a heavy pebble might be arrested.

No luck. Still, he knew that black gold came from *somewhere,* and that somewhere was the focus of his dreams and hopes, and he intended to find it. He saw not another mortal in this juniper jungle, only some ravens circling above. Slowly he made his way uphill, sweating in the autumnal sun, arriving at last at the massive stratum of red granite that seemed to divide the slope into two segments. Above was gray limestone that rose toward the arid ridge where he had found the carbonate silver ore. But that was another world, and another story.

The chances were that the float had eroded from an outcrop in this very granite, probably a quartz vein. But he saw nothing, only the anonymous, smooth-grained, fractured, and jumbled wall of hard red rock that showed not the slightest sign of treasure. He walked along the wall, examining segments of it with his trained prospector's eye, studying the uppermost reaches, the middle range, and the lower parts, paying particular attention to the pebbles that formed talus at its base, and any fracture in the wall.

The chances were that the float had eroded from an outcrop in this very granite, probably a quartz vein. But he saw nothing, only the anonymous, smooth-grained, fractured, and jumbled wall of hard red rock that showed not the slightest sign of treasure. He walked along the wall, examining segments of it with his trained prospector's eye, studying the uppermost reaches, the middle range, and the lower parts, paying particular attention to the pebbles that formed talus at its base, and any fracture in the wall.

Nothing. He hadn't expected it to be easy. Tracing float was one of the most maddening occupations engaged in by mortals.

Still, he had hoped for at least one other sample, some small confirmation that he was on the right track, something to suggest that the presence of black gold on that silent and jumbled grade was more than the freakish result of a passing animal or bird. He also kept a sharp eye for silvery pebbles, because telluride gold was actually silvery deep in its rocky tomb, and darkened only when it was exposed to the elements. But he found nothing.

Tomorrow he would return to his clerking job at the hardware store far above. But this Sabbath he had spent, as he usually did, exploring alone. When the sun dipped behind the distant snow-tipped peaks and darkness threatened to entrap him in a maze of juniper brush, he surrendered and wearily toiled upslope toward a notch in the granite escarpment, clambered up that notch, his heart thudding with the effort, and found himself in another world.

Here the slope was less steep, and an astonishing city of two thousand souls huddled under the drab ridge, its board and batten buildings weather-stained and gray. Along the ridge itself the head frames of half a dozen mines jabbed the cobalt sky. It was not a place where a town should be, and the entire mining camp seemed poised to tumble down that gray slope.

He had acquired the Hard Luck moniker as a result of three calamities. The last and worst disaster had befallen him only recently, but Hard Luck figured he had learned something. That's how he dealt with tragedy: if he had learned something, he could make use of it in the future.

The whole town of Yancey City, and the mining district itself, was named for him. He had located a magnificent body of carbonate silver ore on a high ridge south of the San Juan Mountains, started up the Minerva Mine, named after the goddess of wisdom, and set out to get rich so that he could marry well, since he was as plain as a cucumber.

The raw town soon blossomed just below the Minerva head frame, the whole of it perched on a slope so steep that its buildings were partly dug into notches in the hillside, and half supported on stilts. Eventually some level streets were scraped into the side of that slope, but those were the only places a person could stand without leaning uphill.

The exception was the hospital run by the Sisters of Charity of Leavenworth, located on two acres well below the town in an intimate little plateau notched in a gulch. The flat was watered by a miraculous spring of sweet cool water, which supplied not only the hospital but the entire town. It was the sole source of water for miles in any direction.

It had taken a lot of doing to start the Minerva Mine in a place so lonesome. But Yancey had patiently hired twenty-mule teams to drag the mining equipment up there and start blasting. Everything from heavy timbers to woven cable had to be dragged up there by ox or mule power. He had just as hard a time keeping miners hired. No one wanted to live on a windy ridge, thousands of feet from a spring, scores of miles from the nearest burg, without a level inch of ground in the whole place.

But he persevered, dragged prefabricated buildings up there, put them on stilts, found a good blasting crew, and began driving a shaft. Soon enough the promising mine turned into a bonanza. Not twenty feet in, the silver ore had become fabulously rich and so valuable that Hard Luck could afford to send it to the mill by pack mule and still come out way ahead.

Word of the big silver strike swiftly filtered through Colorado and all the mining camps of the West, and in no time every inch of ground along that ledge was claimed, sometimes by two or three people, which kept the courts entertained. The hard gray limestone of Table Mountain disgorged its silver ore, the town bloomed, and soon half a dozen mines, all in a row, lined that alpine ridge, their head frames stark against blue sky.

It all started well enough. To the right of the Minerva was the Poco Loco, belonging to Alfred Noble and his Rhode Island Syndicate, while to the left was the Good Times, sole property of Gustav Moran, a seedy little bag of tricks with a wounded look in his face.

What Hard Luck's neighbors lacked was scruple, and next thing Hard Luck knew, he was being dragged into the nearest federal court to defend against apex suits. The mining law of the country permitted the discoverer of a mineral vein to pursue it wherever it wandered, provided that it apexed, or surfaced, on his claim, no matter whether the vein found its way into neighboring claims. This made mining lawyers rich, and made the entire mining industry the vassal of powerful law firms. And it broke Hard Luck Yancey.

Moran and Noble had the means to engage nefarious lawyers and butter up fat judges, and soon Hard Luck was fighting a novel double apex suit, never before known to mining law, which claimed that the vein actually surfaced twice, on either side of the Minerva, and that Hard Luck was therefore stealing ore that belonged to the Poco Loco and Good Times.

The judge found for the plaintiffs, declared that Hard Luck owed his neighbors two hundred seventy-three thousand for the value of ore stolen from them, and additional damages to the tune of one hundred thirty thousand for damage to the neighboring properties.

Noble and Moran swiftly attached the Minerva, soon owned it, and Hard Luck was once again euchred out of his property. Like that wretch Henry Comstock, who had sold off his claim for a pittance only to learn he had given his name to a bonanza, Will Yancey had more than once seen a fortune slide through his fingers.

But while poor Comstock drifted from mining town to mining town and never amounted to anything, Yancey always managed to start again. Yancey didn't think the name Hard Luck was very accurate; it wasn't hard luck that cost him the Minerva but neighbors as crooked and ruthless as mortals ever get. So, with each loss, Will Yancey studied on the matter, learned something, and filed away his knowledge for the future. Someday, he figured, he'd be smart. He knew how to discover ore; what baffled him was dealing with ruthless and unscrupulous men. If he could figure that out some day, he might hang on to his discoveries.

That was the thing about Yancey: he was a quiet,

mild, bookish sort. While other prospectors were wandering the hills without knowing galena from fool's gold, or nitric acid from moonshine, Yancey was delving into texts about minerals and geology and chemistry.

While the rest were poking at worthless limestone with picks and shovels, Yancey was learning about hydraulics, explosives, amalgamation, and stamp mills. The result of all this was that Hard Luck Yancey was the most learned and able of all prospectors, and kept finding ore in places that had been passed over by hordes of ignorant sourdoughs. He kept his secrets to himself, quietly studied the brooding hills, and somehow knew or intuited what lay deep within them.

To support himself just now he worked part-time in Mulholland's Hardware Emporium, where his mastery of all things mechanical made him a valued employee. He lived in a modest board and batten cottage, its rear notched into the slope, its front propped up on stilts like most every structure in town. It was the same cottage he had built soon after he started up the Minerva, and far more modest than the elaborate rock eyries erected by the mining moguls who watched car after one-ton car of silver ore emerge from their mines each shift.

The moguls had even tried to take that cottage from him too, but the town's miners themselves had threatened to walk out if they did. Hard Luck was popular among them; he had been a fair and kind employer who paid the going rate of three dollars a day, but saw to it that the drifts were properly timbered and safe.

So Alfred Noble and Gustav Moran contented themselves with stealing a mine, and did not squeeze Hard Luck any further though they claimed that Yancey still owed them seventy-eight thousand dollars. Noble even offered Yancy a job as shift boss, knowing how well he got along with the hard-rock miners who descended into the bowels of Table Mountain each shift and worked in utter darkness save for the pale light of a few lamps. With a foreman like Yancey down there, labor problems would vanish.

But the main reason the miners defended Yancey was that he had donated the ground for the hospital. Any mining town needs an infirmary at the very least, and a hospital if possible, because mining crushes flesh, snaps bones, scorches lungs, burns, cuts, blinds, deafens, chops, breaks, and bloodies men. Yancey saw the need, surveyed the little flat, then turned it over to the Sisters of Charity of Leavenworth, who otherwise lacked the means to set up shop in Yancey, Colorado.

Just ahead of full dark, Yancey reached his weathered cottage, lit a lamp, pulled the black gold from his pocket, rubbed it, and dreamed. Maybe this time he could make his pile without losing it to ruthless men.